BITE THE DUST

CYNTHIA EDEN

This book is a work of fiction. Any similarities to real people, places, or events are not intentional and are purely the result of coincidence. The characters, places, and events in this story are fictional.

Published by Cynthia Eden.

Cover art and design by: Sweet 'N Spicy Designs

Proof-reading by: J. R. T. Editing

CHAPTER ONE

No one should die that way.

Detective Jane Hart stared at the broken body in the middle of Bourbon Street, a doll that had been cast aside. The victim's skin was too pale. Her eyes were wide open — dark — seeming to still show the girl's poor terror.

A crowd had gathered. Hardly a surprise. There was always a crowd on Bourbon Street. Jane could hear the whispers and rumbles behind her as everyone strained to get a look at the body.

The *naked* body. The victim had been dumped, just tossed aside, near the side of Hell's Gate. Music blasted from the interior of the bar, and plenty of folks were still packed inside the place.

How long had the victim been out there, those desperate eyes still open in death as she waited to be found? How many people had just walked past her before someone had actually stopped and realized…

She's dead. Not passed out. Not in some drunken stupor. She's dead.

The fact that her throat was ripped open—that should have given someone a freaking clue.

"Detective Hart?"

It was one of the uniforms, looking green. He'd been the first on scene, and when he'd called in the homicide, she'd been close by. Her captain had sent her over. *My first official case as a homicide detective.* More cops were coming—a crime scene team was on the way.

"There's so much blood," the uniform murmured. Mason. Mason Mitchell. A guy in his early twenties with light blond hair and the horrified gaze that told her he hadn't seen very many bodies before.

Maybe he was new to the beat.

There are always bodies in this city. Once upon a time, the Big Easy had boasted the highest murder rate of any U.S. city.

But things had changed.

Tell that to the girl on the ground.

"Just help me keep everyone back," Jane told him, rubbing at her right side. An old habit, one that she'd never been able to shake. Her fingers pressed hard in that spot, just for a moment, then she squared her shoulders. "I want a closer look at her."

Mason was right. There really was a whole lot of blood. Way too much for a typical scene. It looked as if the victim's throat had been slit wide open, from ear to ear. A horrible way to die but…

Maybe it was quick. The slice of a knife, then she fell.

The victim had been pretty. With long red hair and pale skin. Too young, far too young. But then, there were plenty of girls who were too young on Bourbon Street. They stood in dimly lit doorways, clad in negligees that offered little to the imagination, and they invited passers-by to come in for dances.

Jane crouched over the body, trying to be very, very careful not to touch the victim. The girl was on her back, with her hands spread out at her sides and her legs closed. Perfectly closed. *He posed her at death.*

Chill bumps rose on Jane's arms. The posing was *not* a good sign. *Right, like slitting her throat was a good thing.* Her eyes narrowed. There wasn't any strong light out there, and maybe that was why the girl had just laid there so long.

And not because the people just hadn't given a shit about her.

Jane pulled out her phone and turned on the flashlight app. She directed the light at the girl's neck.

No missing that horrible slice but…

Something else was there. On the left side. About a centimeter above the slice, Jane could see…

Two small holes. Puncture wounds? Yes, yes, they looked like puncture wounds.

Her gaze trailed back up to the victim's face. *No one deserves this death.* Jane wanted to take off her jacket and cover the young victim — *there was just something about her eyes* — but she knew that wasn't possible. She'd contaminate the scene, and the last thing she wanted to do was destroy any evidence.

She heard the cry of a siren behind her, and Jane jumped. She glanced back over her shoulder, her gaze cutting through the crowd, and that was when she saw —

Him.

Tall. Broad shoulders. He was wearing black — a black t-shirt and dark jeans. His hair was dark, too — dark and thick, as it framed his face. A face that wasn't handsome, but rather…dangerous. Intense.

Predatory?

Yes, the way he was staring at the scene was all wrong. The way he was staring at her was just *wrong,* and Jane's hand automatically went to her holster.

His gaze — she couldn't tell what color his eyes were — followed the movement, and a faint smile curved his lips.

What. In. The. Hell?

Her eyes narrowed as she marched toward him.

Other cops were finally at the scene. And she saw the flash of yellow police tape. Perfect. About time that area got sectioned off.

Two uniformed cops hurried toward her, blocking her before she could reach the guy who was *still* smiling.

"Detective Hart—"

"Secure the scene's perimeter," she said, getting straight to the point. "And get those idiots with the camera phones to stop taking their pictures." Yeah, she'd seen those fools, too. Frat boys who were laughing as they recorded. Drunk idiots. This wasn't some show—it was a person's life.

Death.

At her words, the tall, dark stranger glanced over at the frat boys. His smile vanished and she saw his square jaw harden.

Using his inattention to her advantage, Jane closed in on him. She saw his nostrils flare when she was about five feet away, and his head jerked back toward her. Their eyes met—for an instant—and then he backed away. Fast.

Oh, no, you don't.

She surged forward and her hand slapped down on his arm. "Excuse me, sir, but I'm gonna need a word." Her southern accent thickened a bit with those words.

Not a New Orleans accent, because that was a different beast. Mississippi. Gulf Coast. Because once upon a time, she'd been a Mississippi girl.

Until her world had ripped apart.

Her hand tightened on the guy's arm. He'd stopped backing away. Actually, he'd gone as still as a statue beneath her touch. A big statue. About six foot three, two hundred twenty pounds.

Maybe he was the kind of guy who used his size to intimidate people.

She wasn't intimidated.

"I'm Detective Jane Hart." She nodded. "And you are…"

For a moment, she didn't think he'd answer. Her left hand gripped his arm and her right was still poised just above her holster.

"Locke."

She waited, but there was nothing else. Jane let her brows climb. "That a first name or a last?"

His head tilted toward her. "She suffered."

He said it as if it weren't a question. Alarm bells were going off like crazy in Jane's head. The way this guy was acting—it was so *not* a typical bystander response. It was more the response of…

A predator.

A killer.

"Why are you out here tonight, Mr. Locke?" Jane pushed.

His gaze swept over her. She didn't like that. Didn't like him. He was making her feel too on edge, and where she touched him, her skin actually felt warm.

Bad.

Killers could be attractive. Alluring. She knew, she'd sure spent plenty of time studying them. Ted Bundy had certainly used his looks to lure in his victims. Handsome faces could hide horrible monsters, she knew that.

This guy isn't handsome. He's big and strong and dangerous.

"I own Hell."

Her hold tightened on him.

But he motioned to the club behind her. "Hell's Gate, it's mine. So when I heard about the body, I had to come outside. Terrible thing, this. Terrible."

He owned the club. The victim had just been left outside his place of business…right, not suspicious *at all.* "Did you know her?"

"I haven't gotten a good look at her yet."

She didn't believe those rumbling words.

"It's a shame," he suddenly said, his voice dropping, "what some people will do in this city…the lengths they will go to…people want to stay young and strong forever."

Jane looked back at the victim. *Dead far too young*.

"Good luck finding the killer," Locke said.

She turned her focus back to him. "I'll want to talk to your staff. They may have seen something—"

"They didn't."

He was too sure of that.

Her lips thinned. "Do you understand what cooperation is? Because if you don't, you're about to. When a woman's body is *dumped* outside your business, it's bad. Very bad. And when you stare out at the scene like you're some kind of—of—" Words failed her.

He waited.

"You look predatory," Jane said flatly as her hand slid away from him. "There is no sympathy on your face. You seem to be…" *Hunting.* But she didn't say that part, not out loud. She did have *some* restraint. Sometimes.

His head inclined toward her. "I hate this happened to that young woman." Now his words were coated with emotion—emotion that she actually wanted to believe. "It's a waste. A terrible shame. She should still be living her life and now things will just…end. They have to end."

Uh, yeah, about that… "I think they ended when some SOB sliced her throat open."

Mason called her name.

She didn't move.

"I have more questions for you," she said to Locke, a warning edge in her voice.

"I wish I had answers for you."

Okay, that was just a weird-ass response. She didn't have time for weird-ass anything. She glanced over at Mason. "I want you to make Locke comfortable in the back of a patrol car until I can question him again..."

Mason bounded forward. "Make who?"

"Locke." She glanced back at her suspect. "Make him—" Only he wasn't there. Locke had vanished, disappeared in an instant. "Sonofabitch." She surged forward, pushing through the crowd, elbowing her way past the frat jerks with their phones—still filming. Such assholes. *I will so be confiscating those phones later.* She didn't see Locke, not to the left, and not to the right. The guy had slipped away from her.

Jane whirled back to look at Hell's Gate. Did he really own the club? Or had that just been bull?

Mason rushed toward her, huffing. "The ME is here."

"Get in Hell," she told him curtly. "See if a man named Locke is there. If he is, drag his ass out for me."

"Um...do what, ma'am?"

"Drag his ass out," Jane snapped. Then she squared her shoulders. The body wouldn't stay out there much longer. The victim would need to be moved. And she wanted to be there. She wanted to make sure the ME saw those puncture wounds. Jane needed to make sure the victim was taken care of — the victim was her priority. And finding the girl's killer?

Oh, hell, yes, I'm on that, too.

She marched back toward the body. She'd be seeing Locke again. Very, very soon.

Her hand slid down to her right side. Pressed hard. The mark there, as always, seemed to burn...

***

Aidan Locke didn't usually hang out at police stations. But tonight was different. Tonight, there wasn't an option.

So he'd followed the pretty cop — *detective* — back across town. Mary Jane Hart. Though he learned that she didn't allow herself to be called Mary Jane. No, she was just Jane.

And, on the force, she was also all business.

Jane. Not exactly what he'd expected. Small, almost petite. A dancer's body and a warrior's mind. Such an interesting blend.

When he'd seen her earlier, her dark hair had been pulled back, making her eyes seem even bigger. Even darker. Her skin had been a warm gold. And her hand — it had been itching to grab her gun.

As if the gun would have done any good against him.

Meeting her had certainly been interesting. And the fact that she'd instantly looked at him and thought *killer* — well, that had been obvious enough.

And, unfortunately, she'd been dead on.

Before coming to the station, he'd made a little stop at the ME's office. He'd talked to the doctor. Made sure that the right stories were told. The right tests performed on the body that had been brought in to the morgue. He had everything covered. As usual. After all, it was his job to keep the dark secrets of the city hidden.

Someone had to be in charge of the place. And the humans — they just *thought* that they were running the show. No, he was the one pulling the strings. Had been for quite some time. And Aidan would be…for many, many years to come.

The current case was handled. The murdered woman would be forgotten. The matter filed away.

All that remained now was for him to have a talk with the pretty detective. He'd saved her for last. The shadows surrounded him as he waited for her to leave the building.

Someone sure liked working late…Another detail he filed away about the delectable Jane Hart.

All work and no play…

Well, it didn't make for a fun night in New Orleans.

Twenty more minutes passed, and then he saw her. She moved briskly down the police station's stone steps, and her gaze swept around the scene, as if looking for threats.

A threat was there, but she didn't see him. His prey never did.

She hurried down the sidewalk, her stride confident and quick, and he stepped out of those shadows to follow behind her. He didn't make a sound. Not even a rustle and—

Jane whirled toward him, her gun drawn and her body surging with a quick, fluid power. Before he could even blink, her gun was aimed at his heart.

"What kind of idiot stalks a homicide detective?" Jane snarled at him.

The woman had bite. He normally liked that, a lot. But this wasn't about pleasure. This was about business. Strictly business. "Stalking is a very strong word," Aidan murmured, "I was merely…hoping for a chat."

She didn't lower her gun. "So we could finish our conversation from earlier?"

He nodded.

"Conversation…interrogation…I guess you could call it whatever you wanted, *Aidan.*"

Ah, so she'd been digging into his life. He wasn't worried. The cops knew only what he allowed them to know. "Aidan Locke," he said, inclining his head toward her. "At your service."

The gun still wasn't lowering. So, he just stepped forward, and he kept advancing, until the gun pressed into his chest. "I didn't kill that poor girl."

"So your staff at Hell's Gate told me, again and again. The ME said the victim died less than an hour before she was found."

Made sense, considering that Aidan knew the killer would have only hunted at night.

"And everyone who works for you was quick to point out that you'd been having some kind of grand opening bash at that time, and you were right at the bar, serving drinks for all to see."

"Glad you checked out my alibi."

"I checked out *you*." Then, finally, she lowered the gun. But her delicate shoulders remained tense and her chin had notched into the air. "I also sent in one of the uniforms to find you right after that little disappearing act you performed on Bourbon Street, but you were nowhere to be found."

Light from a street lamp fell onto her face. A rather striking face. Not beautiful, but better. Her eyes were a bit exotic, turning up at the corners. Her nose was long, elegant. And her thick hair was slipping out of the ponytail and sliding around her face. Softening her.

Tempting him.

Not now. Business only. Pleasure later.

"I want to help," Aidan said. The words were true enough. He did want to help. He'd find justice for that poor victim. After all, giving her justice was his job.

"Glad to hear that." Jane nodded.

So serious. He knew quite a bit about the new detective. Facts that he'd read weeks ago when she'd first been vetted for the open homicide detective position. Though he doubted the woman realized *he'd* been the one to approve her promotion. When it came to homicide cops in the Big Easy, he always had final say. After all, he didn't want anyone getting in his way.

There was a status to maintain.

"If you're helping," she continued, "then I'd like you to turn over your bar's security footage from tonight. I could get a court order, but that would just take precious time. Time I don't need to waste."

No, he didn't imagine that she liked wasting time.

"I'll help," he said again, nodding.

"Good." She holstered her weapon. "And if we're going to talk, we're going to walk at the same time. I want to see what else the ME has for me."

The walk wouldn't be far. And the ME would have nothing for her. Aidan had seen to that.

But he fell into step beside her, automatically slowing his faster stride to match up with hers. Her scent wrapped around him—something soft. Feminine. Probably one of those lotions that human women were always using. He rather...liked her smell. What was it? He inhaled again.

Apples and...lavender. A nice blend.

Only...there was something more. A deeper, richer scent that was pulling at him. Drawing him closer to her.

Tempting.

"Are you sniffing me?"

He stopped.

"Because that is some weird serial killer shit if you're doing that. Don't make me go for my gun again."

From the corner of his eye, he saw that her hand was already near the holster.

"You smell good," he said, deciding to go with the truth. "But I'll try to stop the 'serial killer shit' for you."

"You'd better." Her steps didn't hurry. She wore boots and jeans. Jeans that hugged her legs and ass ever so well. He'd noticed the ass-hugging earlier, *before* she'd turned with her gun drawn. She had on a jacket, one that looked a bit battered, so he couldn't tell much about her upper body. He suspected her breasts were as perfect as her ass.

CYNTHIA EDEN   18

"I don't want lies from you."

Pity. He only had lies to give her.

"Did you know the victim?"

He shook his head.

"Her prints turned up in the system. She had a...solicitation charge against her. Melanie Wagner, age twenty-one. Just twenty-one. According to the intel I gathered, she was dancing at one of those dives on Bourbon Street." Disgust had entered her voice. "She didn't deserve to be tossed away like trash."

She hadn't been tossed away, though. He'd seen the body and had noticed the care that had been taken to position young Melanie just right.

"I will find her killer." It sounded as if Jane was making a vow. She should be careful doing that. It was never good to make a promise that you couldn't keep.

Up ahead, a small alley snaked away from the street. Darkness filled that alley, and, automatically, his gaze slid toward it. What a perfect hunting spot.

His tongue slid over the edge of his teeth. He could feel them starting to sharpen. "I certainly wish you luck with that endeavor." He started to say more, but then heard a faint rustle of sound. A light noise coming from the alley. Jane wouldn't have noticed it. Most humans wouldn't.

"Forget luck. Give me that security footage."

He stopped walking.

So did she.

Aidan forced a smile. "Of course. I'll call my manager right now and make sure the footage is sent to you." He pulled out his phone, but didn't call anyone. "I hope the ME has news that you can use."

Her gaze raked over him. "I don't get you."

No, she wouldn't. But she should hurry along to the ME's office. The streets weren't safe for her. Or rather, that *particular* street wasn't safe right then.

This problem shouldn't be happening. After he got the test results, the ME should have called in the clean-up team.

"No prior convictions, not so much as a traffic ticket," she said as she tilted her head. More tendrils of her hair escaped from her ponytail, and that scent of hers was seriously getting beneath his skin. "But when I look at you, I *see* you."

He tensed at that, wondering just what she meant.

"You're not some safe guy who plays by the rules. That's a lie. The image you're giving to the world is a lie."

She was hitting far too close to the truth. "So what am I?" *Who am I?*

"That's really what I'd like to know." She shook her head, sending those tendrils of hair sliding over her cheek. "Make that call. I'll be paying you a visit at Hell's Gate come morning."

Morning wasn't that far away.

Jane gave him a curt nod and then headed for the ME's office.

He called his manager and made sure his voice carried as he gave instructions for Graham to send the security footage to Detective Hart. And Aidan watched her walk away.

A truly great ass.

When she hurried up the steps that would take her into the building that housed the ME's office, his attention turned to the alley once more.

He could hear those rustles again. Louder.

And...a cry. A gurgle?

Hell.

The detective was safe, but someone else wasn't. He could smell the blood in the air. His hand reached into his coat, and his fingers curled around the wooden stake he'd hidden there.

Never leave home without a good stake. Advice he'd followed since his thirteenth birthday.

When he rushed into the alley, he saw the victim was struggling, kicking and scratching in the vampire's grip. And that vamp—the vamp was *guzzling* the guy's throat. A homeless man, by the looks of him. A fellow who'd made the mistake of thinking the alley was a safe place to sleep.

It wasn't safe.

"Let him go." Aidan's voice was sharp and hard. Cold with power.

The vamp ignored him. Kept drinking. The homeless man's struggles became weaker.

Shit.

"You're killing him."

The vampire looked up at him. Laughed. Madness burned in that gaze. Madness and power but the vampire *did* actually let go of the victim.

Then the vamp charged at Aidan, rushing forward with fangs bared.

Those fangs never touched him.

The stake drove into the vampire's chest, fast and hard and brutal. Straight to the heart. The vampire cried out and Aidan's arms wrapped around his prey. "It's all right now," Aidan said softly.

The vampire blinked up at him. Death was coming.

Aidan lowered the vamp to the ground. The alley was dirty. It smelled of urine and rotting food. The urine had probably come from the homeless man. During the attack he'd no doubt —

The vamp's hand grabbed tight to him. Like a claw.

Aidan could have broken away. He didn't. He stared down at his prey. When the life faded from the vamp's eyes, he was still crouched there, waiting.

After all, someone should stay until the end. No one deserved to die alone.

CHAPTER TWO

"I don't understand." Dr. Bob Heider pushed the tortoiseshell glasses up on his nose. "Who is it that you are looking for?"

This game wasn't funny. It was seriously pissing her off. "The victim who was brought in earlier tonight. Melanie Wagner. Have you learned anything else about her?"

Dr. Bob's forehead—already impressively high with his receding hairline—seemed to rise even more as he stared at her in confusion. "I don't know any Melanie Wagner."

Jane's temples were pounding. "The dead woman in there!" She pointed behind him, to what she and the other cops called the crypt.

Dr. Bob glanced over his shoulder. "There aren't any bodies in there." But he seemed to be sweating a bit. "Look, I just stepped out to grab some coffee and I-I came back in—"

"In to what?" Jane demanded. "In to find that a body was missing. I mean, come on, Dr. Bob! It's not like a dead body just gets up and walks away when your back is turned!"

He looked away from her. "No new bodies here, detective." His voice was flat.

Okay, fine, so he wanted his turn at hazing the new detective. She'd had her share of pranks played on her this week, but now was not the time. This case wasn't a damn joke. She marched around him and headed into the crypt. "There *is* a new body. *The* woman right—"

No one was there.

There was no body up on the exam table. And when she went to the cold lockers, pulling them open as Dr. Bob protested behind her, she didn't find a twenty-one-year-old woman. "What in the hell?"

"Uh, detective…" Dr. Bob cleared his throat. "Have you been drinking tonight?"

She whirled toward him. "A woman was murdered! Her body was brought here! To you."

He shook his head.

This made zero sense to her.

The guy actually looked confused. Legitimately confused. And that couldn't be happening.

Maybe good old Dr. Bob was the one that had been drinking. Just what was in his coffee mug? She inched closer to him and inhaled, rather the way Aidan had done when he'd gotten close to her. All serial killer style. But the doc didn't smell like booze.

"Look, Doctor—" Jane began.

"It's late," Dr. Bob said, cutting through her words. "I'm going home and getting some good sleep. Even the coffee doesn't work on me anymore." His heavy eyebrows lowered consideringly as he stared at her. "I'd suggest you do the same thing."

He'd suggest she—

Insane.

But…but he took her elbow and guided her out of his office. She craned her neck, looking around, but Jane didn't see Melanie's body. Moments later, she was out in the hallway, feeling stunned and confused.

Maybe…maybe the body had been transferred somewhere else. Yes, that had to be it, right? The body had been transferred. That was all.

She hurried out of the building, her shoulders hunching a bit as she went outside. The night was oddly cold for New Orleans. She hated the cold.

And I hate losing a damn body even more.

She rushed past the mouth of the alley, yanking her phone out. She started to dial her captain, but she heard the soft tread of steps behind her.

Was that Aidan, still tailing her? Had he hung around, waiting for her to reappear?

She spun around, but, this time, she didn't draw her gun. She kept her phone clasped in her hand.

Aidan stared back at her, his body half-hidden by shadows.

"Guessing that didn't go so well," he murmured.

What?

"Trust me, it's better this way."

She wasn't about to trust him. As a rule, she didn't trust anyone.

He stepped closer to her. His hand rose, wrapped around hers and he took her phone away.

"Uh, what are you doing?" Maybe she would be grabbing that gun.

His fingers brushed over hers. That touch — it warmed her. Had her breath catching, and she wasn't a breath-catching type of girl.

"Why do you seek out violence?" He moved even closer to her. "Violence and crime and danger. Why do you want that to be your life?"

It wasn't like that. She was helping people. Helping victims. Making a difference. "Let go of my hand."

But he just stroked her with his fingertips. "Tomorrow, I'll be a stranger."

"You're a stranger tonight." A stranger who was still touching her. Why hadn't she jerked away?

Why did she...like...his touch?

"You never found a body," he said as he came even closer to her. Was it her imagination, or had his blue eyes started to…shine?

She wondered how she'd missed that bright blue gaze before. His eyes were rather gorgeous, really. She'd never seen that shade of blue before. She could probably look into those eyes forever.

If she was the forever type.

She wasn't.

And he was still talking.

"You didn't find the body outside of Hell's Gate. You don't know anything about Melanie Wagner."

Um…

"You were on Bourbon Street, but you were just having a few drinks. There was no murder. No investigation."

His eyes were *definitely* shining. Maybe more like glowing.

His fingers slid over hers once more. "And you didn't meet me." Regret seemed to tinge his voice. "You never met me. Forget me."

He leaned in once more, closing the last bit of distance between them. For an instant, she thought that he might kiss her.

He didn't.

His lips tightened. Anger hardened his face and then he pulled back.

She just stood there.

"Go home." His voice was so deep and dark, wrapping around her. Almost sinking *into* her. "Get a good night's sleep. Have some fucking fabulous dreams." Then he pushed the phone back into her hand and turned away. The guy just started walking away from her.

Really?

"Um…excuse me." She put the phone into her pocket. Pulled out her gun.

He'd frozen in the middle of the sidewalk.

"I don't know what that little speech was about, and, granted, my night is pretty weird so far…"

He was cursing. Cursing and whirling back to face her.

She smiled and lifted her gun. "But you just won the award for the biggest creep factor ever. I'm not forgetting my victim, and I'm not forgetting the murder, and the very fact that you *think* I would…I mean, what, was that supposed to be some kind of lame seduction attempt or something? You were trying to seduce me into silence?"

His jaw dropped open.

His eyes were still shining bright.

"Didn't work," she told him. "But it sure as hell did make me suspicious of you."

He rushed back toward her. She locked her knees and didn't back away.

"You didn't forget."

"No, buddy, I didn't."

"You should have forgotten."

She heard other footsteps then. Footsteps coming up from behind her. She didn't want to look away from Aidan, though, because she was sure he was the threat.

"Humans always forget. It's how things *work* with me."

"We're going into the police station," she told him in her I'm-In-Control-and-You're-A-Criminal voice. "You're going into interrogation and I—"

More footsteps. More people rushing up behind her. She had to look over her shoulder.

Two men were running toward her. Men with eyes that shined nearly as brightly as Aidan's did. What in the hell was happening?

"She didn't forget," Aidan said, sounding horrified. "You were late, I had to take care of the prey …*and she didn't forget.*"

One of the men froze. A thin guy, with rounded shoulders. He was under the street light so she could see the messy mop of his red hair. As she watched, the redhead gave a sad shake of his head and he—he pulled out a gun.

"Then you know what happens…"

The guy was aiming his weapon at her.

Jane whirled to face him. She made sure she brought up her own gun. "I'm a cop!" Jane yelled. "Put down the weapon, *now!*"

But he wasn't putting it down. His finger was squeezing that trigger and she knew the bullet was going to hit her. She had to fire back.

The bullet thundered out from his gun. Her fingers squeezed her trigger.

She expected to feel the slam of impact and —

Aidan shoved her aside. Hard. Her head slammed into the side of the building and Jane went down, moaning. She kept her gun, clinging to it desperately even as the world seemed to go dark around her.

"You asshole!" Aidan bellowed. "Look what you did!"

Aidan was bellowing. That meant he hadn't been hit, right? And neither had she. At least, not by the bullet.

"Jane?" Aidan crouched in front of her. "Jane, you're okay."

Her head was splitting. That pain didn't feel so *okay*.

Was blood sliding down her temple? It felt wet.

"I've got you." And he did. Aidan lifted her up, cradling her in his arms. "Everything is going to be okay. I'll take care of you."

The hell he would. She didn't trust him. Not for an instant. But he was holding her tight and her head was splitting and her eyes wouldn't stay open.

She was passing out. She didn't want to pass out. She had to stop the shooter.

"I've got you," Aidan said again.

And his words…they chilled her.

***

"What in the fuck do we do now?" Garrison Aimes rubbed a hand over his sweaty forehead as he paced in the bedroom.

Jane's bedroom. A bedroom that smelled just like her.

Aidan only spared Garrison the briefest of glances. If he looked at the fool too long, he'd kick his ass. *Idiot – why the hell did you fire at her?*

That was the trouble with guys like Garrison. Third generation punks who thought they knew everything.

They knew nothing. But he'd make real sure that — by dawn — Garrison understood exactly who was in charge. Garrison was just lucky that Jane's bullet hadn't thudded into *him*. But when Aidan had pushed Jane to the side, he saved her *and* Garrison from bullet wounds because Jane's aim had been thrown off.

I bet you don't miss often, do you, sweetheart?

Aidan sat on the edge of Jane's bed. His hand lifted and smoothed over her cheek. She had a cut up on her temple. A big knot had formed around it. She'd hit the wall too hard. His fault, dammit. So it was only right that he make things up to her.

His claws had extended. He sliced his wrist and saw the blood drip out slowly from the small wound. Locking his jaw, he pressed the blood to her lips.

"What in the fuck are you doing?" Garrison demanded.

"Fixing your mistake." Fixing all of the mistakes—the way he always did. Aidan figured this was his third fix of the night, not that he was counting or any shit like that. He'd eliminated the vamp threat, he'd patched up the homeless guy and made him forget his attack and now...now he had to take care of Jane. "Jane, drink."

Her lips opened. She took his blood without any hesitation. Probably because she was concussed and didn't realize what the hell was happening.

I could be giving the woman a smoothie for all she knows.

But as she took a few sips of his blood, Aidan released the breath he'd been holding. Contrary to myth, a vampire's blood didn't have any power to it—well, not the power to heal, anyway. The power to kill? Hell, yeah. It was *his* blood that mattered.

The blood of an alpha.

By the time Jane woke up, there would be no bump on her head. No wound. No concussion.

"And no memory of this night," he said, leaning in close to her. With his blood now linking them, there would be no way for her to resist his command. She'd forget the murder. Forget everything that had happened.

And he'd pay one more little visit to Dr. Bob...just to be sure there weren't any glitches. *That's why I get paid the big damn bucks. To make sure shit gets handled properly.* Only there had been more than a few screw-ups that night. First of all, if the tests had shown that the vic was going to become a vampire, the clean-up crew should have been notified right fucking away. Dr. Bob should have kept the place secure until they arrived.

And I shouldn't have found a vamp feeding in the alley.

Aidan pulled his wrist away from her lips. For just an instant, her eyes opened, and he felt a hard, thick punch to his gut. Her eyes—dark but framed with gold flecks—locked on him. A guy could really get lost in a gaze like hers. Think all kinds of thoughts...

I need to get out of here.

"You don't know me," Aidan told her, his voice almost a caress. "You've never met me." A real shame. Because he was sure that they could have enjoyed the hell out of each other. "Go back to sleep."

Her lips trembled. "But the monsters are waiting."

What? His gut clenched. "No monsters are going to get you. Trust me on that one."

The trembling left her lips, and for an instant, it almost looked as if she were smiling. "Silly...I don't trust...anyone..." Her breath sighed out and her eyes closed.

He smoothed her hair away from her face. Her wound was already healing. She was—

"Uh, yeah, are you gonna hold her hand all night?" Garrison snapped.

E-fucking-nough.

Aidan rose slowly from the bed. He rolled back his shoulders and flexed his fingers. Then, in a blink, he whirled and grabbed Garrison around the neck. He shoved that asshole against the nearest wall and held him there, dangling the smaller man a foot off the ground as he glared at him. "Do you know who I am?"

"Y-yes..." Garrison gasped as he clawed at the fingers around his neck. Like that feeble clawing crap was doing anything.

"Really? Because the way you keep acting all alpha damn tough, it confused me. Made me think that perhaps you believed *you* were the one in charge."

Garrison's face had turned red. Reddish purple.

Aidan brought his nose in closer to the guy. "Let's be clear. I don't give a flying shit who your grandfather was. You're some lame ass punk that I *agreed* to allow in the city, but another screw-up from you, and you won't just be dealing with a banishment, you'll be dealing with death."

Garrison wasn't breathing. Was that due to fear? Or Aidan's grip?

Aidan eased his hold and Garrison sucked in a heaving gulp of air.

Then he let the fool drop.

"S-sorry!" Garrison cried.

"She's the woman you need to apologize to. You *shot* at her. She's human. If that bullet had hit—"

"I-I thought…I was…pr-protecting the pack! Protecting…y-you…She wasn't…wasn't f-forgetting…"

"Humans always forget. Sometimes, they just need a little push." Or a blood bond. "You owe her now. As payment, you'll be watching her back, got it? You'll be making sure that human detective over there is protected." He didn't even know why he was giving this order but…oddly, it seemed important to know that Jane would be watched. Guarded.

New Orleans was a dangerous place. Especially to a woman who might look too hard at—

Monsters.

Aidan glanced over his shoulder at the bed. Jane was sleeping.

Beautiful Jane. Had he not thought she was beautiful before? He'd been wrong. The woman was drop-dead gorgeous.

And her scent was the best sin…

"Watch over her," Aidan growled. "Swear a blood oath on it. *Now*."

"I-I swear! I'll guard her. Never harm!"

Satisfied, Aidan nodded. "Good, now it's time for us to get the hell out of here." He had an ME to see. Dr. Bob should have locked down his damn lab better—so much shit could have been avoided if the guy had just stuck to the original plan. But now…*screw-up after screw-up* tonight.

Aidan couldn't afford to let these screw-ups continue. Vamps weren't going to get a foothold in his town again.

He'd see the ME. Then tie up any other loose ends. There had been too many cops outside of Hell's Gate. A few of them had seen too much. *I'll deal with them.*

Damn. Sometimes, his job was exhausting. Especially when idiots like Garrison made everything harder.

Garrison rushed to the door. His face was still red.

Aidan moved much slower. He peered over at the nightstand and saw a picture there. A picture of Jane, with her arm around the shoulders of a man with dark hair and dark eyes—eyes just like hers. They were both smiling in the picture. Jane looked…happy.

He grabbed the picture. Tucked the frame in his jacket. Taking things that didn't belong to him…he'd always done that. Started back when he was a kid who had nothing. He was usually more restrained but…

She'd forget him, and he'd remember her.

That was the way it worked in his world.

So maybe he deserved a little keepsake for his trouble.

Once more, almost helplessly, he risked a final look back at her. She was snug in her bed. He'd put her gun on the nightstand beside her. He'd noticed that the woman seemed to really like her gun.

Mary Jane Hart.

No, he wouldn't be forgetting her anytime soon.

***

The distant sound of a car horn penetrated the fog of sleep that surrounded her. Jane blinked open her eyes, then moaned at the bright light that spilled through her blinds. *Too bright.*

She rolled onto her side—the side that took her *away* from the sunlight—and her gaze fell on her nightstand.

And the gun there.

Why was her gun there?

She always put the gun *inside* the nightstand drawer. She took the clip out and she put the weapon up securely before she slid into bed. It was her routine and—

And she was still wearing her clothes.

She sat up then, moving fast, damn fast, her heart racing. Her hand lifting, touching her head, and she expected to feel blood on her temple. Blood, a giant goose egg, *something* but…but her skin was smooth.

I was near the alley. An idiot with a gun came up on me and…Aidan. Aidan pushed me away.

The scene played through her mind, again and again. Alley. Gun. Brick wall. But…what in the hell had happened after that?

She licked her lips. They'd gone bone-dry on her.

She didn't remember coming home. Didn't remember leaving her gun out. She *did* vaguely remember—

Bright blue eyes. Aidan, leaning over her. *No monsters are going to get you.*

Jane jumped from the bed. She ran though the small apartment, looking left and right, high and low, making sure that she was alone.

Aidan had been here. She was sure of it, but…but he was gone then. And her mind felt so weird. Foggy. She yanked open the doors that led out to her small balcony, and the blast of sunlight hit her right in the face. Squinting, she lifted her hand to shield her eyes as she headed out onto the balcony. Car horns floated in the wind, and the faintest notes of jazz drifted to her.

It was real. I know it was. But...her fingers slid toward her head once more. She'd hit her head last night, hadn't she? Only it didn't feel sore to the touch. There was no bump. No tender skin.

Her hand lowered. What was going on?

A phone began to ring behind her, the sound was loud, jarring—mostly because she meant for it to be. Jane glanced over her shoulder and saw that her phone was on her nightstand, right beside her gun. The phone was blasting out rock music, a signal that her boss was calling her.

Good. She really wanted to talk with the captain. Jane hurried back inside and swiped the phone before it could ring again. "Captain—" she began.

"We got a murder," Captain Vivian Harris cut her off. "A body dumped right by the ME's office. Can you believe that shit?"

"I—" Yes, yes, she could. Because she'd been at the ME's last night and all hell had broken loose...hadn't it?

"It's a Jane Doe. Uniforms are on scene, but I want you there. You'll be the lead on this one. Your first lead as a homicide detective."

No, it wasn't her first lead. Last night — that case, *that girl* — had been her first run as lead detective. The captain should know that.

"Get there, now. Show me what you can do, Hart."

The call ended.

Her mind was still fuzzy. Things were just…not adding up. But she didn't have time to sit and piss and moan all day. She had a case. A victim who needed her.

Two damn victims.

She'd figure this crap out, but first — *shower. Dress. Haul ass to the crime scene.*

***

There wasn't a crowd waiting this time. This wasn't Bourbon Street and dozens of onlookers — gawkers — weren't trying to stare at the dead body. There was only a thin band of yellow police tape blocking the alley entrance way. And two uniformed cops were standing guard near the tape. One of those cops — he was familiar to her. *Because he was there last night, too.*

The light glinted off his blond hair and when he looked at her, a familiar horror filled his eyes.

Mason Mitchell.

His gaze dipped down to the badge she'd clipped to the pocket on her jeans. "Detective.

The, uh, crime techs are already working. The ME's — he's with her."

Since the ME had been right next door, it was hardly surprising that Dr. Bob had beat her to the scene. She ducked under the police line, then paused. "Is it as bad as last night's scene?" Jane asked Mason.

His brows furrowed. "Ma'am?"

She jerked her thumb over her shoulder. "The victim. Is she cut up like the last one?"

Mason swallowed. "L-last one?"

The guy was way too green. "Never mind." She'd see for herself. Jane turned and made her way down the alley. The place reeked — not from the stale scent of garbage but from death. Blood, decay — and she could see why.

There was a pool of blood near the back of the alley. Thick. Dark. Far too much blood.

Techs were snapping pics of the scene. Dr. Bob was crouched over the body.

The woman on the dirty ground — Jane couldn't see her face, not yet. But she could see her body. Bare toes. Bare calves. *Totally* naked body. Hell, just like poor Melanie Wagner. This wasn't good — two dead girls dumped in a twenty-four hour period. There was a great, gaping hole in the poor girl's chest, and there was —

"Oh, Jane, didn't realize you were already here." Dr. Bob moved back, giving Jane a view of the woman's body. "Poor thing," he murmured. "What kind of freak would do something like this to such a pretty girl?"

Everything stopped for Jane. Just—stopped. For an instant, a thick and heavy silence surrounded her. She didn't hear the traffic, didn't hear the techs murmuring, didn't even hear the rustle of the papers in Dr. Bob's hands. She heard nothing, and she saw only that victim.

A victim with wide-open, dark eyes. With long red hair that spread beneath her head. Skin that was too pale.

A broken doll, cast aside.

Melanie Wagner.

Only…Melanie's throat wasn't slashed open this time. There was no long cut that went from ear to ear. Her throat was smooth. Perfect. It was her chest that had the giant hole.

Dr. Bob frowned. "Jane? You okay?" He tilted his head as he studied her. "You've gone white."

"No, I am not *okay*," she gritted out. Melanie had been an only child. Jane knew that—she'd pulled the records on the woman last night. So she wasn't staring at some twin. And it wasn't someone who *looked* like Melanie.

It *was* Melanie. Straight down to the little mole on the right side of the woman's mouth. "You know her!" Jane snapped at him. "We both do. She was the victim from last night!"

"What?" Dr. Bob just appeared lost.

"The one who had her throat sliced open on Bourbon Street." This was insane. "You were there! You were—"

He stepped closer to her. Alarm flared on his face. "Jane…" Now his voice was low, carrying only to her. "No victims were brought into my office last night. For once, things were quiet." But worry was plain to see on his face. "Are you…are you feeling all right this morning?"

No, she sure as hell wasn't. "She's Melanie Wagner."

"You know the victim?"

They *both* knew her! They'd found her last night. Only…something was wrong. Way wrong. She spun away from Dr. Bob and marched toward Mason. She grabbed the uniformed cop and dragged him closer to the body. "Recognize her?" Jane demanded.

Mason gave a frantic shake of his head. "Did…did someone take her heart?"

"No," Dr. Bob glanced back at the body. "But she was stabbed, right in the heart, by something very sharp."

Stabbed…only last night, Melanie's throat had been slit.

Impossible.

A woman couldn't die twice.

Dr. Bob cast another worried frown Jane's way. Mason hurried back to his post. And Jane tried to figure out what in the hell was happening. "Fingerprint check," she whispered. "She's going to come up in the system." Because that victim *was* Melanie Wagner, she'd bet her life on it.

That poor broken doll was Melanie, and Jane didn't know what the hell was going on.

***

Thirty minutes later, the body had been bagged and tagged. Bob Heider had made certain that the woman was taken care of — after all, it was his job to deal with the dead. Detective Jane Hart had watched every move that he made during his exam of the scene, and then she'd spent far too much time studying the alley.

She's going to be trouble.

Bob watched as Jane marched out of that alley. As soon as she vanished, he pulled out his phone. The crime scene techs were far enough away that he didn't worry they'd overhear him. It wasn't as if he were going to have a long conversation. With this particular fellow, he never did.

The phone rang once, twice.

Bob felt sweat trickling down his spine.

"What the hell do you want?" A deep voice rumbled.

Bob kept his eyes on the alley's entrance. Just in case Jane came back, he wanted to be ready. "We've got a real big problem." And, unless he was wrong… "I'm pretty sure she's headed your way right now."

"What?"

He hunched his shoulders. "*She remembers.*"

"Im-fucking-possible."

So the cocky guy liked to think. "I like her." His breath heaved out. "Don't hurt her."

One of the techs glanced his way.

Bob ended the call and shoved the phone back into his pocket. He forced an attentive expression for the tech even as he thought…

Please, please…don't kill Jane. Because, sure, he might have been lying to her—her and plenty of other cops, but…he didn't want Jane dead.

He didn't want her body coming across his table.

He liked her. She was one of the good people. The kind that cared and tried to make a difference. With her past, hell, it was amazing that she gave a shit at all. But she did and…

Don't kill Jane.

His shoulders slumped and he turned back to the body bag that waited on him.

CHAPTER THREE

Getting into Hell wasn't hard.

After all, it was barely ten a.m. on a Sunday morning. Bourbon Street wasn't exactly plush with tourists right then — most of the folks who'd partied the night before were back in their hotel rooms, sleeping hard and deep. The kind of sleep that the truly hung over often enjoyed.

Hell's Gate waited for Jane. Unassuming. Dark. And with a CLOSED sign at the door. Only that door wasn't locked. When she reached for the knob, it turned all too easily beneath her fingers.

No, getting into Hell wasn't hard…

Her right hand slid toward her holster. She hadn't come unarmed for this little visit.

"Hello!" Jane called out. She took a step inside and goosebumps rose onto her arms. Ignoring the chill, Jane crept deeper into the club. The lights were off. Chairs had been turned upside down and placed on top of the wooden tables. The place had that eerie, complete quiet that one normally found inside…a tomb.

And then…then she heard the clink of glasses. Her gaze shot to the bar. It had been empty a moment before but now, *he* was there. Standing right behind the gleaming bar top. He had what looked like a bottle of whiskey in one hand and a glass in the other. As she stared at him, he lifted the glass up, saluted her, then downed the contents in one gulp.

She pulled out her gun.

Aidan's lips twitched. "Still love that weapon, don't you?"

It was all real. He knows me.

Aidan put down the glass and flattened his hands on the bar's surface. He seemed…bigger. His shoulders stretched the black t-shirt that he wore and his blue eyes were almost painfully bright.

"I want to know what's happening," Jane began.

"You just busted into my club, without an invitation." He lifted one dark brow. "Is this the point when I'm supposed to say…welcome to hell?"

"What. Is. Happening?" She took another step toward him. The floor creaked beneath her boots. "Why am I the only one who seems to remember Melanie Wagner? Why isn't there still crime tape up outside of this place? Why isn't there—"

He smiled. That smile was chilling and it stopped the mad tumble of her words.

There was something about that smile. It was cold and dark and…sad?

She blinked and shook her head and—

He leapt across the bar. Moved in a freakishly fast lunge and was in front of her before she could suck in a breath.

Her gun pushed into his chest. Right over his heart. They'd been in this pose before, hadn't they? The *déjà vu* was overwhelming. "What did you do to me?"

His head tilted. If possible, he seemed even bigger this close. "What do you *want* me to do?" And just like that—his voice was a sensual purr. Temptation.

No way. "You are *not* trying to seduce me now."

His lips curved. Not such a cold smile this time. "To be honest, I wanted to seduce you the first time I saw you."

"There was a dead body at the scene!"

"Was there?" Aidan mused. "I don't remember that…"

"Seems like everyone but me doesn't remember, and I'm calling bullshit on that."

His smile slid away.

"Melanie Wagner had her throat cut last night. Right outside of *your* club. You were here. I was here. And then we both met up later and headed toward the ME's office."

He didn't say anything.

So her words came faster. "Someone ran up behind us—some crazy guy with a gun. He fired at me."

His lashes lowered, covering the brilliant blue of his eyes.

She wasn't giving up. "You pushed me out of the way."

"I saved your life?" he murmured. "How amazingly heroic of me."

"I slammed into a wall. *You threw me* into the bricks." She hadn't needed saving. She could take care of herself just damn fine. "The next thing I knew, I was waking up in my bed. My captain called me, got me to haul ass to a crime scene and guess what I found there?"

"A crime?"

Her teeth ground together. "I found Melanie Wagner. Only her throat wasn't slit. Some sick freak had carved open her chest."

Silence.

She could hear the pounding of her heartbeat. Way too fast. "I'm not crazy." She hated that label. *Hated it.* Because once, so very long ago…a shrink had told her that she was.

She was wrong. I know what I saw. Back then…and now.

"Talk to me." Jane hated the plea in her voice.

He exhaled on a long sigh. "I knew you were going to be a problem." His hand rose and curled around her wrist. His touch was so warm. Strong.

Her hand was tense beneath his as she gripped her weapon. "Why couldn't you just be a good cop...and forget?"

"What—"

He moved again—too fast—a blur. Aidan took the gun from her and pinned her against the wall. They'd moved back at least five feet, in less than a second's time, and now he had the gun pointed under her chin.

"What am I supposed to do with you?" Aidan murmured.

Well, he sure wasn't supposed to shoot her. "How did you do that?"

He leaned in close to her. She saw his nostrils flare, as if he were drinking in her scent.

"You're afraid of me," Aidan said.

"You have a *gun* on me." Fear was a normal response.

"It's your gun. And, besides, I got tired of it being pointed at me." Then he...he dropped the gun. But he didn't back away. The weapon hit the floor and she was damn grateful it hadn't accidentally gone off and hit one of them.

She stared up at him. Those hard cheekbones. That strong jaw. Those...sharp teeth? Holy hell, his eye teeth seemed to be lengthening right before her eyes.

"Tell me, detective..." Aidan said, voice rough and deep. "Do you believe in monsters?"

She stared up into his eyes. That bright blue—his gaze wasn't just bright. His eyes were *glowing*. That crazy memory from the previous night had been true, too. And as he lifted his hands toward her, Jane saw that his fingernails had stretched into long, black claws.

Jane heaved forward and she kneed him in the groin as hard as she could. She thought he'd stumble back so that she could grab for her fallen gun, only he didn't stumble. He didn't even groan.

He did laugh, and then his claw-tipped hand rose to curl around her neck. "I'll take that as a…yes?"

"Get away from me," she shouted at him, rage bursting through her even as fear slid around her heart like a closing fist. *What big teeth you have…what freaking glowing eyes you have…*

"It would have just been so much easier if you'd simply forgotten," he murmured. His hand wasn't hurting her. In fact his fingers seemed to be caressing the skin of her neck, right over the spot where her pulse raced so frantically. "Now this complicates things entirely too much."

"What are you?" *What*, not who. Definitely a what unless this was some kind of bad dream. *Can't be. It feels too real.*

"I already told you that, sweetheart. I'm a monster. The biggest and the baddest of them all." His fingers slid over her throat once more. "And you're a problem."

She shoved against him. He didn't move, and it was pretty much as if she'd just shoved straight into a six foot three wall of stone. His hand was on her throat and she wondered—was this going to be the end for her? After everything she'd survived, was Aidan Locke just going to snap her throat? Take her out in an instant?

No.

Her right side seemed to burn. She'd survived one nightmare before. She could do it again. She *would* do it again and—

"Hey, boss!" A loud voice called as someone approached the entrance to Hell's Gate.

Aidan's head snapped toward the door. He eased a step away from her.

"Where's the pretty detective?" That voice asked as a man—thin, average height, with red hair—strode inside. "Is she already—"

Already what, bastard? Dead?

Because that red-haired guy in the doorway—he was the jerk who'd taken a shot at her the night before. Aidan had turned to fully face him now, and Aidan's inattention was her chance. She flew toward her gun, grabbed it tight, and whirled to take aim at the two men.

The redhead was gaping at her. He'd lifted his hands. "Shit, no, don't shoot!"

Aidan just sighed. "She remembers, Garrison."

Garrison's face flashed blood-red. Nearly as red as his hair "You said humans—they *never* remember!"

"They don't." Aidan tilted his head as he studied her. "That means our lovely detective here is something…else."

He was insane. No, he was the monster in the room. She was the cop. She had to *do* something.

"Are you…are you going to kill her?" Garrison asked, seeming to strangle on the words.

"I'm the one with the gun!" Jane shouted back at him. But…but Aidan was the one with the claws. Claws that were still out.

A man can't have claws! And a man's eyes shouldn't glow and—

Garrison took an aggressive step toward her. Aidan threw up his hand, slamming those claws against Garrison's chest. "The detective isn't dying."

"But—"

"My word," Aidan said flatly. "My law."

Garrison gave a jerky nod.

Aidan's gaze slowly traveled over Jane, moving from her boots, up her jean-clad legs, over to the gun she held then finally, slowly, up to her face. "My town," Aidan said. "My rules." His eyes narrowed on her. "Mine."

Maybe she should just shoot.

"Spread the word," Aidan ordered. "Make sure everyone knows that the detective has been claimed. Anyone going near her will deal with me."

Claimed. She didn't like the sound of that, not at all.

And Garrison was running away. "Hey, trigger happy SOB!" She yelled after him. "I'm the one with the gun!" Since he'd shot at her before, she figured it was only fair that she return the favor.

But Aidan moved to block her shot. "Those bullets won't do much damage to him. Pack silver if you want to take him down. That'll be lesson one for you."

Her temples were pounding. Her world pretty much splintering apart.

"Your old life is gone." He snapped his fingers. "Just like that. If you'd forgotten like the other humans, none of this would be happening. You didn't, though. Because you're not like them." Once again, his gaze swept over her. "And I can't wait to find out just what you are."

She licked lips that had gone far too dry. "Get away from the door." Because she needed to get out of there. Once she was out of Hell, she could think again. And maybe bring back one serious cavalry to this place. *I need back-up. A whole lot of back-up.*

He moved away from the door. "No one will believe you. Not your fellow detectives. Not your captain. They'll just think you're crazy."

She inched toward the door.

"It won't be the first time folks have said that, though, will it?" His voice lowered.

And she knew he'd dug into her past.

She stopped her creeping retreat to the door. Her shoulders flew back and her chin jerked into the air.

"How long did they keep you in that…hospital?"

Not a hospital. A psych ward.

"You saw monsters back then, too, didn't you? Is that why you believe so easily now? Why you aren't screaming and saying that I *can't* have claws coming from my fingertips? You've seen someone like me before?"

No, not like him. Not like him at all.

"You don't want them to say you're crazy again," Aidan continued. "You don't want to lose everything you've worked so hard to gain." His voice was tempting. The devil had probably never sounded quite as tempting. "You keep my secret. And I'll guard your back. That's what a claiming is. You're under my protection because I run this town."

He did? She was so close to the door. "Did you kill Melanie Wagner?"

His lips thinned.

"Did you?" Jane pushed him.

"The first time…" Aidan drawled. "Or the second?"

Her gut clenched.

"Maybe you should go talk to the ME again. All of the blood in that alley…it wasn't just Melanie's," Aidan murmured. "What do you think vampires do?"

Ice coated her skin. *Not vampires. Not!*

"They bite. They drink from their prey. They torture. There's a reason I don't let them in my city."

"She was just a girl." Her fingers were sweating around the gun. And she remembered Melanie's chest. The deep wound.

Was a stake driven into her heart?

"Someone turned that poor girl. I knew it the minute I saw her outside of Hell's Gate. Her throat was slashed to cover up the bite marks."

Bite marks that Jane had seen.

"You still aren't running away, screaming," he said, his voice little more than a whisper. "And I sure have to wonder…*why?*"

Because I do know monsters. I do believe in them. Always have.

"When Melanie woke up again, she was starving. Dangerous. She attacked the first person she saw."

She should walk out of that club. She should run. "And you…you killed her."

"Someone stopped her."

But he'd been that someone. She knew it. Jane gave a sad shake of her head.

"I am so curious…" He took another deep breath. "About what makes you special. But if I'm curious, others will be, too. You'll need me."

She didn't need anyone.

"Running from me isn't the answer."

She was on the threshold of the bar's main entrance. She didn't respond as she ran out to her car. Yes, *ran.* She dove into the driver's side, and she grabbed for the cuffs that she kept in her glove box. Did the guy really think she was just going to flee? Basically knowing that he'd *killed* Melanie? Aidan had all but confessed.

She locked her hands around the cuffs, jumped out of the car and —

He was there. Standing less than three feet away. Watching her with a faint smile on his lips. "Ah, so you're into bondage, too, huh, sweetheart?"

She slapped one of the cuffs around his wrist. "You're coming with me."

Aidan looked at the cuff — a cuff that appeared rather ridiculous around his powerful wrist — and he laughed.

He was still laughing when she grabbed his other wrist, pulled it behind his back, and snapped a cuff on that one, too.

She pushed him forward. Surprisingly, he moved. She'd really expected a fight from him, but when she opened the back door to her car, he—still laughing, like this was the funniest thing in the world to him—climbed inside.

Shaking her head, she slammed the door shut and jumped in the driver's seat.

"You should get a pair of silver cuffs," Aidan advised her. "Like I have at my place."

She did not want to hear more about the guy's bondage issues.

"You didn't read me my rights."

She glanced at him in the rear-view mirror. "You're under arrest for murder. You have the right to remain silent and the right to keep your creepy ass claws to yourself." Her only goal right then was to get him to the police station, then everyone there could see that she wasn't crazy.

She cranked the car and shoved her foot down on the gas pedal. They lurched forward.

He started to laugh again. "This isn't going to work, sweetheart…Bad, bad mistake…"

"Yeah, well, it's my mistake to make. The fact that you pretty much *confessed* to killing poor Melanie Wagner means you're getting a one-way ticket to the police station." She turned the corner. Headed fast down that street. No one was out so she cut right through the city.

"Bad mistake." He wasn't laughing any longer. "Don't make me your enemy. I can help you."

She risked another glance back into the rear-view mirror. "Right. Sure you—"

Another vehicle hit her, just slammed straight into her car with the force of an oncoming train. Jane's words ended in a wild scream as glass shattered and the driver side door of her vehicle came flying back at her. The air bag deployed—a cloud of white blinded her, and dimly...she heard...

The roar of a beast from the back seat.

CHAPTER FOUR

Jane was bleeding. Aidan could smell her blood and that scent pissed him off. The car had been shoved far across the street on impact, and he was trapped in a twisted mass of metal and glass.

He was trapped. Jane was trapped. And some dumb sonofabitch was about to die.

"Get her!" He heard the voice — a man's voice — that sounded from right outside of the wreckage. "Get the woman, now! Before she wakes up."

Wakes up? Jane was unconscious. Jane was hurt — bleeding.

And someone was trying to take her from him.

He growled again, the animalistic sound bursting from him. It was daylight. He was in the middle of the city. This was *not* the place for a full-on shift.

Apparently, it was the place for fools to try and ambush him.

I make the rules. I can fucking break them, too.

Glass shattered again. He heard the groan of metal. The fool outside was trying to get Jane out of the wreckage.

Aidan's hands were still behind his back. Still cuffed. He yanked hard, *harder,* and the cuffs snapped apart.

"Got her!" The soon-to-be-dead bastard yelled excitedly.

"Hurry!" Someone else called. "We need to move before—"

Aidan kicked open the car door—a door that had been barely hanging on. He jumped out of the car and stood there, chest heaving, fury boiling within him, his claws out, and more than ready to attack.

The man who'd taken Jane froze, standing just a few feet away. He had Jane slung over his shoulder and her arms hung down limply. The smell of her blood was even stronger.

"Hurry!" That other voice called out. A woman's voice. Tight. Angry. "I'll stop him!"

Then there was a bang. A sharp pain burned in his shoulder. Aidan looked down—he'd been shot. And the burn he felt told him that, unlike the bullets in Jane's gun...*I just got hit with silver.*

One hit wasn't enough to stop him. Not even close. He lowered his head and he ran—not for the shooter, though, but for the man who was carrying Jane toward a black van that waited near the curb.

The van hadn't hit them. Some piece of shit pickup truck had plowed into Jane's car — and that truck had been abandoned. The van had come up after the wreck. A getaway vehicle. The attack had been well planned.

Just not well enough.

Another silver bullet blasted at him, but he was moving fast and the bullet just grazed his arm. "*Jane!*" Aidan roared. The scent of her blood was driving him mad.

Another bullet came flying at him. This one hit him on the right side, a fast, deep burn.

He didn't look at the shooter. He couldn't take his eyes off Jane. He reached out and grabbed the fool who'd taken her.

The guy screamed and let go of Jane. She started to fall to the ground.

Aidan caught her. He grabbed her and pulled her into his arms just as her gaze flew open. He saw her fear. Her panic and —

Another bullet hit him. His body jerked.

"Aidan?" Her eyes doubled in size. "Did someone just shoot at you?"

Hell, yes, someone had. And now that Jane was safe, that someone was about to pay. He pushed Jane behind him. The man who'd tried to take her had jumped into the van. The driver of that van was yelling as the van flew toward Aidan *and* Jane.

"Shit!" Jane said from behind him. "*Shit!*" She grabbed his hand and yanked Aidan to the side. That yank wasn't going to do it. He grabbed *her* and jumped for safety, making absolutely sure they cleared the street.

When they fell back down, he rolled his body, cushioning her. The scent of burning rubber filled his nostrils, and he saw that the van had braked, just long enough for the shooter to jump in the back. Aidan pushed Jane to the side and sprang to his feet but—

The shooter fired again. The bullet missed but it sent both him and Jane diving for cover.

Someone is playing with the wrong wolf.

The van careened down the street. Giving chase wasn't an option—not with silver burning him and Jane's car a crumpled mess beside him. Aidan rose, glaring at the van. He had Jane's would-be-abductor's scent—a scent that he wouldn't be forgetting—and he'd find the guy.

The fool would pay.

"What just happened?" Jane's fingers curled around his shoulder and she spun him to face her. "And jeez—you're bleeding! They shot you!"

He pulled away from her. "It's just the silver." Silver that was burning like a bitch. He drove his claws into his side and Jane blanched.

"Are you crazy? Stop that!" She reached for his hand.

He dropped the silver bullet onto the concrete. It had burned his fingers when he pulled it out. "Got to get the other…" Aidan gritted. He was starting to get weak. Silver did that to his kind. The longer it was in the blood…the more it drained. His claws sliced into his shoulder, but the bullet there had splintered into at least three parts. It was so hard to get it all.

His knees buckled.

He heard the sound of a siren. Shit. This day was truly just an all-around pisser.

"I'll get help for you!" She squeezed his hand. "I'll get an ambulance and some doctors will stitch you right back up."

He didn't need a damn ambulance. Aidan's fumbling fingers found the last chunk of the bullet. He yanked it out, ignoring the burning pain in his fingers and the faint tendril of smoke that drifted into the air. *Silver is such a bitch.* Aidan tossed the silver bullet fragment. Blood coated his fingertips. "No ambulance. No doctors."

Blood slid down her cheek. She'd been cut just above her eye.

"Someone tried to take you. I wasn't the target. *You* were." The sirens were closer. Maybe some good, upstanding citizen had seen the crash and called the cops.

"Why would someone try to take me?"

That was a damn good question. And he intended to find out the answer. He could feel his wounds closing. That was good. Very good.

He saw the flash of blue lights as a cop car rushed toward him.

"You going to tell them that I'm…"

"Yes." She nodded.

His hand rose. His fingers hovered over her cheek. "They'll think you're crazy."

A second cop car raced up to the scene.

"You killed that woman. You killed Melanie," Jane mumbled, her expression so stark.

She didn't understand. "When a vamp comes at you with the bloodlust riding hard…you have two options. Stop the vamp or die."

"Aidan…"

His fingers fell away from her. "If you'd ever had a vamp come at you, you'd understand. They live only to kill. To destroy. Melanie Wagner…someone else killed her outside of Hell's Gate. They left her body out there for me as a message." He had to talk fast.

"A message?"

"That the vamps are coming into *my* city. A war is about to happen. My kind against theirs. It's been a long time coming, and I have to make sure that I keep these streets safe. If the vamps take over, the city will flow with blood. The humans won't have a chance."

Uniformed cops had jumped from the patrol cars.

"Just what is your kind?" Jane whispered.

He offered her a grim smile.

But he didn't get to answer her. The uniforms were right on them. And they were demanding that Aidan raise his hands. Hmmm…maybe that Good Samaritan had reported that shots were fired. Or maybe they thought he'd been the one driving the pick-up. Either way, he slowly lifted his hands, making sure that his claws didn't show.

"I'm a detective!" Jane said and yelled out her badge number even as she lifted her hands, too. "This was a hit and run! Someone…I think someone was trying to abduct me."

Only that someone had failed.

Would they try again? *We'll just see about that shit.*

Jane glanced over at him, suspicion in her eyes. He'd saved her sweet ass. Did that count for anything? Or was she still about to throw him into a cage? Wolves didn't like to be caged.

He waited, vaguely curious about how this would play out. *Call me a monster, sweetheart, I dare you. Call me…*

"This man saved me." She stepped in front of him. "He needs medical attention."

No, he didn't.

"He saved me," she repeated again. Jane glanced over her shoulder at him. The blood still dripped down her cheek. "So we need to help him."

***

That had been a freaking disaster. The van careened down the road, a van that *didn't* contain Detective Jane Hart.

Dammit. Talk about a major screw-up. And now Jane would have cops looking for the van.

"She saw me!" Eugene Woods ranted as he ran a hand through his hair. "I know she did — she's going to have my face on all the TVs in town!"

Yes, the cop probably would…and that was unfortunate. Virginia Malone looked down at the gun in her shaking hands. They were nearing the warehouse area. An area deserted on a Sunday morning. Sighing, feeling actual regret, she lifted the gun, pointed it at Eugene's panicked body, and fired.

Eugene screamed, but the cry came too late. And in the back of the van, he didn't exactly have room to dodge the bullet.

The driver swore and slammed on the brakes. "Warn me when you're doing that shit!" he yelled back to her.

Eugene had grabbed his chest. He was gasping, struggling to live. He wouldn't be living long.

The driver jumped out of the vehicle, rushed around, and yanked open the van's side door. When he opened that door, she shoved Eugene out. He hit the ground.

He didn't get up.

"Locke is going to follow his scent here. He'll find the body." She looked at the driver. He would understand that they had to get away. *It's always us against the world.* "Can you make sure Locke doesn't find us?" Because she couldn't let Locke mess up this job. Too much was riding on it. Too many lives were at stake.

They'd been hired for one reason. The payout—the payout was going to be freaking huge.

The driver stepped closer. Only…he wasn't just the driver. John "Johnny" Smith was her lover. The only person in this whole world that she cared about. The light glinted off his hair. A mix of brown and blond. A little too long. Rough around the edges.

Just like we both are.

Behind him, Eugene was still gasping.

"No one will find you, baby," Johnny promised her. He caught her hand in his, squeezed. She gave him a weak smile.

"H-help…" Eugene. Still talking. Still living.

She'd put the gun down, but her lover reached for it. He turned, aimed at Eugene and said, "Sorry. Nothing personal, but we can't have you pulling us down."

She jerked at the blast. She shouldn't have been startled. She'd known it was coming. If her lover hadn't done it, she would have pulled that trigger herself. It was just...

He won't ever do that to me. And I won't do it to him. We'll protect each other, always. It's what we do.

Johnny glanced back at her, flashing her a wide smile. "We're gonna have to strike fast. Before the detective has a chance to prepare for us."

Yes, yes, they would.

He pulled the door shut again. She crawled toward the front seat.

When he cranked the van, she found herself looking out toward Eugene. He wasn't moving anymore.

"We'll move fast," Johnny said. "And make sure that wolf doesn't screw things up for us. Hell, even with silver in him, the guy didn't stop."

Because Locke was too strong. Not an average wolf at all.

"We have to make sure he isn't around next time," Johnny said, voice thoughtful. "Get the cop alone, and we have her."

Right. Another job done. And what happened to the female cop once they turned her over to their client—that wasn't Virginia's business. She'd get paid, with more than enough cash to get the hell out of Louisiana. She was sick of the swamps. Sick of that town.

Time for someplace new.

After this last job…

Maybe she could take a break from blood and death for a while.

CHAPTER FIVE

Jane didn't know what the hell had just happened. An EMT had checked out the cut above her eye—he'd put some stinging antiseptic on it and slapped a quick bandage over the wound. He'd tried to get her to go to the hospital so she could get thoroughly checked out, but she'd declined. Yeah, okay, so she'd passed out a minute or two—she wasn't about to be sidelined. If she went to the hospital, she'd lose—

"Locke!" Jane yelled because she saw him trying to slip away. Right. Like she was going to let that happen. "Aidan Locke!" She shoved past the EMT and hurried toward Aidan. Aidan was the one wearing a blood-stained shirt, but no one was trying to push him into the back of an ambulance. Maybe because he looked too…scary. Dangerous?

Wild?

He turned back at her call and he frowned down at her. "Go to the hospital."

She'd never liked being told what to do. Her eyes turned to slits. "Just where do you think you're going?" Over his shoulder, she saw the redheaded guy — Garrison. He had a car waiting at the curb and he was pacing nervously beside it.

"I'm going to find the bastard who tried to take you." Aidan spun away from her.

She grabbed his arm and spun him right back. "Not without me you aren't."

He growled. The animalistic sound should have scared her. This whole nightmare she was living should be freaking her the hell out but, actually, Jane felt oddly calm. *Is this shock?* And his growl...

She found it oddly sexy. Which probably meant she had some serious freaking issues she should work out with a shrink somewhere, sometime.

Only that time wouldn't be right then. Because right then — "How are you even going to track him?"

He flashed her that wide smile, the one that showed his sharp, white teeth. Then Aidan tapped his nose. "Once I've got a scent, I can follow my prey anyplace."

Those words actually sounded like a warning. She filed that warning away for later.

"He touched you. He was sweating and scared and his scent got on you. Now I've got him."

"You can do that?" Tracking a man by his scent seemed as crazy and impossible as…having claws sprout from a guy's fingertips.

"Sweetheart, I can do plenty."

She swallowed and glanced to the right. Garrison was staring at her with wide eyes. "I'm coming with you," Jane announced.

"No, you—"

"I wasn't asking." She marched around him and toward the car. "I'm the cop here. The one with the badge. I'm also the one that freak tried to grab. So if I say I'm coming…" She climbed into the passenger seat. "I'm damn well coming."

She heard Aidan swear, but then he stalked around the car and got in the driver's seat. Garrison jumped in the back.

Aidan turned on the ignition and Garrison leaned forward. Shit, had he just sniffed her, too? She whirled, glaring at him.

"S-sorry about last night," he muttered.

"You *shot* at me."

"S-sorry."

"Sorry doesn't cut it when you take a shot at me."

Aidan was driving through the city. His window was down and it seriously looked as if he were following some kind of scent in the air. She probably should have checked with some of the cops on scene before she hauled ass, but Jane hadn't wanted to risk Aidan leaving her, and she knew he would have.

She needed to stay with him because she was afraid if he found her would-be abductor first...

Aidan might kill the guy.

And that wasn't happening. Jane wanted to question the perp. She wanted to find out just why he'd come for her.

If Aidan hadn't been there, what would've happened?

"I'll make it up to you," Garrison rushed to say.

She glared at him before facing the windshield again. "I need to toss your ass in jail."

"Jail isn't for werewolves," Garrison mumbled.

Werewolves. He'd just confirmed her fear. She needed a drink. Maybe three.

"Can't lock us up with the humans," he continued, voice almost sulky. "It doesn't work that way."

So she was figuring out. "Then how does it work? Who punishes you jerks?"

From the corner of her eye, she saw Aidan's tanned, powerful hands clench around the steering wheel. "I do."

The car jerked forward and she threw up a hand to grab the dashboard, balancing herself. "What? So you're some kind of paranormal law?"

"He *is* the law," Garrison rushed to say.

"Garrison," Aidan snapped the name. "Shut the hell up or I'll dump your ass right here."

She was all for dumping the guy but before Jane could goad Garrison into saying more, Aidan had floored the car. For a moment, the crash flashed back through her mind. Screaming metal. Broken glass. The hard, jerking impact—

Aidan's hand flew from the steering wheel and grabbed hers. His fingers linked with hers, holding her securely. "It's all right."

No, it was actually hard to breathe. Her heart was racing too fast. Her whole chest ached.

"You're scared," Garrison supplied from the backseat. "Your scent changed and—"

Aidan slammed on the brakes. "Get the hell out." He kept his strong hold on Jane.

Garrison scrambled from the car. "But I thought I was supposed to be protecting—"

"I've got her. Get your ass back to Hell's Gate." Then he rushed away with a squeal of his tires.

Breathing got easier for Jane. Why, she wasn't sure. But Aidan kept holding her hand and he didn't mention anything about her scent. Her heartbeat slowed even as the car raced through the streets.

"I'm not going to let anyone hurt you."

Her brows lifted. She should probably pull away from him. It wasn't as if she *needed* someone to hold her hand. Never had.

"I don't understand just what's happening with you," Aidan continued. "What you are, but I figure you'll trust me soon enough, once you realize I'm not all bad."

She swallowed. Licked her lips. Then said, "Not all bad? So what…you're *half* bad?"

She saw the curve of his smile. "At least three-fourths."

Jane got the feeling he was telling the truth. Hell, she *knew* he was. This wasn't some safe, easy guy. No *good* guy. He was dangerous. Not human. And he was still holding her hand. "Why?" Jane forced herself to ask as they headed toward the warehouse district. "Why do I matter to you at all? Why care if someone grabs me or not? I'm surprised you didn't just let him haul me away." This part was the absolute truth, and something that she just didn't understand. "It would've been easier for you. After all, I was dragging your ass to jail."

His head turned toward her. That bright stare met hers, just for an instant. "I'm not letting anyone take you from me."

He didn't *have* her. They were strangers. Sure, she *might* have felt some weird attraction to him, but, honestly, she'd always had a weakness for bad boys. Those dark guys who pushed her. Who made her feel the tiniest bit…

Unsafe. Out of control. On the edge.

Yes, right, another issue to deal with when she finally got around to getting some counseling. If she hadn't been so scarred by her previous encounter with a shrink—so very long ago—maybe she would have tried the therapy route.

Maybe not.

"Fuck," Aidan suddenly snarled and he spun the car hard to the right. Her gaze shot around the area and she saw the body—and the blood.

Fuck, indeed.

She barely waited for the car to brake before she was lunging out and running toward the body. One look, and she knew it was the man who'd tried to take her. He was sprawled on the ground, eyes closed, chest bloody.

Her hand flew to his throat. No pulse.

"Two shots," Aidan snapped. "They wanted to make sure he was dead."

"They?"

"The driver of the van. Whoever the hell shot *me.*"

She patted down the dead man's body, but he didn't have any ID that she could feel, and she didn't want to touch him too much—if there was DNA or other evidence on him, she didn't want to destroy it.

"Can you find them?" Her gaze flickered over the dead man's face. An average face. Not handsome. Just…bland. Round chin. Thin lips.

Heavy brows. "The ones who were with him, can you get their scent, too?"

He put his hands on his hips. Turned to the left. To the right. He didn't answer her.

"If they killed him, their scent has to be here, right? You *can* track them." He didn't even need to try jerking her around.

His eyes gleamed. "I can track anyone."

Good. She glanced back at the dead man. A shiver slid over her. *What is happening in this town?*

***

Ditching a werewolf wasn't easy, Virginia knew it. So when they dumped their van and stripped their clothes at the edge of the mighty Mississippi, she knew they were going for a swim.

The water was breath-stealingly cold when she jumped in. And swimming—it was harder than she remembered. This job *sucked*.

The stinky water sloshed toward her mouth as she followed Johnny. They'd get back to land soon. Get clothes that would be waiting for them—they had planned for situations like this one, after all.

Get clothes. Get dry. Get in a new ride.
And get that bitch detective.

The water hit her in the face. Werewolves were such pains in the ass.

***

Night had fallen once again. Aidan stood on the second story balcony of Hell's Gate and looked out at the city. This city — people loved the night here. They loved their drinks. They loved their music. They loved raising some hell.

Only until that hell takes your soul.

He hadn't been able to find the others who'd been involved in the attempt on Jane's life. He'd tracked them to the river's edge. Found their dumped van — and their clothes. Clothes for a woman and a man. They'd jumped — ass naked, from the looks of things — into the river.

Obviously, it hadn't been their first time to flee from a werewolf.

Music pumped below him. He watched the bodies on the street. Men and woman. Young and old. So many careless humans.

And...her.

He'd been aware of her, of course. Her scent had gotten beneath his skin. *In* him, and he didn't know why.

Jane Hart stood in the middle of the street. Her head was tilted back. That dark, thick hair of hers slid loosely over her shoulders. She wore her battered jacket and the jeans that fit her round hips and long legs like a second skin. Her eyes were locked right on him.

She hadn't tried to tell her captain about the big, bad werewolf. She was keeping his secret. For the moment, anyway.

He leaned forward, wrapping his hands around the wrought-iron railing of the balcony as he stared down at her. She made for quite the enticing picture, did she realize that? Such incredibly tempting prey.

A man rushed up behind her, and he put his hand out, reaching for her shoulder.

Every muscle in Aidan's body tensed and he pushed forward onto the balls of his feet, ready to jump over that balcony and rip the guy away from her.

But…

"Not interested," he heard Jane snap as she pushed the guy away. The guy stumbled back into the crowd, and she looked up at Aidan once again.

Just what…he wondered…*would* it take to interest a woman like her? His hand tightened around the balcony's railing.

She gave a grim nod and then started walking toward Hell's Gate. Anticipation flooded through him. He'd puzzled over her that day. He'd reassured some fucking panicked werewolves that she wasn't a threat. That he was handling her. That she was his problem. *His.*

He'd figure out why she was different. He'd take care of her.

Aidan headed down the stairs, and when he reached the landing on the bar's first floor, he saw that she was only steps away from him. She looked small and fragile, human, but he was willing to bet his sexy little detective had a gun tucked under her jacket.

Had she heeded his advice, though? Had she gotten herself some very much needed silver bullets? In this town, if she was truly going to step into *his* world, she'd need to better arm herself.

Knowing that eyes were on him—they always were—he stalked up to her and put his hands on her shoulders.

"All right, Locke," Jane began, her voice sharp. "We need to—"

He kissed her. Mostly because he'd been curious about the way she would taste. He'd wondered how her lips would feel beneath his. He'd wondered…would the connection he felt for her wane with a taste? Or would it grow?

It fucking grew.

Because her lips were parted. His tongue could slip right inside, and it did. He pulled her closer, and her head tipped back. Her hands flew up and grabbed onto his arms, but she didn't push him away, a good thing considering the eyes on them in that club.

Her small nails sank into his arms. And her sweet tongue—it tasted him, too.

The kiss wasn't soft. Wasn't a kind little public peck. He kissed her with a ferocious hunger, as if she were already naked in a bed under him. And she kissed him back with the same wild need.

He hadn't expected it.

Hadn't expected to feel the beast within him practically howling in pleasure because he'd found someone he wanted. Craved.

Someone he *would have.*

His cock shoved against the front of his jeans and since he was holding her so tightly, there was no way Jane missed his hard-on. A few more seconds, and he wouldn't care about their audience. Hell, right then, he didn't care. He wanted her clothes gone. He wanted to taste every single inch of her, and his beast sure wanted to *take.*

She shoved him back.

He went back, but only because he needed to get his splintering control in place. His heart was racing too fast. His breath heaved out, and his claws—he'd barely stopped them from springing out in that crowded bar.

"What in the hell are you doing?" She touched her lips. Lips that were swollen and red from his mouth.

He caught her hand. Laced his fingers through hers. "Missed you, too, sweetheart," he murmured.

Her eyes widened. "What—"

Aidan pulled her through the crowd, heading for his office. People wisely got the fuck out of his way as he passed by them, pulling Jane in his wake. She was muttering behind him, and he even found her mutters cute, which meant he had a huge problem on his hands.

But where Jane was concerned, what else was new?

He let her hand go and shoved open the door to his office. Not really surprising him, Jane froze, not crossing that threshold. Her dark gaze cut suspiciously toward him.

He gave her a smile. A bit hard, considering the way his dick still shoved against his jeans, but he managed a wry, "Come into my lair," for her.

Her eyes slid toward his office. Then back to him.

"Promise," Aidan added. "I won't bite."

Unless you ask. Then I'll be happy to oblige.

CHAPTER SIX

She crossed the threshold. Aidan followed her, making sure to lock the door because he didn't want anyone else coming in after them. The office was sound-proofed, a very necessary precaution when other werewolves were in the area — their super sensitive hearing could mean secrets got spilled.

He wasn't in the mood to spill secrets.

He saw Jane touch her lips again as she paced in front of his desk. "What was that about? Why did you kiss me?"

Propping his shoulders against the door, he leaned back and let his gaze sweep over her. "I want to fuck you."

She stopped pacing.

"I thought the kiss made that pretty clear." He lifted a brow. "Was I too vague? Should I try again?"

"You're not supposed to say things like that." Her voice had gone hoarse.

She obviously had him confused with a human. Her mistake. "What am I supposed to say? That you're beautiful? That you charm me? That I look at you and ache?" His laughter was rough. "Those lines are for mortals, not for me. That isn't the way I work."

After drawing a quick breath, she took a step toward him. "How do you work?"

"I'm a very primitive kind of guy." That was the flat truth. "When I see something I want, I take it."

"I'm not something. I'm *someone.*"

"And I'm not the flowers and candy type. I am the type who'll give you so much pleasure you'll scream until you're hoarse."

She stared at him. "Got it. You're the way too overconfident type."

He laughed. Damn, but she was fun. "You can judge for yourself if I deliver on my promise." Aidan pushed away from the wall and reached for her.

"No!" Jane gave a sharp shake of her head. "Don't touch me! That's just—that's not why I'm here." She frowned at him. "And I think you're just trying to throw me off track."

Maybe he was. Maybe he'd kissed her because he wanted her—he did want to fuck her until she screamed with pleasure—but he also wanted to protect her. Kissing her in public like that, showing the other wolves there just where he stood with her…

No one will hurt her. At least, not until he figured out just what secrets lovely Jane was hiding from him. Secrets would come out, they always did.

"Why are you here?" Aidan asked her, keeping his voice soft.

"Melanie."

His back teeth clenched. "She's gone, and she won't be coming back." *Again.*

"You said she was a vampire."

Aidan tapped his chin. "Is that what I said?" Actually, he thought he'd said that vampires—

"I called the ME. Didn't get into the whole bullshit fight about why he didn't seem to remember seeing Melanie the *first* time she was on his table."

He didn't let his expression alter.

"I just demanded a report," Jane said. "He told me wood splinters were found near her heart, *in* her heart. So I'm guessing she'd been staked, just like a vampire."

They needed to be clear on this. "Melanie Wagner died the night you found her outside of Hell's Gate. Whatever was in that alley—it wasn't her any longer."

Her shoulders squared. "Tell me everything. I want to know it all."

He didn't speak.

"Now you get quiet?" Her hand brushed through her hair. "Tell me what's happening in this town. Vampires, werewolves—let me know what I'm up against! Because I'm not just going to give up. Melanie is *my victim.* My job is to give her justice. I need to stop her killer."

"You're willing to go up against a vampire?"

She swallowed. He caught the change in her scent, the quick flash of fear. His wolf liked that scent, but the man—Aidan didn't like for her to be afraid. In fact, he wanted to make sure that she never experienced another moment of fear for the rest of her life.

"Tell me," Jane said again. "Tell me everything I need to know."

She needed a drink for that. Good thing he kept some whiskey handy. After all, he did own a bar. Without a word, Aidan went to the cabinet near his desk. He grabbed for the whiskey— twenty years old, and a gift he'd gotten when he'd come into power in New Orleans—and he poured her a glass.

She crept closer to him, and when he offered her the drink, her brows furrowed.

"Sweetheart," he drawled, "I'm about to rip your little world apart. Take the drink, you'll thank me for it."

"Like my world hasn't been ripped apart before." Jane swiped the drink from him and then she just tossed it back and downed it in two fast swallows.

"Uh, you were supposed to sip that," he said.

She slammed the empty glass down on the cabinet. "Maybe I wanted more than a sip."

Mental note—the woman could definitely handle her alcohol. She hadn't so much as blinked when she downed the strongest whiskey he had.

Now she was tapping her foot, being all impatient and—still—sexy.

"You're a werewolf," she said.

"Guilty." He flashed her a wide, wolfish smile.

"Do you...do you become an actual wolf?"

"If the mood is right." If he got angry enough and the beast took over. If he let his control go just enough, then yeah, he'd shift. But most werewolves wouldn't go that far. Most *couldn't*. They got claws and sharp teeth, enhanced senses and extra strength. Only a precious few could actually shift. The bloodlines had become too weakened over time. "But I'm the exception, not the rule. For a modern day werewolf, you're mostly looking at a guy with extra strength and amped up senses."

"What about that little talent of making people forget?"

He stared at her.

"I was supposed to forget, remember? Is that something that all werewolves can do, or just you?"

"Most werewolves have a certain talent for…persuasion." Her suspicion was plain to see so he added, "But my gift is stronger. I don't just persuade, I control."

Usually.

Not with her.

"How many werewolves are running around this city?"

"About fifty."

"Jesus."

"They're just like humans—they look like humans. So they get angry or aroused and a bit of their beast side comes out, nothing to worry about. Werewolves actually *want* to stay hidden. They want to live with humans."

She nodded. "Keep talking."

"Werewolves aren't the problem here. I handle them."

"Because you're the werewolf police."

Was she mocking him? He couldn't tell. He poured himself a whiskey and sipped the hell out of it. "I keep my city in line. I make sure no werewolves get too caught up in—"

"*Persuading* humans to do things?"

Yes. Because power could be too addictive. "Persuading. Going wild and using claws. The usual."

She paled.

"It's not the werewolves that humans need to fear. It's the vampires. We've been keeping them out of this city for a long time now." A really hard task considering the way the vamps flocked to New Orleans. Like there was some kind of beacon for them.

"So…" She licked her lips, a quick swipe of that sexy pink tongue. "When you say vamps…are we talking turning-into-bats, burning-in-sunlight, I'll-drink-your-blood creatures? Or are they different, too?"

Vampires were his natural enemies. When a werewolf came around a vampire, the urge to kill exploded within him. There was no reason. There was no sanity.

There was just instinct.

Normally, the fights were brutal. Vicious. Last night, with Melanie, he'd held back. Only because he was strong. He'd felt a stirring of pity for her, and he'd ended her hell quickly.

"They're different," Aidan told her. If she was stepping into this world, she needed to be ready. Better to be armed with as much knowledge as possible. "Sunlight doesn't do anything to them. They don't ignite if the light hits them. They're just—they're stronger at night. The dark gives them strength, so most vamps come out then. They drink blood. They have an insatiable appetite for blood, especially the newly transformed." Pity stirred within him once more as he remembered Melanie. "Those are the ones who don't have a shot. All they know—it's bloodlust. It consumes them. I've seen a newly turned vamp kill his own mother, his father, his sister—and never stop." Not until Aidan had stopped him. He wouldn't ever forget that carnage. The scent of blood had drawn him to the little house at the edge of the swamp. He'd gone in and walked into a bloody nightmare. The vamp had still been feeding on his sister.

A kid, maybe ten or eleven.

The vamp? He'd been hardly more than eighteen. Not even old enough to buy alcohol.

"How does someone become a vampire?"

"A few are born that way." Those were the really scary bastards. The too-powerful vampires that were very, very hard to put down. Now, he was careful as he told her, "Genetic throwbacks, to a time long gone. They age normally unless…"

"Yeah, okay, don't trail off like that."

"Unless they die violently in the prime of their life. Something happens then. A trigger. Adrenaline kicks up their dormant genes, and they come back. They wake up—and they're vampires."

"So some people are just walking around with ticking time bombs inside of them?"

"Very few." Precious fucking few. "Most are made."

"How." Not a question.

"A vamp feeds. Gorges. Takes enough blood to kill his prey, but right before that prey takes her last breath, the vamp gives her some of *his* blood." He knew this had been the way for Melanie. "Those few drops are all that's needed. The prey will die, for just a short while, and wake up to the bloodlust." And he pitied anyone who got in that vampire's path.

"That's why you were at the morgue last night. You knew Melanie would wake up and be a vampire."

He nodded. "I suspected she would. I saw the bite marks on her neck, same as you." But bite marks didn't mean a victim automatically became a vampire. Thanks to advances in science, there were ways to tell if a new bloodsucker would rise. He'd gone and talked to the ME. The plan had been to keep Melanie's body secure until they were *sure* that she would change. Garrison and the rest of the clean-up crew had been given the job of tying up that loose end, only —

I wound up being the one who had to stake Melanie.

Her hand rose and slid along the slender column of her throat. "You put a stake in her heart."

"She was killing a man when I found her. She came at me, fangs bared, eyes wild. I stopped her." His hands clenched into fists. "Or should I have let her keep going? Vamps get an extra power rush when they have werewolf blood. She could have fed from me and then gone out and killed ten humans. Maybe twenty or—"

"Stop it." She spun away from him.

"*I've* been keeping the vamps out of this town for a while now." And he'd been keeping the body count to a minimum. "I'll find the guy who did this to Melanie. I'll stop him."

Jane glanced over her shoulder. "Because you'll stake him?"

"Stake him. Take his head." Another sure fire way to kill a vampire. "Burn his ass to ashes."

Jane flinched.

"Those are the three ways that work best. Otherwise, a vamp will just keep coming at you."

Her shoulders hunched. "Vampires. Freaking vampires."

Don't forget the werewolves, sweetheart.

"That whiskey wasn't even nearly enough for me," Jane said. Slowly, she turned back to face him. "Who else knows about all this?"

He didn't let his expression change.

"I'm guessing there are people in power here who know, right? Government officials in New Orleans? No way everyone is in the dark. No way you *persuade* everyone to forget."

There were some secrets he could share with her, and some he couldn't.

When the silence stretched too long, she let out a frustrated sigh. "And what was up with the dead guy? I mean, I'm supposed to buy that it's just coincidence that right after I meet you and learn about all this craziness — and have to deal with a staked vampire — I suddenly have someone trying to abduct me? Someone who winds up dead, with silver bullets in him."

His gaze flickered to her.

"The ME confirmed that to me. And since your fingertips were burning when you dug the bullet chunks out of your body earlier — a truly crazy thing to do by the way — I'm guessing the person who shot you is the same one who shot the man we found."

He'd figured the same thing. "His friends turned on him because they knew I had his scent. I was tracking him. You'd seen his face — you could ID him. He screwed up, and the guy paid for it with his life."

"His friends? They hardly sound like friends to me." She wrapped her arms around her stomach.

Aidan inclined his head. "They were probably more like business associates."

"Hired to do a job." Her voice lowered as she mused, "And abducting me was the job? Why?"

Now he went to her, taking his time about it. Jane backed up until she hit his desk. Aidan kept closing in on her. He didn't touch her, though, but he leaned in close and put his hands down — palms flat — on either side of her body, caging her between him and the desk. Her scent wrapped around him. Tempted him far too much. "Maybe someone else found out that you were…special."

"Because you couldn't make me forget?" Her words were a husky whisper. "How would they even know that?"

"Someone saw you." It was the only thing that made sense to him. "Probably outside of Hell's Gate, when you first found Melanie. Someone saw you there, and then that same person saw you when you found Melanie the second time. The watcher realized you'd forgotten nothing."

"Someone is stalking me? Is that what you're saying?"

"Someone is…interested in you, now."

Her eyes were so wide and dark. "Melanie's killer."

That was who he suspected. "It would make sense the vamp would want to go back and find his new creation. Only Melanie wasn't out feeding—she'd been put down."

"She wasn't an animal. You don't put down people!"

She wouldn't understand. Jane still didn't grasp the way the paranormal world worked. "She was rabid. She would have killed anyone in her path."

Tears glinted in her eyes. Tears of rage. "She wasn't an animal."

But I am. His hand lifted and stroked over her cheek. A tear had spilled from her eye, sliding in a little twisting path over her skin. He caught that tear on his fingertip. "Be careful," Aidan warned her. "Caring too much can be a dangerous thing."

"Why would her killer want me? So I didn't forget, so I—"

"I told you about vampires who are...born."

"Right, yes. They have to die violently— otherwise, they don't even know they *are* vamps and—"

"There are a few tell-tale signs." His finger stroked over her cheek. Then down, to her lips. Such plump lips. So soft. And her teeth were white and perfect. Not as sharp as his.

Not yet.

"S-signs?" Her breath blew against his fingertip.

"Um." His finger slid away from her delectable mouth. Down, down his hand went until his fingers were curled around her throat. He held her carefully, feeling the fast, desperate beat of her pulse beneath his touch.

"What signs? Aidan, just spill it, already."

"The number one indicator would be...a werewolf's persuasion doesn't work on a born vampire."

Her pulse sped beneath his hand. "What?"

"No matter how strong the werewolf is, a born vampire can resist the persuasion."

He saw the understanding flare in her eyes seconds before she said, "I'm *not* a vampire!"

Not yet, you aren't. Because if she was, he wouldn't be stroking her skin so tenderly. The beast in him would be trying to rip out her throat.

Can't happen. He dropped his hand and stepped back.

"What are the other signs?" Jane asked.

He shrugged.

"Aidan…" Her voice sharpened.

"Do you have any allergies, sweetheart?"

"Everyone has allergies."

"Vamps can't handle garlic. That part of the legend is true."

She swallowed. "Garlic is nasty as hell. So I don't like it on my pizza. That doesn't mean I'm some kind of-of vamp-in-waiting."

No, it didn't.

"It means I just don't like garlic," Jane continued doggedly.

He took a slow breath and could almost taste her. The woman's scent was truly delectable, and he'd come to crave it. *Another dangerous sign.* "I'd suggest a new career path for you," he told her, seriously. "One that doesn't have you running around with a gun all day and possibly dying a most violent death in the line of duty." That would sure lessen her chances of waking up undead.

"I'm not a vampire." She stepped forward.

He didn't back up.

Their bodies brushed.

He wanted her mouth again.

"That's what other werewolves will think, too," he said because she needed to be aware of what would happen. "That you're a vamp-in-waiting." She'd actually hit on the exact term for her kind — or rather, what he strongly suspected her kind to be. "They'll be threatened by you."

"Why? It's not like I'm going out to hunt them!"

"Vampires and werewolves are natural enemies. I told you that already. When a vamp gets around a werewolf, the instinct to attack, to kill, it's a primal force."

"But I'm not a vampire," her voice had turned hushed. She tried to step around him. He just moved to the right and blocked her path. Frustration flashed across her face. "Do you want to kill me?" Jane asked him.

He laughed "Thought we covered this…"

"You want to fuck me."

On the desk would be nice. Or against the wall. If she insisted on a bed, he could do that routine, too. As long as he had *her*.

"If the others see me as a threat, how come I'm still walking around?"

"Because you have my protection. They won't challenge me." They'd be fools to try. There was more he could tell her, more about alpha werewolves and vamps-in-waiting and the strange chemistry that could burn between them.

You want the one thing that will destroy you.

But he'd told her enough. For the moment.

Besides, maybe she wasn't a vamp-in-waiting. Maybe she was something else. Soon enough, he'd know.

"They won't touch me, but the vampire out there—he wants me?"

He can't have you. "Jane—"

Her hip vibrated. Not her hip, her phone. The vibration was followed by a fast blast of rock music. "That's my captain." She yanked out the phone and turned away from him. "Hart. What's happening?"

When her shoulders stiffened, he knew the news wasn't good.

"Where?" A beat of silence. "On my way. Yes, yes, I can be there in fifteen minutes. I understand." She hung up the phone and whirled for the door.

Once more, he blocked her path.

Her hands flew up and pushed against his chest. "Stop doing that!"

"You need me."

"No, what I need is for you to get out of my way. I have a job to do, and I'm going to do it."

He held her stare. He'd easily overheard her conversation with her captain.

Hart. What's happening?

Detective, we've got another one. Another damn blood-covered female victim on the streets.

Where?

Right behind the St. Louis Cathedral.

On my way.

I need you there fast, understand?

Now she was ready to rush off on her own. Ready to find another body. But if this victim truly had been killed just like Melanie... "You know I need to see her, too," Aidan said flatly.

Because he'd be the one who had to stop her, if this victim woke up, too.

He thought Jane would argue. He could practically see the wheels turning in her mind, but after a moment, she gave a grim nod. "Fine, but you don't get in my way."

What? Did she think he was some kind of amateur? "I'm the one who saved that sweet ass of yours earlier today. Don't worry about *me* getting in the way."

Her eyes narrowed. He thought about kissing her again. Instead, he backed away, unlocked the door, and got ready to hunt.

No vamps are going to turn this city into a bloodbath. Not on my watch.

***

"That was easy enough," Virginia Malone said with a quick smile as she tossed the phone to her lover.

"Baby, you are a true chameleon."

Her cheeks tinted. She actually *was* a chameleon, in a really weird way. She couldn't change her face or her body, but she could change her voice, a talent she'd discovered when she'd been an eight year-old-girl living in a foster home and pretty much hating life. She'd been trying to imitate her foster mother's furious yells and suddenly, Virginia hadn't been speaking with some squeaky kid's voice.

She'd been using a deep, smoker's voice, one rich and husky, and her foster mother had stared at her as if she were some kind of demon.

The woman had actually even gone to a priest and tried to get an exorcism done on her.

I wasn't the demon, crazy bitch. Virginia still wasn't sure exactly what she was, but she'd teamed up with Johnny when she'd finally run away from her last foster home — she'd been fifteen then — and she hadn't looked back.

Johnny pocketed the phone she'd tossed his way, a phone that he'd swiped from some captain at the PD. It took balls to pull off a move like that, and her Johnny, he'd never shied away from those types of snatch and grabs. She actually thought he liked stealing from cops, that he got an extra rush from those jobs.

"She'll be here in fifteen minutes," Virginia said, rubbing her arms. It was dark behind the cathedral, and being there, it kept reminding her of that stupid would-be exorcism. Her foster mom had held her down on the bed, and the priest had poured holy water all over her.

Had he even been a real priest? Did real priests nearly drown little girls who were screaming and begging to be let go?

Her gaze slid to the back of the cathedral. At night, with the lights shining on the back of the Jesus statue, a big, intense shadow covered the back of the cathedral. That shadow was in the pose of Jesus, reaching out his hands. And it was...

Intense.

Scary?

Yeah, the whole place was scary.

"If she's coming, then we just have to be ready for her," Johnny said with a nod.

Right. Ready. She was supposed to get on the ground and play the victim, and Johnny was going to wait in the shadows. When the detective got close enough to Virginia...*I'll tase the bitch. Then Johnny will grab her.*

"Do you ever wonder..." Johnny's voice was mild. "Just what you are?"

She laughed at that question, but Virginia could hear the nervousness in her own voice. "I'm a woman, John. You of all people should—"

"I'm talking about the way you can change your voice. There's a reason I just called you a chameleon."

She was growing more nervous by the moment. "What are you talking about?"

"The guy who hired us—he knew what you could do. Said your chameleon talent would come in handy." He shoved his hands into his pockets. "Made me wonder…does he know what you are?"

She wanted him to stop saying that. She was a woman, nothing more, nothing less.

"I mean, you never knew your parents, right? What if they were different, too? What if they had your power?"

Changing her voice was hardly a power. "They dumped me, so it doesn't matter what they had," she threw back. But even as she said those words, Virginia was aware of an ache in her heart. That ache had always been there.

"I'm just saying…vamps are real. We're working for one, aren't we? And werewolves are strolling around like they're freaking bad asses. Other things have to be out there, too. What if you're one of those other things?"

She crouched on the ground. "Showtime is coming. We need to get ready." She was just supposed to sprawl there, with the Taser hidden under her side. Seemed easy enough. Hesitating before she stretched out, Virginia asked, "What if she brings the wolf with her?" The whole point had been to make a grab for the detective when the big guy wasn't around.

"That's why we've got back-up, too."

Wait, what? She hadn't been told about any back-up.

Then she heard it—the soft pad of approaching footsteps. A man was coming from the shadows—big and strong and menacing.

For an instant, Virginia almost forgot to breathe. Their employer. The vampire. Johnny had called him? She wished he'd told her. Because the guy coming toward her...he made her nervous. Her stomach knotted more with every step that he took.

Automatically, she reached for her gun but she didn't have it. Johnny did. Johnny had given her the Taser, and that was the only weapon she had.

Like the Taser will do any good on him.

"She's coming?" Their employer asked.

Virginia forced a nod.

"Good, but...if she's looking for a dead body..." The vampire's voice was deep and dark and oddly sexy. "Don't you think we should give her one?"

It took an instant for his words to sink in. One long, terrible instant. And then she tried to use the Taser. Virginia yanked up her arm as the vampire charged her and she fired at him.

But he was too fast and that Taser, when it hit him, it didn't even make him hesitate. He grabbed her, locked his hand around her neck, and yanked her toward him. Virginia tried to scream…*Johnny! Johnny, help me!* Only no sound came from her. His hold was too tight.

"Johnny asked for a bonus payment," the vamp revealed. "Seems he wants you to live forever…"

"Baby, it's going to be okay." Johnny's voice was high and nervous.

"Since you're bringing me such a special gift, I agreed." The vampire's breath was hot on her cheek. Vampires weren't cold, despite the stories that she'd heard. They were hot. Too hot. As if they'd just stepped out of hell.

Her gaze frantically tried to find Johnny. He had to stop the vamp. This—this couldn't happen.

"It's going to be okay," Johnny said again, but his words sounded hollow, uncertain.

Johnny wasn't usually uncertain. He was cocky, assured. He was the one—the only one who'd ever cared about her. He was—

Fangs tore into her throat. The bite hurt so much, and she could feel her blood spurting out. The vampire was gulping and laughing as she fought him.

Johnny didn't help her.

"Relax, Ginny."

Johnny was the only one who called her Ginny.

"You'll live forever, baby. You'll change, then you'll change me and we'll both have eternity…and a fat load of cash to keep us riding high."

She clawed out with her nails. But the vampire wasn't letting her go. Johnny wasn't helping her. Her neck was wet, her shirt was wet and she was—

Sprawled, on the ground. Her body was twitching, and she couldn't stop those wild trembles. She couldn't lift her hands or roll her body over. She could only stare above her. *He* was there, grinning down at her. Their employer. The vampire who'd just fed on her. "Doesn't hurt anymore, does it?"

Yes, yes it did.

She tried to speak again but only managed a weak moan.

"This will make it *all* better." He shoved his wrist to her mouth. She attempted to turn away, but he just held her locked in a grip that threatened to shatter her jaw.

Then…there was nothing. The vampire backed away. She kept staring straight up. She didn't hear Johnny anymore. Didn't hear his lies about how everything was going to be okay.

She was staring at the back of the cathedral, and she could see the Jesus shadow back there. The arms were reaching up to the sky.

And death—death was reaching for her.

CHAPTER SEVEN

When Jane arrived at the Saint Louis Cathedral, she expected to see the flash of police lights. She thought uniformed officers would be waiting. That police tape would be up.

But…there was nothing.

Aidan crept behind her as she advanced. The cathedral wasn't open for visitors, not then. Jackson Square was closed down for the night. The area was dark and quiet—almost tomb-like. *This isn't right.* Her hand reached for her gun as she began to slip down Pirate's Alley, the narrow street that slid along the side of the cathedral. *If you could even call it a street.* More like an old pathway left over from days long gone. One tied to myth and legend. Ghost stories.

But she wasn't looking for ghosts that night. She was looking for her victim.

And the whole set up was making her nervous.

"I smell blood." Aidan's voice was a bare whisper in her ear. She shivered. She didn't smell blood but if the werewolf said he did…

"A lot of it," Aidan added.

Hell. She couldn't keep inching along when someone was up there, hurt. Why weren't other cops out there?

Her grip on the gun tightened as Jane made her way to the back of the cathedral and then — then she saw the body. A woman. Curled on the ground, with a heavy pool of darkness beneath her. *Not darkness, blood. That's blood.*

The woman was alone. No cops. No Good Samaritan who'd supposedly called in the attack. Nothing.

And she was— "I think she's still alive!" Jane said. Because she'd seen the faintest movement of that woman's chest. At that sign, Jane leapt forward even as Aidan called out sharply behind her. She didn't stop, though. She ran fast toward the fallen woman and when she got closer —

Her neck. Oh, God.

The woman was choking on blood. Her lips were moving as she tried to speak, and her eyes were wide open. Those eyes immediately locked on Jane when she crouched next to the woman.

"It's going to be all right," Jane told her. Oh, jeez, that was such a lie. The woman was bleeding out right in front of her. Jane put down her gun and pressed her fingers over the gaping wound that was the woman's throat. You were supposed to apply pressure in situations like this one, right? Supposed to apply pressure and try to stop the blood flow.

Why isn't an ambulance here? Why isn't someone else here?

"Aidan!" Jane yelled. She didn't see him. The werewolf had been right behind her, but he wasn't there now. "Aidan, I need you! Call an ambulance!"

He didn't answer. Shit. She kept one hand on the woman's throat. The woman—that choking sound the lady made was horrifying. The victim was struggling so desperately to live. Fumbling, Jane pulled out her phone and dialed for an ambulance. The phone clicked and the operator picked up. "I need an ambulance," Jane began. "I'm Detective Jane Hart, badge number three-three-two-eight—"

Something hit her. Not something, someone. Hard and fast. The phone flew from her hand and shattered on the pavement and Jane slammed into the pavement a second after it. She rolled, spinning, and found herself staring down the barrel of her own gun.

"Hello, Detective Hart," said the asshole holding her gun. A stocky, shaggy-haired guy who had just made the top of her enemy list. "I was waiting for you."

His fingers began to tighten around the trigger.

***

Aidan's claws had burst from his fingertips. His teeth had sharpened, and every instinct he possessed was screaming one thing.

Kill. Destroy.

A vampire was close by, and Aidan's beast had sensed the bastard. He could smell the male, could catch the scent of blood and death that clung to him. Aidan knew exactly why the leech had come out that night—

You want Jane.

Too fucking bad. Because Aidan had decided he wanted her, too.

So while Jane rushed to help the victim, Aidan turned to follow the vampire's scent. Every step he took had him sliding away from the cathedral. Away from Jane. And toward the vampire. And every step…it made the man he was lose more control. The beast was reacting too strongly to the vamp. The beast knew its job, knew its instincts.

A vamp was close.

Kill or be killed.

Aidan was the law in that city. He was supposed to be in control, always. And vamps *weren't* supposed to be turning this city into a fucking blood bath.

Another sharp turn and he was in a narrow alleyway. It reeked of garbage and stale beer but the scent that dominated the others—blood.

Vampire.

Mocking laughter drifted in the wind. "You think you've got me."

Aidan could see the vampire. A male. Close to Aidan's height. Broad shoulders. Powerful build. His eyes were green, bright, and his face was oddly familiar to Aidan.

Where have I seen this undead bastard before?

The vampire lifted his hands, as if to say…*Come and get me.* Aidan realized then why the vampire's scent had been so strong. The vamp was bleeding. He'd cut himself and then used that blood trail to draw Aidan right to him. The wolf Aidan carried hadn't been able to resist that scent. It had launched him straight into attack mode.

The rush of the shift swept over Aidan. The beast knew his job, all right, and he was going to do it. Bones began to pop and snap. Aidan could feel the power surging just beneath his skin.

"A throwback, are you?" Now the vamp was interested. "Oh, but your blood will give me a nice boost." Then the vamp leapt toward Aidan. He grabbed Aidan and jerked his head to the right, baring his neck.

The beast inside of Aidan snarled and the man—well, it was Aidan's turn to laugh. His claws sank into the vamp's chest. The vamp yelled and jerked back.

Aidan wasn't done. He was just getting started. "Time for your trip to hell." There was a reason his club was called Hell's Gate. He was the one who sent bastards like this vamp on to their next freaking life.

Primitive instinct built, blocking out rational thought.

Vampire. Kill. Destroy.

The scent of the vamp's blood was stronger now—now that Aidan had sliced the guy open. And the vamp hadn't fought back. Still wasn't fighting back. It was almost as if he wanted to keep bleeding. As if he wanted—

Me, here, with him.

While Jane was...

A gunshot rang out.

Aidan's head snapped to the right.

He wanted to go to her. And his wolf—

He wants to kill the vampire.

"Always wondered," the vamp murmured. "Who has the control? The man or the beast? Bet you fucking hate being owned by a dog."

Another shot ripped through the night.

"Guess what happens..." The vamp's words were such a damn taunt. "If that sweet piece of ass dies violently..."

He didn't have to guess. Aidan whirled and lunged toward the mouth of that alley.

But the vamp had moved — with freaking way too fast speed — and was in front of him. Vamps and alpha werewolves both were gifted with enhanced speed. The vamp shoved his hand against Aidan's chest. "If she dies violently," he said, flashing fangs. "She's mine."

"Not going to happen," Aidan gritted out. Speaking with a man's voice was hard. The words were little more than a rough growl.

"Let's just see about that." Then the vamp lifted his hand — and Aidan saw the glint of silver. Like that was supposed to impress him. The knife sliced toward him, but Aidan caught the vamp's hand and held it in a steely grip.

Then Aidan bared his teeth.

"Animal," the vamp sneered. "That's all you ever — "

Aidan snapped the guy's wrist. Screw staying civilized — time for a blood battle.

**

When the first bullet had thundered out of the gun, Jane had been surging up, desperate to stop the shooter.

But the bullet hadn't hit her. Because *someone* had tackled the shooter right before he'd fired. That same someone was rolling around on the ground with the attacker, and Jane caught the distinct sound of a growl.

Only…that wasn't Aidan's. Her eyes squinted as she tried to see in the dark. She rushed forward and scooped up the gun—*her* gun—that had been dropped in the whole tackling moment.

"Freeze!" Jane yelled.

The tangle of limbs that was two men—they kept fighting.

"Freeze!" She yelled again. And then—she fired. The blast shocked the men and they finally listened to her. Both of them froze. She saw her rescuer's face in that instance and surprise ripped through her. Garrison? That guy had come to her aid?

She pointed her weapon at the other fellow. "Get to your feet or I will shoot you right now."

He laughed. "Cops aren't supposed to shoot unarmed men."

Cops also weren't supposed to get ambushed behind dark cathedrals. "*Get up!*"

He rose and Garrison shadowed him. Were Garrison's claws out? It looked as if they might be.

"Garrison, that woman needs help," Jane said. "She's still alive." *For the moment.*

Garrison took a step toward the woman on the ground, then he hesitated.

"She needs help!" Jane yelled. *Move!*

"Vamp blood," Garrison mumbled. "It's too late."

What? No, no, it wasn't. "Garrison, either hold the gun on that jerk or put your hands on the victim and stop the bleeding! Help me!"

Garrison lurched forward. He bent over the woman. From the corner of her eye, Jane saw him put his hands on the woman's throat. His claws were *definitely* out, and he seemed to be shaking. His whole body was trembling.

"V-vamp blood…" He said again, voice thickening.

"That's a mistake," the man who'd attacked Jane snapped. "He can't be around her. Do you have any freaking clue how werewolves react to vampires?"

So Aidan had told her. "You're no vamp." If the guy was, then Garrison would probably still be locked in some kind of epic death battle with him.

The fellow laughed. "Nah…The boss is, and he's got your wolf. Getting himself a pelt right now. Then you'll be alone. Easy pickings." He glared toward Garrison. "Should've been alone…didn't see that dick coming…"

She hadn't seen Garrison, either, and she had no clue why he'd followed her but…

Getting himself a pelt. Her attacker's words echoed in her ears.

Not all werewolves could shift. Aidan had told her that, too. He could, though. He was one of the few and…*oh, God.* "Garrison! Where is Aidan?"

"I don't think she's going to make it…" Garrison muttered.

"She has to!" Because if the victim had been given vamp blood and she died right then…

She'll come back. And I can't kill her. Killing a victim like that just seemed too many twisted shades of wrong to her.

Her gaze flew around the dark area. "Aidan?" No answer from him.

Her attacker was laughing.

"Aidan!"

No way was anyone taking his pelt. Right. Right?

"She's—she's not breathing!" Garrison called out. "What do I do? *What do I do?*"

Jane wrenched her gaze to him.

The woman had gone deathly still. There was no more terrible choking noises. No more gasps. Nothing. Jane rushed to her.

And the attacker's thudding footsteps sounded too loudly in her ears. He was fleeing, just leaving that woman behind to die.

"Stop!" Jane shouted. She lifted her gun. "Stop!"

He didn't stop.

She could give chase. She could shoot. Or she could try and help that woman on the ground…

Victims matter. Victims come first.

Garrison raced past her, going after the fleeing man. And Jane reached for the woman. The victim's body was still warm. Her eyes were open and she—

The woman gasped.

She's still alive.

A siren blasted in the distance.

***

"Aidan?"

That was Jane's voice. Calling him. Needing him.

"Aidan!"

But he wasn't a man any longer. He was a wolf. Fully shifted, attacking. The vamp was far stronger than he'd expected—obviously not some newly turned human. The vamp had the enhanced strength that came from being born, not made, and he wasn't going down easily.

"I planned this, you know," the vampire said as he and Aidan circled each other.

Aidan snarled back at him.

"I wanted to get her out into the open. Lovely Jane. I needed her alone, though, away from you." Slashes covered his chest. Slashes from Aidan's claws. "And those gunshots tell me…it's time to collect my sweet prey."

Kill. Destroy. Take—

Other scents hit him then. More vampires. Closing in. Coming in fast.

The wolf howled as fury grew in him.

"Didn't think I'd come alone, did you?" The vampire taunted. A sliver of moonlight fell on his blond hair. "It's not as if wolves are the only ones with packs."

Aidan spun toward the mouth of the alley. Three vamps were there. Men, young. Fangs bared. They—

Smell fresh.

Newly turned. And too eager to attack. All three of them launched at Aidan at the same time. He leapt right back at them. Fangs and claws and snarls filled the air.

"And I'm done here." The blond vamp's voice was satisfied. "Time for Jane to meet her fate."

The vampire ran from that alley.

And Aidan...*Kill. Destroy.*

The man couldn't control the beast, not anymore. The three new vampires screamed as they died.

***

EMTs raced toward Jane. "Hurry!" she yelled. "The victim is barely alive." But the victim *was* still living. She didn't know where Garrison had gone or where Aidan was—she needed the victim to get help so that she could give chase after those werewolves.

One of the EMTs swore when he got a look at the injured woman.

He took over for Jane, and she grabbed his shoulder. "Keep her alive," she ordered him.

His expression said he didn't know if it would be possible.

It had better be.

She pushed up to her feet and ran past the ambulance. Garrison had gone to the right when he'd given chase. She needed to get after him.

"Detective Hart!"

A uniform was shouting for her.

"Detective Hart, what is happening—"

"Suspect fled on foot," she yelled back to him. "Adult male, stocky build, about six feet tall, hair came to his shoulders, and he was wearing dark clothes and—" *Being pursued by a werewolf.* "He fled on foot! I'm going after him!" She didn't stop to say anything else. Her focus was already on the bastard she *would* catch. The man who'd lurked in the shadows while a woman died.

Her feet pounded over the pavement. She cut across the street, and when she came to a seemingly dead end, she zipped down a nearly invisible alley and through an old, broken down building. *Must have come this way. No other choice.*

But once she burst out of that building, Jane stopped, glancing to the left, to the right.

Where was Garrison? The road diverged up ahead. Crap. She was sure she'd come the right way so far, but…*now where do I go?* Her breath sawed in and out of her lungs as her heart raced.

Howls reached her ears. The actual full-on howls that a wolf would make. Her blood chilled and she gripped her gun tighter.

Then, stiffening her spine, she ran toward those howls. Aidan had said that not many wolves could do a full-on shift, so maybe that was just Garrison really getting his beast on, in a non-shifted way, but howling way and—

Blood. Bodies. Death.

She staggered to a stop in front of another too-thin alley and Jane stared straight into the too-bright blue gaze of a wolf. A freaking *massively* sized wolf.

"Oh, shit," she whispered as the wolf crouched low to the ground. Its fangs snapped together and it lunged at her. "Aidan? *Aidan?*"

The beast slammed his paws into her chest. She went down, but she didn't drop her gun. She kept that weapon, a weapon that was loaded with silver bullets, per Aidan's instructions, and when they crashed to the ground, she almost pulled the trigger.

Almost…

Despite what Aidan thought, she wasn't gun happy. Quite the opposite. She only shot when there was no choice.

There was seriously almost no choice.

But he hadn't sank those fangs into her throat, and though she could feel his hot breath on her cheek, he wasn't attacking.

He was...sniffing her.

I sure as hell hope I don't smell like a vampire.

Three bodies were on the ground. There was blood on the werewolf's mouth. She *should* shoot. His gaping mouth came closer to her throat.

Tears stung her eyes. "I'm sorry." Because she was getting out of that alley. She was—

Something was snapping. Popping. *He* was snapping and popping. His bones were reshaping. The fur on the beast's body seemed to be melting away. He fell away from her and she scuttled back, moving like a crab as she watched him in horror. The wolf's body had contorted, elongated, and the form of a man reappeared. A man with long, strong legs. Muscled thighs. A broad chest, a rippling stomach, and chiseled abs. His broad fingers grabbed for the ground as his claws vanished, and the muscles in his arms bulged as he drew in deep, gulping breaths. "Next time..."

He was naked. Completely naked.

Right. That made sense, though. If he'd turned into a wolf, his clothes had probably gotten shredded during the shift. But what in the hell was she supposed to do with a naked man right then? Cops were going to be swarming this area soon.

"Next time," he said, his voice thick and rumbling, "shoot me."

"Figured you'd been shot enough in the last twenty-four hours," she said.

His head turned. He peered over one broad shoulder at her. His gaze was still that eerily bright blue. "Shoot me. If I ever come at you again…"

"You didn't go for my neck with your uber sharp teeth. You just got all sniffy." She marched away from him and toward the bodies. *Don't focus on the naked werewolf. Focus on the bodies.* "Now what in the hell happened here?"

"Ambush. Vamp lured me out here with his blood. Thought he was planning a grab on you."

Staring at the remains on the ground had bile rising in her throat. So much blood. And they'd been killed by—claws.

Aidan's hand curled around her shoulder and she flinched away from him.

"Easy." His voice was still a rumble. "They weren't human. They were vamps. If you look at their teeth, you'll see that."

She'd already noticed the extra-long incisors.

"A vamp's fangs sharpen when they're in their predatory mode. And when they die, they stay that way."

She kept her gaze *up* on his face. And not on other things. *Dead bodies. Naked werewolf.*

"Their job was to kill me," Aidan rasped. "Too bad for them, I wasn't in the mood to die."

"So you took out all three of them? By yourself?"

His lips twisted in disgust. "They were newly turned. Doing the Vampire Master's bidding. He got away."

Um, okay, that made one against four. And he'd still taken out three vampires?

So he was as kick-ass as he'd wanted her to believe.

"His buddy got away, too," she said, turning from the bodies on the ground. Aidan had said they were vampires, but…they'd been people before they were turned. They'd had lives. Families. And staring down at them hurt her heart.

I need to find the vampire who is turning these people. I have to stop him.

"His buddy?"

Her gaze cut over him. "We have got to find you clothes."

"What buddy?"

"The one who was waiting with the victim. He tried to attack me, but your pal Garrison stepped in." She gave a wry shake of her head. "This time, Garrison saved my hide instead of aiming to take my life."

Aidan grunted. "Cause that's his job. He's supposed to protect you."

He was? Since when?

"Company," Aidan suddenly barked as he whirled toward the entrance to the alley. She got a quick view of his ass — nice — and then he was surging toward the man heading their way. A man in a police officer's uniform. A man who was — crap, Mason. It figured they'd run into him because this area was on Mason Mitchell's beat.

"Freeze!" Mason yelled. "Hands up! Hands — "

Aidan didn't freeze. He rushed forward and locked his hands around Mason's shoulders. She was surprised Mason's gun didn't go off but then Aidan started talking…

His words were so low. She couldn't hear them clearly so she inched forward and then she caught the order of… *You never saw me. I wasn't here. Go back to the main road. Search to the left.*

Mason just nodded, face a bit slack, then he turned and left the alley.

Her goosebumps were way worse. Jane hadn't signed on for this — mind control. Dead vampires. Werewolves who lost their clothes.

Aidan glanced back at her.

"You shouldn't do that." Anger stirred within her. "It's not right to play with people's minds."

"You wanted me to let him call in back-up? Wanted me to explain why I'm naked with three dead men?"

"The bodies—"

"*My* city, remember? When it comes to the paranormals, I'm the law. My pack will take care of the vampires."

But would his pack give them justice? "They were humans once."

Humans who might not have asked to be changed.

"They'll get justice when I track that Master Vamp who used them to make his own army." He glowered at her. "Now where is Garrison?"

I wish I knew. "He gave chase. When the other guy fled from the cathedral, Garrison went after him." She brushed by Aidan, marching to the front of the alley. "Look, you need to get the hell out of here before anyone else arrives." *Get out, get clothes, and let me figure this shit out.*

"No way," Aidan said flatly. "You're the target. That bastard wants you."

"Me?"

"He wants you to die, Mary Jane."

"Jane," she whispered. "Everyone always calls me Jane. Not Mary Jane, got it?"

"He wants you to die, and I'm not letting that happen."

"*I'm* not letting that happen, okay? I know how to protect myself, and I will." She also had a job to do, one that didn't involve her cowering because she was afraid some big bad *vampire* was coming for her. "You have to get out of here, do you understand? I don't want you playing mind games with cops." And if they all saw the naked werewolf… "Just *go*. We'll meet up later."

"You think I'm leaving you on your own?"

She shook her head. "I think we're wasting time. Cops are here." She could hear them closing in. "Get out of here. I get that you're some kind of paranormal boss, but I'll handle the humans."

Voices rose, coming toward them. More cops. "Go," she said again.

"I'll be close."

"Yeah, well, be dressed while you're close." She rushed out to face the cops. She would have to stall them, if she could, and they were coming in fast. More uniforms who must have given chase after she'd left the cathedral. "Hurry," she said as she glanced over her shoulder at Aidan.

Only…he wasn't there. The alley—a dead end alley—was empty. There was a wall at the back of that alley. A big, brick wall. Had to be at least fifteen feet high.

"Detective Hart!"

She sucked in a deep breath and whirled to face the cops. "Secure the scene," she barked. "Get the ME out here, *now*. And we need to make sure every available unit is on the streets—our killer is out there. He is close, and we have to find him."

Before more blood filled the streets.

CHAPTER EIGHT

Garrison Aimes chased his prey, rushing fast through the city. For a human, that asshole he was after could sure move fast.

But I'm faster. He was catching up. He could see the fellow up ahead, rushing through the crowd.

Garrison pushed people out of his way. He followed his prey around the nearest corner and then—

The scent of a vampire hit him. Strong. Overwhelming. Blood and death, and his beast bellowed within him. Garrison stopped his chase and spun around. His gaze scanned the street. His nostrils flared. The vamp was close. *Hunting me?*

He knew he was supposed to catch the human who'd been after Detective Hart. Distantly, he heard the guy's thudding footsteps as he kept racing away. But Garrison wasn't following him any longer. Instead, he was tracking the vampire. Following that blood scent.

Vampires…they'd killed his parents. Nearly killed *him*. He'd been just a kid. A dumb, helpless kid who hadn't even realized he was any different from his friends. He hadn't even known he *was* a werewolf, not until that day. Not until claws had burst from his twelve-year-old hands as he fought to defend himself. They hadn't expected him to fight back.

Maybe that was why he'd lived.

Since then, his grandfather had been grooming him, always training him—*kill or be killed*. The old werewolf motto. Only the fierce survived.

He guessed that his parents hadn't been fierce enough.

His hands curled at his sides as he followed that vampire's scent. An ambulance rushed by him, its lights flashing in a sickening swirl. New scents hit him as that ambulance careened down the street. Blood and death. And…

Her. The woman who'd been broken on the ground. Her scent was different. Earthier. Richer.

Her blood was still on his hands. He'd tried to help her. As his fingers had become soaked in that woman's blood, Garrison had remembered that he'd tried to help his mother in the same way. He'd put his hands on the wounds, those terrible wounds that had ripped open her throat, and he'd tried to help.

But he'd been too late.

The ambulance was gone.

The vampire's scent was strengthening. The guy was coming closer. Moving fast. *Does he think to hunt me?* Garrison would prove he wasn't weak, not the runt of the litter, the one who'd survived by chance.

He stepped off the curb and then—

A motorcycle revved. His head whipped up and he saw a black clad figure on that motorcycle, hurtling toward him. The vampire wasn't on foot—he was on a freaking motorcycle, and he was coming straight for Garrison.

Garrison didn't jump out of the street. His beast wouldn't let him. The vampire was coming at him, in a straight and deadly game of chicken.

He wouldn't back away.

His claws burst from his fingertips. A snarl lifted his lips.

The motorcycle's engine roared, louder and louder, coming closer and—

He could smell the scent of burning rubber. Could see the green gaze of the vampire. It was a gaze he'd seen before. A face he'd seen before.

Fucking murderer.

His control vanished in that instant. The past rose around him, so much fury and hate and pain. He screamed as he ran toward that motorcycle, toward that bastard who'd haunted his nightmares and robbed him of a family. He

screamed with his hate and he knew he'd battle
to the death right then. He would *not* stop.

The motorcycle sped toward him, faster and
faster. He leapt into the air, trying to hurtle over
the front of the bike. He swiped his claws across
the vampire's chest—a chest that was already
bloody but the motorcycle's front wheel slammed
into Garrison, and he fell back. The motorcycle
barreled down onto him, and he rolled quickly,
spinning, but the wheels caught his left leg and
he heard the bone snap.

The motorcycle flew past him.

He heard humans gasping and yelling.
Others had seen the attack. He should get up. His
hands pushed against the street. Pain throbbed
and burned in his smashed leg.

The motorcycle braked.

His head lifted and he saw the vampire turn
his bike around. Turn around and then gun the
ride again—*he's coming at me once more.*

Garrison tried to stand, but his leg gave out.
The humans close by were still screaming, but
none of them were helping. None of them were
coming to help drag his ass out of the street.

Because they don't want to die.

He started crawling. He hauled his damn
body and realized his leg was far more savaged
than he'd realized. Not just broken, bones were
shattered.

The roar of that motorcycle was close. Too close.

Then…Jane was there. She jumped in front of him and lifted her gun. "Everyone get down!" Jane yelled.

The humans were huddled on the street corners. They pretty much *were* already down.

"Stop!" Jane shouted at the motorcycle driver.

He didn't stop. If anything, the vampire just drove faster. *Of course the freak is coming faster, he wants her to die, too.*

And she was going to die. Die while trying to…

Help me.

"Not…worth it," Garrison yelled. "Go!"

The motorcycle was too close. Jane fired. The bullet slammed into the front tire. The woman had some fucking good aim.

She fired again, another direct hit and the bike spun to the right as the driver lost control. The vamp jumped from the bike as it turned onto its side, sending a bright spray of sparks into the air as the metal scraped across the street.

Jane spun back to him. She grabbed his arms and dragged Garrison out of the street. She was groaning with the effort, and some of the other humans finally came forward and helped him.

"What in the hell just happened?" Jane demanded once he was pressed to the side of a nearby building's wall. "What were you doing? Death wish much?"

Only some days.

He peered over her shoulder. The motorcycle had stopped its deadly slide. It now lay in the middle of the street, twisted, on its side.

The driver…

"Where is he?" Garrison demanded, ignoring the pain that burned in his leg.

Sirens were blaring. Uniformed cops pushed their way through the humans. Why did humans huddle so?

"He's crumpled in the road," Jane said. "I'm getting him, don't worry." She slapped her hand on his shoulder. "And…don't look at your leg, okay? Just…don't."

Hell.

She jumped up and ran back to the street. He glanced down at his leg.

Sonofabitch.

***

Jane pushed through the crowd. Garrison's leg was a twisted mess of bone and muscle. The motorcycle had obviously driven right over it, and she didn't know what the hell was going to happen to him. *Don't let him lose the leg. Don't.*

She turned to the street — but the man who'd been on that motorcycle wasn't there. The street was empty.

Jane rushed out and spun around, looking to the left and the right. She wished she had a shifter's nose so she could track the guy. Maybe sending Aidan away hadn't been the best plan ever. Hell. She could sure use him right then.

As she stood there, Jane felt as if someone was watching her. The hair on her nape seemed to stand on end. *Hunted.* That was exactly how she felt.

Only Jane didn't want to be the prey. She wanted to be the hunter.

Hurrying, she made her way back to Garrison's side. A cop in uniform was trying to help him. She slid in close to Garrison and whispered in his ear, "Do you still smell the vamp?"

Sweat dripped down his face. "Gone." Anger beat in that one word.

Dammit.

"But he'll…he'll be back." Garrison's head turned and he stared into her eyes. "For…y-you."

***

Aidan didn't spend much time in hospitals. He had a normal clean-up crew who came for any wounded or dead werewolves. But this time…this time was different.

He stalked through the halls of the hospital. Human doctors couldn't help Garrison. When they tried, they'd just do more damage. He walked briskly forward, two of his most trusted pack members right at his heels.

Graham Faulkner, his second in command and the manager at Hell's Gate, was tall and lethal. His blond hair was shoved back from his high forehead and a slashing scar cut across his cheek.

Paris Cole, Aidan's right-hand man, didn't so much as stalk as the guy glided. He was a werewolf who moved like a jungle cat. His dark coffee skin was a sharp contrast to his light, golden eyes, and women were often charmed by the guy. They didn't see his danger, not until too late. Paris's pretty boy features tended to blind them. They should learn that death could look a lot like a GQ ad.

Paris and Graham didn't speak as they followed him. They'd gotten the call about Garrison, and about the Master Vamp who was playing in their town. They were just as pissed as Aidan, and when werewolves were pissed…

It is never a good thing.

He turned to the right and ignored the nurse who jumped up and shouted, "You're not allowed back here!" Aidan just kept walking right past her and into the emergency room.

"Of course, we're allowed, sweets," Paris said, his voice all charm. "We've got family back there."

Family. Pack. To werewolves, it was always the same thing.

Aidan shoved open the swinging doors in front of him. Pandemonium. Chaos. Not just one room — but a series of beds housing about half a dozen patients. The patients were sectioned away from each other by thin, white curtains.

"I'm not losing my freaking leg!"

He didn't need Garrison's shout to find the guy. Aidan had already been following the younger wolf's scent toward the last curtain. He yanked it to the side and saw Garrison — too pale, too weak, and with one hell of a mess that was left of his leg. Two doctors whirled at Aidan's approach.

"You can't be here!" One sputtered. "Get out, you —"

Aidan wrapped his hand around the guy's shoulder. "Other patients need you. Go see about them."

The guy nodded and walked off.

"What the hell?" The other doc demanded, a guy wearing green scrubs and with a face mask concealing his mouth and chin. "You can't —"

Aidan stepped in front of him. "You never saw this patient. You never saw me. Go help someone else."

The man's brown eyes blinked once, twice, and he nodded.

Jane would be pissed with him. She'd say he shouldn't control humans.

Jane.

She was in that emergency room. Aidan could smell her. Her sweet scent blocked out the blood and antiseptic and stirred him deep inside. She wasn't hurt—no blood from her. But she was afraid.

"Get Garrison out of here," he ordered Paris and Graham. Because they always took care of their own kind, and in order to save Garrison's leg…hell, they'd have to be very, very careful.

Garrison couldn't heal like Aidan. His power was so much lower and his body would take a much longer period of time to repair itself. But he *could* heal. Provided human docs didn't screw him up by inserting bolts into his leg—or by cutting the leg off.

Once they had him out of that hospital and in werewolf hands, Garrison could be given some of Aidan's blood to help with the recovery. Aidan's blood was always kept on hand in case any of the pack members were severely injured.

The others stepped forward. Aidan turned away. Jane's scent was calling to him. She was—

"It was him."

Aidan's shoulders stiffened at Garrison's words.

"It was the vamp who killed my parents. "

He looked back at Garrison. "Are you sure of that?" He'd thought the vampire had looked familiar...and if it really was that bastard...

Thane. Thane Durant. He wasn't some newbie vamp. Thane Durant was an ancient with one hell of a lot of power. There was a reason vamps like him earned the title of *Master.* Power flowed through the guy's whole body. Every kill increased his strength. And he loved draining werewolves. Loved causing chaos.

And I have wanted to end his sorry existence for years. Ever since Aidan had rushed into Garrison's home and seen the carnage left in the vamp's wake.

Thane had gotten away that night, and Aidan had only caught a fleeting glimpse of the bastard.

Pain had darkened Garrison's face. "As if...as if I could forget that..." Garrison said, breath heaving as Paris pulled him from the bed. "It was...him."

Aidan nodded. "I will deal with him."

"N-no...my family, my — "

Aidan crossed to him in an instant. "How did you survive tonight?"

Garrison's gaze dropped.

"You think I haven't heard? You think I don't know? *She* saved you." Jane. Putting herself at risk. "He was coming at her because she became a shield for you. You were supposed to protect her, but she saved your hide." And she could have died.

"My family —"

"Get him out of here," he snapped again because the scent of Jane's fear had just ratcheted up higher. "*Out.*"

Then he whirled and rushed back through the maze of the ER. And then…another door. Another nurse who tried to get in his way and —

Jane.

She came to him. She shoved open swinging doors and froze when her gaze locked on him. Her dark stare was stark. Desperate. And she just looked so hurt and sad. He wanted to pull her close. To never let her hurt again.

This woman…she was dangerous to him. Too dangerous.

"She didn't make it," Jane said. Her hand pushed against the heavy curtain of her hair. "I thought…I was praying…" Her hand fell limply to her side. "Too much blood loss. She fought, but there was…the doctor said he couldn't save her."

He wasn't the sort to comfort. Gestures like that weren't part of his life yet he found himself walking to her. Lifting his arms and wrapping them around her shoulders. She was stiff at first, but then she leaned into him. His head lowered over her and Jane's soft hair brushed against his cheek.

"I wanted to save her," she said, as if confessing a deep, dark secret. "Now…" Her hands had closed around his shirt, balling the material into her fists. "Now what am I supposed to do?" Her voice was so low, just for him alone. "Kill her, *again,* when she wakes up as a vampire?"

He wasn't sure she would wake up. Maybe she'd be one of the lucky ones who just died. But since Thane did enjoy his chaos…*odds are that he turned her. I bet Thane gave her his blood. The bastard seems to be making an undead army.* His lips brushed over her cheek. "She isn't human any longer. That means she isn't your problem." He stepped back. "You do nothing. I'll handle everything."

Alarm flashed in her eyes. "No, don't!"

There was no choice.

"Aidan, there has to be another way."

He caught her hand in his. Such a small hand. He lifted her fingers to his mouth and brushed a soft kiss over the back of her hand. "There isn't. She's *gone*, sweetheart. If she rises, only a monster will be in her place."

She pulled her hand from his and moved, putting herself in front of those swinging doors as if she were physically blocking him from getting to the vampire. "How long will it take? When will she turn?"

He glanced over his shoulder. If they weren't careful, others would overhear. "Not immediately. It usually takes a few hours." Long enough for the bite's power to spread through her body. To reanimate her. She'd be transferred to the hospital's morgue, and there…well, he'd make sure she didn't have the chance to hurt anyone else.

"You can't do this," Jane whispered.

It was what had to be done.

A group of nurses and doctors swept out of the ER. He smelled the blood on them.

One of the doctors stopped near Jane's side. "I'm sorry, detective."

So am I, sweetheart. Because he would do what was necessary. If that woman woke up, she would be a dangerous threat. One that had to be stopped.

He *would* stop her. Aidan turned and left Jane with the doctor.

***

Johnny Smith waited outside of the hospital, hiding in the shadows. Every time an ambulance approached and the flash of those swirling lights lit up the night, he tensed.

Ginny was in that hospital. The docs wouldn't save her, at least, he didn't think they would. She'd looked…bad. So bad, on the ground. For an instant, he wondered if he'd done the right thing. But…

Eternity. Once she changed, she'd have eternity. They wouldn't have to worry about growing old and their bodies falling apart on them. His Ginny would always be strong. *He* would always be strong, once she turned him. They'd be together.

Forever.

She'd just…she'd been so pitiful on the ground, choking, twitching.

She'll be strong now. He skirted around to the back of the hospital. His gaze slid to the entrance for staff. He hurried inside, taking time to grab some green scrubs from a locker and don them as quickly as possible. He knew where they'd be taking Ginny. As soon as they were done with her…

His steps quickened as he headed to the morgue. He'd be waiting on Ginny to arrive.

When he entered the morgue, the place was cold. Icy. And there was some big, fat asshole who roused at his approach. "What's happening?" The guy asked, frowning. "Where's your ID badge?"

Johnny reached under the edge of his borrowed scrub even as he flashed a smile at the fellow. "Right here." Then he moved fast, bringing up his knife and shoving it right into the guy's throat before the fellow could make a single sound.

The guy's thick, big fingers tried to rise up and fight him, but Johnny just jerked the knife hard to the right. Then he let the dumbass fall. Blood poured from the wound. He stared at it a moment, thinking. Maybe Ginny would like that blood, once she woke up.

He grabbed the guy's legs and started dragging him. The man grunted, still alive. Well, he wouldn't be alive for long. Johnny dumped him behind the desk. Then he just sat down in the man's chair, the wheels rolled back beneath his weight, and he made himself comfortable. Soon enough, Ginny would be coming right to him.

He couldn't wait to see her again.

***

When Aidan stalked down the hospital corridor, Jane watched him with desperate eyes. The victim *was* dead. She knew that—but, killing her again? No way did that seem right.

Her breath eased out slowly. She had to stop Aidan. To do that, she'd have to buy herself some time. How *much* time, well, that just depended on how good Aidan was with his mind control routine. "Stop that man!"

Everyone in the hospital turned to glance at her—everyone, including the security guard and the two uniformed cops who were near the emergency room exit.

Even Aidan glanced over at her.

She lifted her badge, like they needed the reminder of who she was. "Stop him!" She stared straight at Aidan. "That man needs to be taken down to the police station for questioning."

There was a roomful of people watching them. Surely he couldn't do that mind control mojo on them all at the same time?

The uniformed cops hurried toward him.

"Take him in your patrol car," Jane instructed. "Get him out of here."

One guy locked a hand on Aidan's shoulder. When Aidan tensed, so did Jane. *Don't pull out your claws. Don't.*

He didn't. He *did* glare at her. "This isn't what you want to do."

No, it wasn't, but she didn't have too many options and just stopping the guy at that moment was right at the top of her list. Stop him, distract him, and then she could try and handle their victim/vamp-to-be. Jane nodded curtly. "Take him." Though she didn't know how far they'd actually get with him. Aidan wasn't turning on his beast mode right then, so that was good. Maybe he'd save the mind control bit for later, but to be safe…

She hurried away from him. She wanted to get to the victim. She needed to see her. Jane pushed through those swinging emergency room doors. "The victim! Where is —"

"They've already taken her down," the nurse told her, sympathy on her face. "You'll get a full report, don't worry. But that is going to take time."

Time wasn't something she had and the report wasn't something she wanted right then. So she rushed by the nurse, running for the stairwell that she saw on the right. Jane knew the bodies were kept below in the morgue, and she had to get down there.

Before Aidan does.

***

Aidan didn't put up a fight, at least, not with every eye in that ER on him. He had to hand it to Jane, she'd played him well.

Just not well enough.

As soon as he was outside and the only eyes on him belonged to the two cops, he whirled around. He grabbed the cop on his right and slammed him back against the side of the hospital. The cop on his left fumbled for his gun.

Aidan caught his hand. "You don't need that."

The man stared into his eyes.

"Go back on patrol. Forget me."

The fellow nodded. And his partner…well, he was rising.

"Kenny, you crazy? Attack that asshole!"

Aidan sighed. He let go of cop number one, and turned to fellow number two. "Kenny *isn't* crazy." And that guy had lifted his gun, too. "You don't want to do that…"

"Get on your knees!"

Ah, now, he didn't do that for anyone.

Aidan flew forward and slammed the guy into the wall once more. He felt the power of the beast bursting inside of him. *"Don't piss me off."*

The young cop shuddered.

"Go out on patrol," he gritted. "Forget me."

He waited for that message to be received, and then, when the guy's eyes glazed over, Aidan stepped back.

Jane, why the hell are you doing this? He'd gone over the rules of the paranormal world with her. And now she was going to play games? Fuck, no, that couldn't happen.

He wouldn't let it happen.

***

Jane shoved open the swinging doors of the morgue. "I need to see the woman who was just brought in!"

Silence.

"Um, hello?" Jane advanced toward the desk. An empty desk. Oh, jeez, but the place reeked. It smelled of antiseptic and, well, death. "A body was just transferred down here!" She called out. "I need to see her, now." Aidan had said she had a few hours, but Jane didn't want to push things. The sooner she got the victim, the better.

But no one was in the morgue. The place was icy and…

Was that blood on the floor?

Jane peered down, and, hell, yes, it was. She followed the trail. It looked as if someone had been dragged…and —

Jesus.

A body was crumpled far behind the desk. An older man, wearing blue scrubs, and with an ID badge that identified him as Dr. Ken Loft.

His throat had been cut wide open.

I am so tired of that sight.

The doors squeaked behind her as they opened. She spun and found Aidan standing right there. His face was tight with fury as he reached for her. *"You can't trick me, Jane."*

Um, she could. She had. But right then, they had a bigger problem on their hands. "The guy who runs the morgue is dead."

His nostrils flared. "Yeah, I smelled that."

Right. Werewolves. Sharp noses. Blood. Whatever. "Did…did she do it?"

He glanced over her shoulder. "The vamp won't be awake yet. I told you that."

She wasn't awake. She wasn't there. She should have been. "Where is she?"

A muscle flexed in his jaw.

"Can you track her?" Jane asked him. "Can you find her?"

"*Now* you want my help? Ten minutes ago, you were trying to get the cops to lock me up." But he'd already pulled away from her and headed back for the door.

"Aidan!'

He paused. His hands were clenched at his sides. "I've got her scent. Let's see where it leads."

Her breath heaved out as she rushed to catch him. Just as she reached for the door, he captured her hand in his and held tight. "You owe me, Jane."

"I—"

"And never, *ever* betray me again."

"It wasn't a betrayal." Not really. Someone needed to relax. They'd address that whole betrayal business later. Right then… "Find me the body."

***

Johnny shoved his foot down hard on the accelerator. How fucking convenient. Someone had just left an ambulance out for him to use at the back of that hospital. The perfect getaway vehicle.

"Don't you worry, baby!" he called back to Ginny. "I'll get you someplace nice and safe for you to wake up. I'm going to take care of everything." She'd wake up, change him, and they would fucking be invincible. "Don't you worry," he said again as he drove faster. "I've got you." And he would never let her go.

CHAPTER NINE

It was nearing four a.m. when Jane stormed into her apartment. They hadn't found the victim. *Dammit.* Aidan had lost the trail once the victim — and the guy who'd taken her body — had apparently high-tailed it away in an ambulance. Video footage had shown her the guy's face — and it had been the same bozo who'd attacked Jane behind the cathedral. Stocky, long hair, gaunt face.

Aidan told her that the fellow they were after had disguised his scent, that they weren't looking for some kind of paranormal amateur.

Like she was supposed to tell her captain that crap. *"No, captain, you see…we're dealing with a man who really understands beasts. Real beasts. And so he took the body and managed to elude the werewolf that I have on his trail."*

Her captain would have sent her in for a psych evaluation. Since she wasn't in the mood to go down that particular path again, she'd kept out the details about beasts and vampires. Now her captain believed they were looking for some guy who either had a serious issue with necrophilia or—more likely in her captain's book—had taken the body because he believed evidence was on it that would incriminate him in the victim's murder.

Either way, Jane was still missing a body.

And she had to deal with a very pissed off werewolf.

She knew Aidan was pissed, all right. He'd still been muttering about betrayal when he left her at the hospital. Then she'd had to calm down her captain and talk with the other cops and try and create some kind of protected crime scene in the morgue.

But at least the poor guy who'd been killed in there wasn't going to turn into a vampire. According to Aidan, no vamp scents had been detected in the morgue. Dr. Ken Loft's death was a simple case of murder—the kind she *could* deal with.

She yanked off her jacket. Tossed it aside. Kicked away her shoes and felt every ache in her body. Jane knew she needed to crash and crash hard. She'd need to hit the streets running in just a few hours. Since she apparently had some kind of Master Vampire after her, it made sense to hunt for him during the day, if he was weaker then. It made sense—

A fierce pounding shook her door. She whipped around, her heart racing.

The pounding came again, even harder than before. She inched forward, already pulling out her gun. Jane put her eye to the peephole and saw Aidan's still pissed visage staring back at her. No, *glaring* back.

"Open the damn door," he snarled. "I know you're right there. I can hear you."

Someone was a bossy werewolf. She put the gun down on a nearby table. She took her time about it—

He pounded again. *"Mary Jane!"*

Her hand flew over the lock and she quickly opened the door. "I have neighbors. Nice, normal people who like to sleep at four a.m. in the morning. They don't need you shaking the whole building with your angry fists."

His blue eyes glinted. Jane thought she caught a hint of fang. Was she supposed to be scared? Her chin notched up. "And didn't I tell you? It's Jane. Just Jane. Not Mary Jane." She only let one person in the world call her Mary Jane, and Aidan wasn't that guy. Not that she'd seen that particular man in a very, very long time. *Because it's safer that way.*

Aidan crossed the threshold and stalked way too close into her personal space. She backed up, but only because she didn't want him touching her. When he touched her, her body got all hot and achy, and, okay, turned on—all responses that she *shouldn't* have to the guy.

He kicked the door shut behind him, but didn't look back.

Shaking her head, she slid around him and locked the door. As if just closing it was going to do any good. "I thought you guys had to be given invitations to enter a home." She'd seen that on a TV show.

"Vampires," he said, shaking his head in disgust. "That's some vampire BS on TV. Not real. I can go anywhere. Vamps can go anywhere." He tossed a glare over his shoulder as his gaze dropped down to the lock she'd just flipped. "And that flimsy ass lock is not going to keep out a Master Vampire. All it would have taken was one good kick from me, and your door would be on the floor."

"Um, yeah, you say that as if I'm supposed to *thank you* for not destroying my door." She marched around him, heading for her balcony because suddenly, it was hard to breathe in the apartment. Why did the guy seem to take up so much space?

Before she could reach that sliding glass door, his fingers snagged her wrist. Sure enough, heat pulsed through her at his touch.

"You didn't stay at the hospital. You didn't stay with the other cops." He made those words sound like an accusation.

She swung toward him. "You have got to relax. I'm a big girl. I can manage to go across town and back to my own home just fine."

"Master. Vampire." Aidan gritted out the words.

"Homicide. Detective," Jane gritted right back. "That means I don't get the luxury of hiding and pretending that bad shit isn't happening. I have a job to do, and I'm going to do it."

"This isn't about some human job—"

"You're right," she cut him off. "It's about human lives. Justice. You say you take care of your pack? Well, I take care of the people here, and that's what I'm going to keep doing. I'm going to keep right on protecting them."

"She died because of you."

Her heart stopped beating. "Wh-what?" And the past was there, surging toward her. A woman's scream. A man's broken voice, begging.

For you. All for you, little one.

His hold tightened on her. "She was bait, don't you see that? The Master Vamp asshole was trying to lure you out. He wanted to take you. He knows that I'm protecting you, and he tried to separate us so that he could get to you."

She died because of you.

A dull ringing filled her ears. The past wasn't leaving her alone. And the pain from the present was suddenly ripping into her. *Not again. Not. Again.*

"He's going to keep coming," Aidan growled. "He knows what you can become, and he isn't going to stop."

She jerked free of him. "You need to leave."

"Mary Jane—"

"*Jane!*" Her voice was a yell. Great. Now she was the one waking the neighbors, but he'd pushed her too far. *She died because of you.* "Get the hell out."

He blinked. "You're…hurting?"

What did he think? That she was celebrating?

He reached for her hand again, but she stepped back in a fast move. His brows shot up and she could see the confusion in his eyes. "I didn't mean to hold you too hard…" His words came awkwardly. "Sometimes, I forget how strong I am. I don't usually spend a lot of time with female humans."

"Your touch didn't hurt me. Your jackass words did." She drew in a deep breath. "Thanks for adding more guilt onto my soul, exactly what I always wanted." Jane pointed toward the door. "Like I said, leave."

"Guilt?" He blinked. "I didn't…my words were to warn you. Not to make you feel guilty."

He was making her want to scream, again. "How did you think it would make me feel to learn she died…oh, wait, what were you words?

Because of me. I want to help people, not get them killed!"

He stepped toward her. Stopped. Looked helpless. "I…misspoke."

His words were low, guttural.

Her eyes narrowed on him. "Want to try that again?"

"I. Am. Sorry!" Now he was back to angry. Or, gruff. Or something. "I just wanted you safe. I wanted you to understand your peril."

"Consider the peril understood." She was still pointing to the door.

"He killed her. She meant nothing to him. Human life means *nothing*. He won't stop. He will just keep coming until he gets what he wants."

Her mouth had gone dry. "And I'm what he wants." Because he thought she was some kind of born vampire creature. Ready to sprout fangs and drink blood once she'd gotten the pesky matter of her violent death out of the way.

"You are what he wants." Aidan's hands clenched. "And you are what he cannot have." He drew in a deep breath. "She didn't die because of you. I-I didn't mean that. My words with you…they aren't the best."

So she'd noticed.

"She died because he was trying to *get* to you. And he'll keep trying. You aren't safe on your own."

Her hand lowered. Not because she didn't want him to leave, she did. Really. But…her hand couldn't stay up forever. "So what are you proposing? I already have a basic plan, you know. I'm going to find him. Hunt him. *Stop* him. I'll see that he pays for what he's done."

Aidan shook his head. "Human justice—"

"Right. I know. We've been through this before." She still planned to find the vamp. "But being a sitting duck isn't my idea of a good time."

His gaze swept over her. "I won't let him have you."

"*I* won't let him have me." She had silver bullets and even a wooden stake at the ready. There was no way she'd go down without a fight.

"You aren't safe with him out there. He can make more vampires. Can send them after you. A trusted friend can become a predator."

How had life gotten so out of control? She strode away from him. Opened her sliding glass door and stepped out onto the balcony.

"I'm staying with you."

Of course, he'd followed her.

Her spine was so stiff and straight that it hurt. "I don't think that's a good idea."

She could feel him behind her. Heat and power. Her hands curled around the balcony's wooden railing. Then his hands were there, too. Not touching hers but…resting right beside hers.

Curling along the railing, too. His hands were so much bigger and darker than her own.

"Why not?"

When he asked that question, his breath blew lightly over the curve of her ear. Jane shivered. What was happening? One moment, she was screaming at him, and the next, her body was far to primed. It wasn't normal and it wasn't right. "You're lying to me."

Behind her, she felt him stiffen. She exhaled slowly and fought to keep her voice level. "You think I didn't realize it? You're doling out information to me so carefully. I'm not a fool, Aidan. I get that you've been manipulating the people in this city for years." Cops. Government officials. Every-damn-body. She pulled her hands away from the railing and turned to face him. His hands stayed up, still holding tight to the wood behind her, so she was trapped in his embrace. "I'm not going to let you manipulate me."

His eyes seemed to see straight into his soul.

"So how about we don't play games? How about you don't come over here telling me what I'm *going* to do? How about you talk to me? Honestly. Tell me what you're holding back."

A muscle flexed along the hard line of his jaw. "You don't want to know…"

"I'm asking. I want to know."

"Jane…"

"Truth only, got it? When I ask you a question, respond honestly."

Grimly, he nodded.

"Did you really lose that guy's scent tonight?"

"Yes." Flat. Bitter.

"Do you think the Master Vampire is going to come for me?"

"I think he plans to kill you…but only so you can come back like him."

An insane killer. Hardly the life she had planned.

"And you being with me." She stopped, cleared her throat. "You think you can stop him?"

"I think I'd fucking die trying."

This was the part that she just didn't get. "*Why*?"

His lashes lowered, shielding his eyes from her.

She put her hands on his chest. Her fingers balled around the fabric of his shirt, making two small fists. "Truth, remember? Why does it matter to you? Wouldn't I become just another vamp for you to stake? Why go to all of this trouble? You don't know me."

Silence. She needed him to answer her. To stop with the games and just say —

"Because I want you."

Her heart thundered in her ears.

"I want you more than I can damn well ever remember wanting anyone. I look at you, and I ache. I want to take and take until you scream as you come for me."

Breathing was hard. Real hard. And her fists tightened even more around his shirt.

"There's a little known fact about alpha werewolves and…women like you."

Weren't *most* facts about werewolves "little known" to people? Or else, the whole world would realize monsters were real.

"Your scent…attracts."

Wait, *what?*

"That was another sign. Another way I knew what you were."

No wonder he'd been sniffing her so much. "What?" Jane asked as she stared up at him. "Do I smell like some kind of aphrodisiac to you?" The question was sarcastic.

But he nodded. Then he said, "You smell…like you were meant to be mine."

She should let him go. She should really get her ass off that balcony.

"It's a physical instinct. You feel it, too, don't you? Back in the old days…" And now his laugh was bitter. "The *very* old days, a woman like you was given a protector. A werewolf alpha who would make sure that she never died that violent death, that she lived a long life — one full of happiness and a hell of a lot of kids."

She knew where this was going. "Werewolf kids?"

"I said most werewolves weren't like me. That they couldn't shift fully. Do you wonder why there *aren't* a lot of alphas like me running around? Because there aren't a lot of women like you any longer. The bloodline is stronger when it's someone—" He stopped, but he didn't need to say anymore.

When it's someone like me.

So that was it. He wanted her because she could be some kind of magical genetic aphrodisiac to him? Some great breeder *for* him? That wasn't exactly…sexy. Or overwhelmingly romantic.

It also just wasn't damn fun. *Not* words a woman wanted to hear.

Aidan drew in a ragged breath. "An alpha's job is to protect."

Ah. So much made sense now. Like how he'd suddenly been extra hell-bent on protecting her. When before, it had just been about making her forget.

"Nature designed us to fight vampires. No other being is physically capable of fighting them. We are natural enemies…enemies who sometimes want the same thing."

Okay, now something new was worrying her. "So you guys—you alphas—you find women like me. You stick with them, protect them, try to

make sure that they live long, healthy lives."
Minus the violent ending.

He just watched her.

"But what happens..." Jane asked, as an ache grew in her heart. "If you don't manage to keep the women safe? What if they change? What if they become vampires?"

His jaw hardened.

"Only say it doesn't happen when you first meet them." Her words shot out in rapid-fire succession. "What if you've made some of those super alpha babies you mentioned...and then, after the woman has the kids, *then* she's murdered and becomes a vamp." Jane had always played the *What if* game too much. Her mother used to tell her that she borrowed trouble. Jane just liked to think that she was trying to prepare herself for coming danger. "What happens in that situation?" The ache in her heart got way worse. "Or *has* that situation happened before?"

Aidan backed away from her.

Oh, crap, that was an answer, wasn't it? "The alphas...they still kill the vampires, don't they? You told me they were driven to kill. So even if the alpha had a child with that woman, if she became—"

"Vampires are monsters. No souls. Just evil. They live to destroy everything and everyone around them. A vampire who turned like that would kill her own child in a heartbeat."

He's saying the alphas killed their mates.

"I *won't* let that happen to you," he promised. But there was something about his voice. A darkness. A pain…

I think he's holding back with me again.

And she decided that if they were playing the truth game, he deserved plenty of honesty from her, too. "I don't know what scares me more. You…or the vampires out there."

"I'm not here to hurt you." Intensity deepened his voice even more.

"Not right now you're not, no." She rubbed her chilled arms. "But I can't count on the fact that you'll always be on my side." As long as she stayed human, yes, but…

Her arms fell. Her hand brushed against her right side. It was a habit that wouldn't die. And it reminded her of a nightmare that would never end. Aidan didn't get it. He thought he was just protecting her from a threat that was just unfolding around them. He didn't realize…

Monsters had been in her life for a very long time.

"I think you should go now." She made her voice sound brisk. "I'm exhausted and I've got a long day of vamp hunting ahead of me tomorrow. A girl needs her beauty sleep if she's facing undead monsters who want to take her soul."

His hand lifted. Jane tensed as his fingers slid over cheek. "It's when you do things like that, when you say things like that…" His own voice was gruff. "That you make me want you even more."

Her lashes lowered. "We just talked about why we are so very wrong for each other."

"I want you."

Her heartbeat needed to slow the hell down. "You aren't having me."

His lips tilted just a little and what could have been a dimple flashed in his left cheek. "We shall see."

Arrogant werewolf.

Then he sauntered back inside. She followed, more than ready to get him out of her apartment. Only…he still wasn't leaving. Did werewolves just have issues getting the hell out? As she watched him in mounting horror, he eyed her lumpy sofa, looked disgruntled, but finally stretched his too-long length across the cushions. His legs dangled over the arm rest.

"Um, what are you doing, wolf?"

He looked up at her. "Getting comfortable. Unless you wanted to share that bed of yours?" Now he sounded hopeful.

"Get comfortable in your own home."

He looked hurt. And…hot. Dammit.

Aidan gave her a quick smile. "There are actually women who would kill to have me right here. They think I'm rather sexy."

"I think you're rather a pain in my ass."

His sigh was long and rough. "My Mary Jane—"

"*Jane.*" She was sure he did that just to mess with her.

"A Master Vampire knows who you are, so it stands to reason that he knows where you live, too. I'm staying here, in case the bloodsucker gets the idea to come for you tonight. When dawn arrives, I'll leave you be."

"What are you going to do? Stay here every night until he's stopped? Sleeping on my couch?"

"I'd prefer your bed. Or we could always go to my place."

Insane. "I had a normal life two days ago." She whirled away from him.

"Did you?" His voice followed her.

No, I was just pretending. I always knew I was different.

"Normal is boring," he said, before she could respond. "I promise you, sweetheart, life with me won't be boring."

She was bone tired and the bed was calling—screaming—her name. And maybe, just *maybe*, it wasn't so bad to have a tough werewolf on the premises, at least not until she figured out how powerful that Master Vampire actually was.

Jane yanked open the closet and grabbed the quilt there. An extra pillow waited on the shelf up top, and she snagged that, too. Then she hurried back toward Aidan.

But as she approached, the guy began to appear seriously...alarmed.

He sat up quickly. "What are you doing?"

Her eyes did a little roll. "Giving you a pillow. And a quilt." She tossed the pillow at him, but held a little tightly to the quilt. "A warning, wolf. Do not mess up this quilt. My grandmother made it for me right before she passed away, and I freaking treasure it, got that?"

His gaze took note of the way she was caressing the quilt. "If it matters, why give it to me?"

"Because you need a cover. And I have it." She offered the quilt to him.

He didn't take it.

"Aidan..."

"I appreciate your kindness," he said gruffly. And when he took the quilt, his fingers brushed over hers. "I will take care of it for you."

Right. Good. Great. *Why does his touch slide right through me? Is it really just that genetic mumbo jumbo he was talking about?*

Or is it something else? Something more?

She turned away from him.

He caught her hand. His fingers slid over her knuckles and his thumb brushed against the inside of her palm. Until that moment, she never would have thought that her palm was sensitive. Definitely not some kind of erogenous zone. But as he rubbed his thumb into the center of her palm, her breath came a bit faster. "If you ever want to let yourself go," Aidan said. She glanced at him and found that bright gaze locked on hers. "I'll be close by."

She had to swallow. Twice. "I'd think letting go with a werewolf would be a dangerous thing."

His thumb stroked harder against her palm. Her breasts were starting to ache. Did he know what he was doing to her? Just with that touch?

"I wouldn't hurt you."

"Not unless I became a vampire."

Another hard caress, and then his hand slid from hers. "I give you my word. I will fight hell to make sure that never happens to you."

She needed to get away from him. Just back away.

So why was she standing right there? "I can fight my own battles."

"But who says you have to fight them alone?"

Her lips parted. His gaze slipped to her mouth. "You taste so sweet. So good. I'd love to taste you…again."

She licked her lips.

He growled.

No, dammit, she had *not* meant to lick her lips. Wrong move. Very, very wrong.

She took a big step away from him. "Good night, Aidan." She hurried for her bedroom. Just as she was at the threshold to her room, she heard him say —

"Good night, sweetheart."

Jane shut the door. Her back slid against the wood as she tried to get her body back under control. He wasn't a man. He was a werewolf. Incredibly dangerous. And she shouldn't want him so much.

But she did.

Dammit, she just did.

CHAPTER TEN

The werewolf was there. In her apartment. In her bed?

Fucking werewolves. He hated the slobbering beasts. Always thinking they were so perfect. So strong and unstoppable.

They were nothing more than animals, hiding behind the bodies of men.

He kept watch from the shadows. He couldn't get too close to the building. The mangy werewolf might catch his scent. And not just any werewolf, either. An alpha.

Which made him even fucking madder as he saw the lights turn off in his prey's apartment.

The werewolf should have been dead. If he hadn't been an alpha, he *would* have been dead in that alley. Drained and then ripped apart by the vampires so that they'd enjoy the power of his blood. Every last drop. Only things hadn't ended that way.

And now the werewolf was fucking *his* vamp-to-be.

The foolish beast probably thought he was keeping her safe. Locking her away from the big, bad vamp. But he didn't have to get inside that apartment in order to get to her.

I can make her come to me.

He slipped deeper into the shadows and watched as two humans skulked around her building. Humans, ah, but they could certainly be useful. He'd paid them just the right amount of money, and, no questions asked, they'd agreed to the job. In this instance, he knew it was smarter to use humans and not vamps. The alpha wouldn't even think twice when he caught the scent of humans in her building. The humans would be able to get close enough to do the job he needed.

And he could watch. See hell come alive. All before the sun rose.

You thought I was done for the night? Think again. He couldn't give the werewolf time to hunt him. He had to keep attacking. Had to claim his prey.

It was a good thing that, after death, a vamp-to-be like the pretty detective could regenerate. Because her death wasn't going to be pleasant.

For her kind, it never was…

***

The dream came again. Dream. Nightmare. Memory. All one and the same for Jane. She was young, barely eleven, and tied down. The rope cut into her wrists and her ankles, and no matter how much she begged, no one would let her go.

When she turned her head, she could see her mom. Tossed on the floor, her limbs all twisted and a big pool of red underneath her body. Her dad…he was there, too. Another quick turn of her head showed Jane her dad's form.

His eyes were still open, but she didn't think he saw her, not anymore.

"There, there…no need for tears, little one. It's all for you." That voice was back. The voice she hated. Mean and cold and cruel and she wouldn't look at him. She just *wouldn't*.

"We waited a long time for you. You'd better not disappoint."

She looked back at her dad. This was her house. Her mom's house. Her dad's house. These people—they didn't belong there. They should never have been inside.

"You can scream if you want," that mean voice told her.

It was all the warning she got. Pain came then. So hot. Burning, branding. She screamed and screamed but it didn't stop. And she could smell something—something funny. Something—

It's me. I'm burning.

Her voice broke and her cries stopped.

"Good girl."

She didn't want to be good. Not if he liked that.

"I'll be back soon." He stroked back her hair, and his green eyes gleamed down at her. "We'll take a little break. Let you get a bit of strength back so that we can finish things up." His blond hair was swept away from his face. A face that seemed so normal.

It isn't. He's not normal. He's evil. Monster. Monster. Monster!

There were no tears on her cheeks. She'd stopped crying after...*Daddy.*

The green-eyed man — *monster* — shut the door on the way out. Her home. He had taken over. *They had.* In the middle of the night, monsters had come for her. Her mom had told her that monsters weren't real. That she should never be afraid of them.

Her mom had been wrong.

She heard faint squeaks. The softest of rustles. Her eyes had closed. When had they closed? She should look around. See what was happening.

But she was afraid and she didn't think she wanted to see anything else.

Her right side kept hurting. Throbbing.

"Mary Jane..." A soft voice. "Mary Jane...are you okay?"

Don't be here. Don't. Run away.

"Y-you didn't tell them I was here."

Now she did cry. One long tear slid down her cheek.

"I'm gonna…I'm gonna get you out."

She shook her head and kept her eyes closed. But she felt him pulling on the ropes that held her ankles down. There was a faint sawing motion. It sounded so loud to her ears. She was afraid *he* would hear. "Stop." The barest of whispers.

But the rope gave way. Her legs were free and her feet *hurt* because it felt like needles were shoved into them. She bit her lower lip as hard as she could, trying to hold back her cries. Now wasn't the time to scream. She knew that.

Her eyes opened.

Her dad's sightless eyes stared back at her.

No, look away. Look away!

Then the rope was gone from her wrists. Sawed away. He'd cut her wrists with the knife he had, but she didn't care about that. Then he was pulling her, pushing her toward the window. Such a small window. They were in the basement. And that window was up high.

"I'll go through first," he said. He shimmied up and vanished.

I don't want to leave mom and dad.

"Mary Jane!" He reached down for her. His hand was small, barely bigger than hers. Dirty. Bloody. "Come with me, Mary Jane!"

Had he been hiding, during everything? Hiding and waiting?

She looked at his hand and she—she heard the basement door opening. The faintest of clicks from the top of the stairs. He was coming for her again.

She grabbed for the dirty little hand, and he pulled her up, yanking with all of his strength. Her body slid through the narrow opening. Her shoulders. Her chest. Her stomach. Her—

The monster grabbed her feet.

"No!" she screamed.

***

Aidan's eyes flew open at Jane's shout and he bounded off the lumpy couch. Two strides had him at her bedroom door. It was locked when he reached for it, but he just kicked out, shattering that lock. The door flew open beneath the force of his kick and it bounced against the wall.

Jane was sitting up in bed. Her eyes wide and horrified. Her breath heaving. She looked terrified.

But no one else was in the room. He froze at the foot of her bed, wanting nothing more than to reach out and wrap his arms around her. "Where's the threat?" Aidan forced those gravelly words out.

"In my own head."

Her reply was so soft, but a werewolf could hear the softest of words. The barest of whispers.

Were those tears on her cheeks? *Yes.* And at the sight of those tears, he was moving toward her, helpless to stay away. He sat on the edge of her bed, but when he reached for her, she flinched.

That was when he realized that his claws had come out.

Aidan shoved his hands behind his back. He wanted to touch her more than he wanted to draw a damn breath, but he hated her fear. And right then, the scent of her fear was surrounding him.

Her hair was tousled. She wore a black tank top, one that had slid half-way down one slender shoulder, and her covers were pooled at her waist. Jane held those covers tightly, more like *death-grip-tightly* in her fists.

"Do werewolves have bad dreams?" Jane asked.

He nodded, then realized she was staring down at her covers, not him. "We do."

"And when you have them, what do you do?"

"Find something to make me forget them."

Her head lifted. Her eyes met his. There were fucking tears still glinting in her gaze. "Make me forget."

And he did — the only way he could. Aidan leaned in toward her. He couldn't touch her, not with his claws because he didn't want to freak her the hell out any more than she already was. So he touched Jane with his mouth. Just his lips. He kissed at the tear tracks on her cheeks.

She stiffened.

First his lips feathered over Jane's left cheek, then her right.

"Aidan…"

Her lashes had lowered once more. He kissed those lashes. Hated her tears. Hated that she was afraid.

He pulled back, just for a moment. Her lashes lifted.

Giving her time to tell him to get the hell away, he slowly lowered his mouth toward hers.

Only she didn't tell him to get the hell away.

She leaned toward him. She closed the last bit of distance between them. She…

Kissed him.

Her lips were so soft beneath his. She tasted like heaven and sin. The best kind of temptation. Her mouth parted and her tongue swept out to slide along his lips.

She was going to drive him crazy.

He moved closer to her. Kissed her harder. Deeper. Let her feel his desire. Her every breath, her every sigh just drove him on. Just made him want her so much more.

He'd had plenty of lovers, but he'd never wanted anyone this way. So badly that he was aching. So badly that one kiss had him stretched hard and ready to erupt. He grabbed the covers near her. Yanked them back because he wanted to feel more of her. See more of her.

Her legs were long and bare. Insanely sexy. She wore a pair of panties—not bikini panties or a scrap of lace but panties that almost looked like shorts. Small and mind-blowingly sexy in a bold red color.

The black tank top covered too much of her. *Time to ditch that.* He kissed her neck. Let her feel the faintest edge of his teeth and when she moaned, his cock jerked in anticipation.

So fucking good.

His hand slid to the hem of her shirt. He felt the softness of her skin beneath his touch. *Don't scare her. Stay in control.*

"Aidan…there's forgetting, and then there's fucking."

The woman knew just how to talk dirty to him. A grin curved his lips. "Oh, sweetheart, I am more than happy to fu—"

He saw her scar, high on her right side. Every muscle in his body clamped down. It wasn't the kind of scar one would get from a surgery. Not even from a knife wound. And not some gunshot she'd taken while in the line of duty as a cop, either. The scar was old, it curved. It twisted.

And…

The curves of that scar are too precise. Not an accident. Something deliberate—

She yanked her tank top back down and shoved him back. "Stop."

He'd only seen half of that scar. Just half. Enough to piss him off. His beast was snarling inside. "Someone...marked you."

Jane jumped from the bed. "I had a nightmare. I'm fine now. Go back in the den." Her gaze flew toward the window. "It's still dark outside. We probably barely slept an hour, maybe two."

He was still on the bed and still battling his rage. "You were young when it happened." His mind flew back over what he'd learned about her. "When your parents died?"

Jane sucked in a sharp breath. "I am not talking about this with you." She pointed to the door.

Aidan rose, slowly. "I know what kind of mark that is." Because he'd seen others like it before.

"Good for you." She gave a hard shake of her head. "Look, maybe werewolves need to work on tact because it is not cool to talk about a woman's scars." Her hand hovered over that scar, and he realized that he'd seen her do that same movement before. Seen her palm press to her side, but he hadn't realized what hid beneath her clothes. "But in the human world, it's just tacky to point out a person's flaws."

"You have no flaws."

Her eyes widened, then she blinked. Laughed. "Trust me, I have plenty."

Actually, he thought she was pretty perfect.

Except for the whole potential to become a vampire thing. But he was working on that.

But her laughter — as sweet as it was — faded. Suspicion swept over her face. "How do you know about my parents?"

Because I had a wolf dig into your past. Paris was particularly good at unearthing secrets.

"You investigated me, didn't you?"

He rolled his shoulders.

"Seriously? I'm a *cop!* I'm a detective and —"

"Someone had to make sure you'd be a good fit as detective."

She leapt toward him. "What?"

Hell. He hadn't meant to say that. But he was still so pissed about her scar, about someone *marking* her that way. No, not marking. Branding. Because that was exactly what it was. Her skin had been burned. The scar had been too careful, too curved and precise for anything less.

She hurt, and I wasn't there.

"Why the hell are you acting as if I'm a detective because of *you*?" Jane demanded. "I didn't even know you until that night on Bourbon Street."

"Just because you didn't know me, it doesn't mean that I didn't know you."

Her eyes widened. "*What?*"

"I told you before, sweetheart. I run this town."

"The paranormal parts!"

All parts. "You think I was going to let just anyone start investigating deaths in my city? There are procedures that have to be followed. And background checks by *me* are part of those procedures."

"More secrets," she said.

Yes. "Jane…" His gaze dropped to her hand, the hand that was still pressed to her right side. "I want to see the scar. All of it."

"Why?"

"Because I think there was more to your parents' death than you realize." Or maybe she did realize it, and he wasn't the only one keeping secrets. Maybe…

"Fine." She grabbed for the hem of her tank top.

But before she could lift the top, he heard the sound of breaking glass, the distinct shattering was far too close — coming from her den. Then there was a *whoosh* and the scent of fire had his nostrils twitching.

"What in the hell…" Jane began.

He was already running out of her bedroom. He made it to the den just in time to see another bottle hurtle through the glass door that led to her balcony. The bottle crashed to the floor, exploding on impact and sending flames racing across her floor.

Her den was already on fire. The smoke billowed as the flames greedily attacked everything in their path.

Another burning bottle came flying into her den. *Freaking Molotov cocktail.* A tactic that he'd even used before, when his pack had tried to smoke out vampires.

He lunged for the bottle, but it crashed before he got there, sending another trail of flames racing across her floor.

"Aidan!"

He whirled. Jane was behind him, staring in shock at her burning home. He saw that she'd taken the time to yank on a pair of jeans and grab some shoes. Her hand was clutched around her phone.

"Get out!" Aidan yelled. The flames were building too fast. And the asshole outside was launching another one right then. He could see the attack coming. "Get out *now!*"

But she shoved her phone into her back pocket and ran into her little kitchen, grabbing a fire extinguisher. In seconds, she was back. Jane used the fire extinguisher and shot it at the flames—

The fire is too big. She can't stay.

He grabbed her as she sprayed white foam all around them. His arms locked around her stomach as he pulled her toward the door.

"No!" Jane yelled at him. "This is my home, I have to—" She started coughing, choking on the thick smoke. The fire was spreading too damn fast. As if it had been given a little *paranormal* help.

Some flames burn hotter than others. He knew that truth.

"You need to get everyone else out of this building." Because she had human neighbors who needed to be protected. "Help them!" He wrenched open the apartment's front door and pushed her outside.

Her eyes were huge as she nodded, then she whirled and rushed across the hall. She lifted her fist and started banging on the door. "Mr. Jenkins, we need to get out of here, *now!*"

Aidan ran back into her home. The fire was eating every fucking thing. Blazing out of control. The flames were dark orange, burning so bright and hot. *I know those flames. I know who made them.*

Someone who would be paying, in blood.

He fought his way to her balcony doors—the glass had been shattered by the bottles and the heat. He peered down at the street and saw the two men gazing up at the building. Did they think the shadows would save them? That he couldn't see them as they hid?

Dead men.

Because they'd tried to harm Jane.

And now those men were out there, waiting…for her? If the flames didn't take her, were they planning to grab her outside? The fire crackled behind him.

He spun back, stared at the engulfed room. *They won't take her.*

He ran toward the flames.

***

The stairwell had filled with smoke. Jane had never seen a fire spread so quickly. She coughed a bit as she helped Mr. Jenkins down the last of the steps. The building's entrance was just a few feet away. She pushed him forward and, once she was sure he was going to make it out, she turned and pounded on the door to the right. Her downstairs tenant was an artist, Roth Sly, and he didn't usually come home until dawn, but she wasn't about to run out without checking to see if — for once — the guy was there.

Why didn't any of the buildings' alarms go off? The smoke detectors should be blaring! But they weren't.

Her fist thudded into his door. "Roth! Roth, *open up!*"

No answer. She glanced up — the top of the stairs were a blackened mess of smoke.

She grabbed for the door knob, trying to twist it and get into Roth's apartment, but the thing was locked. She kicked at the door, wishing she had some werewolf strength right then. "Roth! There's a fire!" She kicked again.

And the door flew open. Roth blinked blearily at her. "Jane?"

She grabbed his hand. "Fire!"

His eyes widened and he stumbled out after her. His chest was bare and a pair of jeans hung low on his hips. Tattoos covered his chest and piercings slid up the side of his left ear. When he got a look at the smoke upstairs, he double-timed it with her to the exit. She looked back, though, because she was missing a werewolf. "Aidan!"

The smoke funneled down the stairs.

Roth yanked her outside. "I can hear the flames!"

So could she and what she *needed* to be hearing was the siren of a fire truck. All of the buildings on that block were too close together. If one went…they all could burn.

When she stepped outside, fresh air hit her, and Jane gulped it greedily. "Nine, one, one!" She snapped because Roth might have forgotten his shirt, but his smart phone was in his hand. "Call them!"

Her gaze flew around the street. *Werewolf…werewolf, where are you?*

"Jane!" Her name was a roar.

Her head jerked at the sound, such a powerful cry to carry over the flames, and she saw Aidan standing on her balcony. But he wasn't staring at her. He seemed to be looking behind her. "Jane, they're coming!" he bellowed.

They?

Then hard hands grabbed her. Hands that bruised and yanked as she was pulled back. Her head jerked toward her attacker, and she found herself staring at a guy in a black ski mask.

Not just one asshole in a mask.

Another guy tried to grab her feet—another jerk in a ski mask. She kicked him right in his ski mask-covered face, and when she heard bones crush, Jane gave a cold grin.

The other bastard still had her arms. Was *twisting* them. So she slammed her head into his. The hit was hard, but she ignored the pain even as he cried out. His hold slackened on her for a moment and he stumbled back.

"Bitch!"

Her hand flew to her holster—a holster that wasn't there. Hell. She let her body go immediately into a fighting stance because she knew he'd be coming at her again. He was bigger, but she'd be faster. She had taken down plenty of big guys before.

The bigger they are…the harder I will make them fall.

He swung at her again, but she blocked the blow with her left hand, then she did a fast jump kick right to his head.

And you fall.

But his buddy was rising, now, and he'd just pulled out a knife. The blade glinted in the night.

"Jane!"

She was rather busy, but her head still whipped over at Aidan's call because she'd last seen the guy standing on the balcony of her burning building.

He wasn't on that balcony any longer.

He was flying right *over* the balcony.

No, seriously, *no.* "Aidan!" The werewolf was going to break his neck. "Aidan—"

The knife came at her, and she had to dodge back. She dodged even as Aidan jumped down to the ground. His knees barely seemed to buckle. He was holding something—something that was burning a bit—and he quickly slashed at the flames with his hands to put out that bit of fire.

And that knife is slashing at me.

She grabbed the attacker's wrist and twisted until he dropped the knife. He made the wise decision to drop it about two seconds before she would have broken his wrist. "I'm a cop, dumbass," she hissed at him.

"You're dead," he threw back at her, his voice muffled behind the mask.

She yanked his arm behind his back. Jane grabbed for his other hand and pushed him down until his knees hit the pavement. She held the jerk just like that but—

Ski Mask Number Two was up and at them—charging for her. *Can you jerks not just stay down?*

His hands were out, but he didn't touch her. Because Aidan was there. He stepped into the assailant's path and drove his fist into the guy's gut. The fellow flew back into the air, a good five feet, and he crashed into the ground.

Aidan whirled toward her. "You're all right?"

"Fine." As long as she didn't look at her burning home. "These guys attacked—"

"They set the fire. They're after you."

Yes, right, she'd rather figured that part out for herself.

A siren broke through the night. Loud and long and she was so glad that help was coming, even if that help was arriving too late to save her apartment. At least the other buildings could be saved. *I hope.*

She could see the swirl of lights in the distance. Not just fire fighters but cops. They'd get these two men taken into custody and she'd find out why they'd targeted her. *Did the Master Vamp send you after me? Another damn trap?*

She kept her tight hold on one of the ski mask-wearing SOBs and made sure that he wasn't about to get away from her. This guy was going to be her key—

"Jane!" Aidan's roar came one second before she heard the impact.

A whistle.

A thud.

And the man she'd been holding went slack before her.

Hit. Shot.

Aidan flew at her, tackling her to the ground. She heard another whistle—and someone cried out, a fast, guttural cry.

Then she heard screams. More shots.

"Get off me!" Jane yelled. She shoved against Aidan, but he wasn't moving. Not so much as an inch, and the guy was like solid rock above her. His body completely surrounded hers.

"Can't. He'll shoot you, sweetheart."

"There are other people out there!" She punched against him, as hard as she could. "Stop! Let me go!"

"You're the only one that fucking matters to me."

Jane stopped struggling. "They matter to me."

His head lifted. He stared down at her. Glared. "Fuck me…"

He got off her. Ran toward a cowering Mr. Jenkins and yanked the guy behind a truck.

Jenkins wasn't the target. If he had been…he would be dead.

She dove toward Roth. He'd just poked his head from his hiding spot—behind a street sign. Like that little sign was protecting his six foot two frame. She shoved him down onto the ground behind the truck, right next to Jenkins.

Then she ran back toward the two men she'd intended to take into custody. She put her fingers at the neck of the first fellow…

No pulse.

The fire truck braked at the scene, and two patrol cars came to skidding halts. "Active shooter in the area!" Jane called out, warning them. "Be on alert!"

The cops immediately pulled out their guns. Her gaze swept to the right. Aidan was by the other downed, masked man. Aidan gave a grim shake of his head.

The shooter took out the men who would've led me back to him. He doesn't care who he hurts. Everyone is expendable.

And he was still out there, damn him.

CHAPTER ELEVEN

The fire was out. The shooter was gone. And Jane—Jane was staring up at her blackened building with eyes that were angry and a face that was smudged with soot.

Aidan approached her slowly. The shooter had been smart. He'd stayed far enough away that Aidan hadn't caught his scent. He'd fired — using a rifle—and taken out his targets from a safe distance back.

Did he tell you fools…if you don't succeed, you die?

Aidan rather doubted that their deaths had been part of the deal that the men had made.

One of the fire fighters approached Jane. It wasn't hard to overhear his words. "We stopped the fire, detective. Didn't spread to the other units, but your place…it's looking like a total loss."

She didn't flinch. Didn't say anything. Just gave a solemn nod. Her gaze was on her balcony.

The guy put his hand on Jane's shoulder. "The fire marshal will be here soon." He squeezed her. "I'm sorry."

Aidan's eyes turned to slits. The comforting fire fighter could move the hell on. There were still some smolders that he needed to address.

Aidan stepped forward. The guy looked at him. Aidan looked back, then he made a very slow process of glancing at the guy's hand. A hand still curled around Jane's shoulder.

The fire fighter snatched his hand back and went to go take care of the smolders.

"What did you do?" Jane murmured. "Flash some fang?"

He sidled closer to her. "Hardly."

"Did you already make Roth and Mr. Jenkins forget that you jumped off the balcony and didn't even get a scratch on you when you landed?"

She wasn't looking at him. Just still staring at the balcony. Aidan cleared his throat. "They didn't notice, so nothing to explain." The two men had been dazed at the time. Dazed and *not* helping Jane fight off her attackers. The older guy — Aidan got that Jenkins might be too weak to fight back. But the Roth jerk? *When a woman is getting attacked, you help her. You don't run for cover and leave her vulnerable.*

Even if the woman knew how to kick some serious ass. Everyone could use some back-up.

"My whole life was in that apartment." Her voice hitched with sorrow.

"You'll stay with me."

She kept her gaze on the smoking balcony. "You have this serious tendency to dictate instead of *asking*. I'm going to assume that's an alpha thing? 'Cause you're used to giving orders to your pack?"

"Yes."

"I'm not part of the pack. So ask with me." Her gaze finally slid to him. So dark. He wished he could read all of the emotions in her eyes. "You need to—" Her words ended in a little gasp. "Is that my grandmother's quilt?"

He lifted it up and, keeping his voice expressionless said, "*Will* you stay with me?"

Her hands reached for the quilt. She stroked it carefully, lovingly. "It's my quilt."

Like he'd risk the fire for anyone else's quilt. He'd gone into the flames before he jumped off that balcony *just* to get the quilt for her. His lips curved. "I'm afraid it might be a little smoky." And unfortunately, it *had* caught fire on his way out, but he'd hit at the flames once he'd made his way to the ground and he'd knocked out the fluttering fire. "But nothing a little repair work won't fix."

She stared up at him, her eyes so wide. "Thank you."

His heart ached. "It wasn't hard to bring with me. No big deal."

"It is a big deal." She paused. "And you know it."

He'd just wanted to…*make her happy.*

"You stayed in the fire to get this, didn't you?"

Aidan swallowed. "It mattered to you." He was discovering that when things mattered to her — no matter how small — they mattered to him, too.

The silence stretched between them. He wished all of those fire fighters weren't there but…hell, screw them. Aidan leaned forward and kissed her. Not a rough and hard kiss, the kind he was used to. The kind he normally enjoyed. But…careful. Savoring her. Enjoying her. *Just being damn glad no one took her from me.*

Now he understood the stories that he'd heard growing up. How some alphas had nearly become obsessed with their mates. That need was easy to understand now because when something mattered so much, you would do anything to protect—

To keep.

To claim.

He lifted his lips from her mouth, but his forehead tipped down and pressed lightly to hers.

"I *will* stay with you," Jane murmured. "And thanks for asking so nicely."

That ache in his heart spread.

"I want to be clear on this," she added. "I'm not doing this as a way to jump your bones."

The smoke drifted in the air. "How disappointing."

"Roth and Mr. Jenkins could have been killed tonight. Human casualties don't belong in this war. So if the vamp is going to keep coming after me, then I want to be sure I put as much distance between myself and any other potential victims as possible."

"The guy doesn't care much for collateral damage." His gaze darted to the right—to the two bodies being loaded in black body bags.

"I care," she said grimly. "So I'm thinking your *place* will come with plenty of paranormal protection?"

"You can count on it."

"Good." She swung away, and, holding tight to her quilt, she began to march toward the patrol cars.

"Mary Jane…"

She stilled. "Jane."

"Just wanted to say…you can always feel free to jump my bones."

Jane glanced over her shoulder at him.

"Always."

A faint smile curved her lips. Then she walked away.

He rather liked her smiles.

***

"Baby, we're safe." Johnny said as he opened the back door of the ambulance. He pulled out the gurney, being real careful to put down the legs on that contraption so Virginia's body wouldn't bounce and fall to the hard cement flooring.

They were in a deserted warehouse, one right near the river front. He was supposed to meet the boss there just before dawn—and it was nearly that time, now. *And I don't see the vamp anywhere.*

His fingers shook a bit as he unzipped the body bag. Virginia's skin was chalky, her eyes closed. She wasn't breathing. Her beautiful face was too still. He touched her lightly, amazed by just how cold she truly was right then.

"The hard part is over," he told her. "You'll wake up, the boss will have some food for you, and then everything else will be easy. You'll transform me and—"

Her hand flew up and clamped around his wrist.

"G-Ginny?"

Her eyes opened. The color was darker. Deeper.

He started to smile.

Then she yanked his hand to her mouth and Virginia sank her fangs into his wrist. It wasn't a gentle bite. She ripped and tore right through the skin and veins and muscles. She gulped and drank so deeply and he frantically tried to pull away.

But she was too strong.

Footsteps echoed around him. Faint, mocking laughter filled the air.

"I guess our girl woke up early…"

The boss was there.

His thudding heartbeat filled his ears and sweat pooled down Johnny's back as he jerked his head toward the guy's voice. "Help me! She's *hurting* me!"

"She's drinking. It's what new vampires do." The footsteps came closer, and the voice continued, ever so calm and unconcerned, "They have a hunger, you see. A great, voracious hunger that they must sate. They have to drink and drink until that hunger no longer screams in their mind, obliterating out all other thought or care."

His knees were trying to buckle. "Ginny, baby, I'm sorry…" Johnny was sorry, but he had to do it. He punched her. Right in the face. As hard as he could.

She let him go. He stumbled away from the gurney, but she leapt up, jumping from the body bag and *onto* him in one move. They hit the ground with a bone-shattering impact. In a flash, Virginia's legs pinned his arms down and her hand yanked his neck to the side.

"No!" He yelled. "You have her food—"

That had been part of the deal. The plan. The vampire was going to bring Ginny a victim.

Ginny's teeth sliced into his throat.

"I do have the food. *You're the food.*" The guy's footsteps shuffled closer.

Ginny was drinking from him, gulping down Johnny's blood and he couldn't get her off him. He couldn't make her stop. She was supposed to transform him, but not like this. *This* wasn't the plan.

His body shuddered beneath her. His nails scraped across the concrete around him. "G-Ginny…"

She didn't stop.

And soon it was hard to fight. His body became limp beneath her. Each breath was a struggle. He was cold. But at least he didn't feel pain any longer.

"So…good…" Ginny whispered. Her head rose.

Johnny blinked and made himself stare up at her. Blood soaked her lips and dripped down her chin. Her eyes seemed so dark. *Hungry. Cruel.*

She wasn't his Ginny. He tried to talk but only a rough groan came from him.

At that sound, she blinked, and some of the mania seemed to leave her face. "J-Johnny?"

His body wasn't shuddering any longer.

"Johnny! God, Johnny!" She scrambled off him. "What happened? *What did I do?*"

She needed to give him her blood. If he got her blood, he'd live. Right? Wasn't that the way it worked?

He'd...

There was no more cold. No more pain. There was nothing.

"Johnny!"

***

Thane Durant smiled as he watched the human take his last breath. The blood had spread beneath him in a wide pool, gleaming in the night.

"Johnny?" Virginia's voice was so broken. She looked broken as she crouched over the still human. Her hands were rushing over him, trying to bring him back. It was too late for that.

Just what he'd wanted.

Thane liked to give all of his new vampires a little test. It was important for them to understand—from the very beginning—that they would have no other attachment in life. Well, in their afterlife. No friends, no family, no lover—no one would be more important than he was.

So he liked to provide those newly turned a special meal.

A meal that went straight to the heart.

Virginia yanked her hand up to her mouth and sank her new fangs into her wrist. Oh, such a sweet gesture. She thought she'd be able to save the human with her blood.

Before her bleeding hand could go back to the dead one's mouth, Thane leapt forward and caught it in a steely grip. "It's such a pity to waste good blood."

She looked up at her. She was crying. Wasn't that adorable? He knew that she and Johnny had been involved with plenty of crimes. Kidnappings. Even murders. But she was crying over his dead body. She'd truly cared for her human, as much as she was able to care.

"I have to bring him back," she whispered.

"He's gone. Long gone." To come back, the guy would have needed the vamp blood *before* he drew his last breath. "Nothing will bring him back." Perhaps a bit of voodoo magic, but *no one* would be able to control the guy then. "We need to leave. The sun will rise soon."

He let her go.

She instantly shoved her hand to the dead man's mouth.

Sighing, he watched her. Such a foolish gesture.

"Drink! Drink, *please!*"

Thane rolled his eyes. "The dead don't drink. They decompose."

Her head snapped toward him. Her eyes flared with fury. "*You did this!*"

Now he had to laugh. "I didn't slash his throat in a frenzy of bloodlust. That was *you,* love."

She leapt to her feet and charged at him. Before she could strike, Thane caught her hands and held her tightly. All of his amusement fled. "Do I fucking look like someone you get to hit?"

Memories from his past flashed through his mind. A big fist. The snap of bones. *No one hurts me now.*

"You attacked me!" She cried out. Blood was still dripping down her chin.

He really did hate for blood to go to waste.

Using his grip on her arms, he lifted her up. She screamed but he leaned forward and licked that blood off her chin. "You, love," he whispered. "You killed him, not me." He licked away that blood, kissing her chin and enjoying the sweet coppery taste as she tried to wrench her head away from him.

"*You killed me!*" Virginia shrieked.

He lowered her back to the ground, but didn't let her go. "That was your dead lover's idea. He wanted you to be a vampire. Seems he thought you were getting old. You both were. And he wanted to stop time." He didn't spare another glance for the dead man. "Consider time stopped." *For you both.*

Tears trickled down her cheeks. "I didn't want this."

"I could've killed you both." His original plan. Until he'd realized that she was something he didn't understand, not yet. The way she could change her voice—it was fascinating to him. A talent he could use. So he'd decided to keep her around, for the moment. Besides, he'd lost a few of his new recruits to the werewolf alpha. She'd be needed, soon. *An expendable vampire.*

"You should've killed me."

He let her go. "Does the blood taste good?"

Her gaze was on the body. "*Yes.*"

"Want more of it?"

She shook her head no, even as she had to whisper, "Yes."

Because the bloodlust would rise in her again. It was always that way for the newly turned. No control, just hunger. So much hunger. "I'll take care of you," he promised her. He offered his hand. "Come with me or stay with the dead."

Her shoulders shook as she kept staring at her lover's savaged throat. "Johnny, I'm sorry."

"Why? He sold you out first." Thane kept his hand up. "The sun will rise any moment. Do you truly want to be alone then?"

Slowly, so slowly, her hand lifted toward him. Her fingers slid over his skin.

"Good choice," he told her.

***

Since she'd met Aidan, her life had truly gone to hell. Jane stood inside his office at Hell's Gate, glancing around nervously. She'd been shot at, ambushed behind the cathedral, her apartment had been set on fire…what would be next?

She wasn't sure she wanted to know. And if she didn't get a few hours of sleep, she was going to collapse. Simple fact. She wasn't some supernatural powerhouse. She was a human. Humans needed to sleep in order to survive. They also needed food. It was pretty hard for her to remember the last time she'd eaten, but the need to fall into an unconscious heap was going to take precedence for her.

Jane eyed the leather couch. It would work.

She'd just settled onto the cushions when Aidan opened the door and strode inside. "We could've gone to my home," he grumbled. "It's far bigger than this place."

Jane was sure it was, but he'd also told her it was out in the swamp, and she'd wanted to stay in the city. Her eyes closed as she sank into that soft leather. Serious heaven…in hell. If she'd had the energy, she would have smiled at the thought. Instead, she pulled her quilt up around her body and let out a long sigh.

"I have a perfectly good bed there," he added as the floor creaked beneath his footsteps.

No doubt, he probably had a monstrously huge bed.

"It's a four poster," Aidan continued, voice deepening a bit. "Made of solid, hard wood. Perfect for all kinds of…things."

She wasn't going to touch that one, not then. "Just need a few…hours…" Jane said, her voice already slurring. "Can crash here…then come up with a new plan…"

There were leads she had to run down. Witnesses to question. A killer vamp that she needed to stop.

Jane felt the light touch of Aidan's fingers on her forehead as he brushed back her hair. His touch was oddly soothing. Strange to think of a werewolf as someone who could soothe.

"Crash with me anytime, Mary Jane," he murmured. His fingers slid down her cheek.

She forced her eyelids to open, even though sleep called so temptingly to her. He'd knelt beside the couch, and his mouth was incredibly close to her. Was it so wrong that she wanted him to kiss her right then? A kiss good night?

Not that it was really night any longer. The sun was rising.

Just a few hours of sleep. Maybe two or three, then I'll be okay.

He leaned forward. "Sleep well," Aidan said, his voice deep and rumbly. A werewolf's voice. His lips pressed to hers. Tender. He could be tender when he wanted to be.

Her lashes began to slip closed once more. Even though she needed to tell him… "Sorry…"

"For what?"

Sleep had her, and it wasn't letting go. "If…I…scream…"

***

Why would Jane scream in her sleep?

Aidan stood as he watched her. Her face was so peaceful. Beautiful. Her lashes cast shadows on her high cheeks. Her breath came softly as she cuddled beneath her quilt. It smelled of ash. Once she wakened, he'd get the quilt cleaned for her, but he wasn't moving it then. Jane seemed to need it, and he wanted her to have everything that she needed.

He wanted to be all that she needed.

So for a time, he didn't move at all. He just stared down at her, making sure her breathing stayed soft and even. What gave Jane her nightmares? What made her scream out? Was it her parents' death? Or something else?

And what in the hell could he do to stop her screams?

When he was sure that she'd slipped far away from him, Aidan marched back to his office door. He opened it, softly, and saw Paris waiting a few feet away, one shoulder propped up against the wall.

When his friend saw him, Paris raised his brows. "I'm guessing the sexy detective is out now?" He inhaled, his lips curving. "She does smell rather delicious…"

Aidan flashed fang. "Do not even *think* it."

"Hey, ease up! I'm not alpha, so it isn't like her scent screws with my head. At least, not the way it does yours." He straightened away from the wall. "But I've got to know, is it like the stories say? Does it pull you right in? Obsess you? Make you not even able to *think* of anything else?" His voice lowered dramatically as he continued, "Should I go get you a chair? Do you need to sit down because you aren't close to her anymore and you just damn well might freaking die if you don't see her precious face?"

Muttering in disgust, Aidan flipped him off. "I need you to do a job, asshole." But even as he growled at the guy, there was faint humor in his eyes. Paris was pretty much the only one in the pack who would dare say any shit like that. He and Paris had grown up together. Been through more battles than he could count. He'd saved

Paris, Paris had saved him, and Aidan knew, beyond any shadow of a doubt, that Paris would kill — or die — to protect him.

Just as Aidan would do for him.

There was, quite simply, no one he trusted more.

"I *am* doing a job," Paris said, sounding a bit offended. "I'm the one who got that dumbass Garrison out of the hospital and into a werewolf safe house so his leg could get proper treatment. You're welcome, by the way."

Aidan waited.

"What?" Paris crossed his arms over his chest, and, slowly some of the humor faded from his golden eyes. "What am I missing?"

"It's something *I* missed." He glanced toward his now shut office door. "About her."

"Well, yeah, if you'd gone to talk with the woman before you approved her promotion to homicide detective, you would've known she was some kind of vampire and werewolf honey that would draw you in like mad but —"

"No, something else." He exhaled slowly. "This doesn't go beyond us."

Paris took a few steps closer. Suddenly, he appeared very serious. Unusual for Paris.

"She has — Jane has a scar. It looks like it was made with a soldering pen." And he'd seen vampires use those pens before. Vamps could heal very fast, from anything but fire. So since tattoo ink wouldn't last on them—their bodies just flushed it out of their systems—they'd started using fire to mark themselves. Or rather, the fire of a soldering pen. They branded their bodies to show their affiliation with a certain vamp sector. To show their power.

And unless Aidan was wrong… "I think a vampire bastard marked Jane." And he wanted to *destroy* the fool.

Paris sucked in a sharp breath.

"She was young when it happened. Probably little more than a kid." And this is what bothered him the most. "We know her parents were killed when she was eleven." That had been in the preliminary paperwork on her background investigation—material that had come to him when she'd been vetted for the detective position. "But our intel said it was a botched home invasion."

"My team got that intel," Paris said carefully.

"Right. And usually, your team knows their shit."

"Not this time?"

"They need to go back and dig deeper. No, not *they*." He gave a grim nod. "*You*. Just you. I want you to dig into her past personally. Learn more about the attack on her. She was taken to a hospital afterwards, right? Find the doctors and nurses who took care of her. Get them to tell you exactly what they remember about that night."

"Long time ago," Paris muttered. "Humans might not remember anything from back then."

"Then bring someone to me who was there," he said as his fingers tightened into fists. "And I will make the person remember."

Because no one fucking marked Jane. No one.

Paris nodded. He started to turn away, then he stopped. "What did her scar look like?"

"I only saw part of it." He would be seeing the rest. She would show him.

"But, we need—"

"I need to know who hurt her. And I need them to pay." Simple. "Tell no one else. Come back to me when you learn more."

"Understood."

Aidan turned away and reached for the doorknob. He could feel Paris still watching him, though, so he glanced back over his shoulder. "What?"

"You didn't answer my questions from before," Paris murmured as he tilted his head to the right and studied Aidan. "You okay…with her?"

Is it like the stories say? Does it pull you right in? Obsess you? Make you not even able to think of anything else? Should I go get you a chair? Do you need to sit down because you aren't close to her anymore and you just damn well might freaking die if you don't see her precious face?

Paris had been mocking, but yeah, he was fucking being pulled in by her. And with his particular past, he had to tread very, very carefully. "Get me answers." He needed them, fast.

Before they were all in too deep.

He opened the door and headed back into his office. Jane continued to sleep and a faint furrow had appeared between her brows. Aidan made sure to lock the office door and then he went to her just as she—

"*Don't burn me,*" Jane whispered. "I won't tell…"

She whimpered. The cry was high and sharp. It was a child's cry.

His claws slid from his fingertips. The vampire who'd hurt her would *pay.*

"Don't—" Jane cried out.

Carefully, Aidan pressed a kiss to her cheek. "No one will burn you, sweetheart. It won't happen." Not on his watch.

Had the vampire tonight been trying to send a message with his fire? Had the flames stirred up memories of Jane's past?

A home invasion gone wrong…that had been the story in the papers and in all the old police files. Robbers had broken into Jane's home. She'd escaped, but her parents hadn't been so lucky.

Her whimpers faded away. Jane. So fierce when she was awake. So strong. And asleep…

I will destroy any threat to her.

"Sleep well, sweetheart," Aidan said as he pulled a chair closer to the couch. He knew that he wouldn't be leaving her side. Jane might not get it, but protecting her was his number one priority.

Now, and, he suspected, always.

CHAPTER TWELVE

Jane rolled to her side, stretching slowly. Her arm rose above her head, sliding over the smooth, velvety surface of leather, and her eyes opened.

He wasn't watching her, a good thing. If she'd opened her eyes and found Aidan staring back at her while she slept, that probably would have scared the shit out of her. *Serial killer style.*

He was close, though, sitting near her, and Aidan had his laptop open on his lap. She studied him a moment as full wakefulness slid through her. He had a sexy stubble growth lining his hard jaw, his hair was tousled, his gaze narrowed in thought and—

"You didn't scream."

He seemed totally focused on the laptop— but now she realized he was actually focused on her.

"You didn't scream while you slept."

Jane swallowed. "I didn't? That's good." She sat up, her fingers automatically moving to stroke over her quilt.

"You did say something, though."

Oh, crap. "What?"

"You asked not to be burned."

Her fingers stilled.

Deliberately, Aidan shut the laptop and put it on his desk. Then he came back and focused that laser-like stare on her. "Want to talk about that, sweetheart?"

She licked her dry lips.

His gaze fell, followed the movement, and heated.

"Not really," she said and was surprised that her voice came out so breathy. She hadn't meant that, had she?

"Too bad." He leaned toward her. "I want to know who the fuck marked you."

Marked?

"I've been sitting here, trying to get some pack work done, but I keep thinking about *you*. How young you must have been when some bastard gave you that mark, when he hurt *you*." Fury flashed on his face. "He's a dead man walking."

"I-isn't that what all vampires are?"

He blinked. "Jane…" Aidan growled.

"I don't remember a lot about that night." Her words tumbled out. "When I tried to tell the people at the hospital, they said I was delusional. Too much stress." A child psychiatrist had been called in to talk with her, though she hadn't realized that was the lady's job, not back then. The woman had talked to her for hours, telling her that Jane was "trying to make a terrible, terrible tragedy into something that was a nightmare."

Only it hadn't been a nightmare. It had been real.

That had been Jane's first run-in with a shrink, and it hadn't ended well. Instead of being helped, the woman had sent a kid off to a psych ward.

And she'd told me the only way out was to stop talking about monsters.

"I won't think you're delusional."

No, he wouldn't. He couldn't. After all, he was a werewolf. "The man who—who burned me was tall. Blond. He had a perfectly normal face." A good-looking killer. "What I remember most though—I remember his teeth." She swallowed and confessed, "They were fangs. He was a vampire." *There, I said it. Finally.*

Aidan absorbed that revelation in silence. "No wonder you didn't have a full-on flip out when I told you about monsters."

"I've known about monsters for a long time." *Since one killed my parents.* "I just thought it was smarter to stop talking about them, until I had more proof." That was something else the shrink had told her. *If you keep telling these stories, I'll have*

*to make them lock you up again. You don't want that,
do you, dear?*

She'd hated that shrink.

"Tell me about him."

"I already told you what I know. He was tall
with blond hair. And…and he had green eyes."
She remembered his eyes. "I can't forget him
because I keep seeing his face when I close my
eyes."

Aidan glanced away from her. Had he
stiffened when she described the vamp? "It will
be easy enough to forget the dead," he said.

"No." She rose and carefully folded her quilt.
"Forgetting them isn't easy." Life might be
simpler if it were. "And right now, I have a dead
woman who needs justice. I have to go out and
see just which vamp decided to end Melanie
Wagner's life."

He rose, too, and blocked her path. "What
about the attack on *your* life last night?"

"Well, I'm sure guessing that attack and the
vamp who turned Melanie…I'm thinking they're
related." Everything had spiraled *after* she found
Melanie on Bourbon Street. "So I start with her,
and I work my way back. I'll find the link to the
vampire through her. I'll get him."

His gaze became hooded. "Turning him over
to your cop friends isn't an option. Prisons
weren't made to hold vampires."

"Finding him is priority one. Stopping him from hurting anyone else? That's number two. Jailing him…" She ran a hand over her face. "I'll figure that one out along the way." Jane sidestepped around him.

"I made arrangements for new clothing and shoes to be brought to you." He gestured toward his desk and she finally took note of the bags there. Fancy bags from stores that she normally avoided because she'd rather spend all of that cash on, like, food. A week's worth of food — two weeks — equaled one shirt from some of those places. Jane knew that for certain because she'd gone in some of those shops before, just to look.

A woman could always look, right?

"You can use my bathroom, too," Aidan murmured as he pointed to a door on his right. "Shower is in there. In case you want to freshen up before you go out to question witnesses and fight for the dead. You know, your deal."

She slanted a narrow-eyed glance his way. Was he making fun of her? Then she thought about the shower and tried to casually smell her shirt. Okay, so she *maybe* smelled like fire. And probably looked like hell. A shower and a change of clothes wouldn't be the worst thing ever before she hit the streets. Hesitant, she inched her way toward the bags on his desk. "How did you know my size?"

"I touched you. I know your body."

That was so cocky. And, oddly, sexy. Maybe it was the way his voice had dipped when he said he knew her body. Kind of made her feel a little melty. She scooped up the bags. "I'll try them on, *after* I shower. And I'll definitely be paying you back for everything."

"More bags are coming."

She gaped at him.

"The fire took your belongings. I'm giving them back to you."

Insurance would cover that, right? "I'll pay you—"

A muscle flexed along his jaw. "You have trouble with gifts."

"I have trouble with strings."

"I don't see strings." He lifted his hands. Big, powerful hands. He looked at them, then her. "I just see you."

His gaze had heated and that melting she felt was getting worse. He wanted her, she knew it, and she wanted him. She could admit that. The guy wasn't some heartless jerk—he was so much more and he was getting to her. Sinking beneath her guard and she was nervous.

Afraid.

His nostrils flared a bit. "You don't have to be."

She backed toward his bathroom, holding the bags tightly. "I don't have to be what?"

"Afraid. Not of me."

The door was just inches away. "What makes you think I'm afraid?"

"Because I can smell your fear. I can smell when you're happy. When you're mad. When you're…turned on."

So embarrassing. Her cheeks burned. She was hitting on fear, anger, and arousal right then, all at the same time. And the wolf would know it. "Guess I don't get any secrets, huh? Hardly seems fair."

"When you want to know how I feel, just ask." He paused a beat. "Like right now, I want you."

Her gaze jerked to his.

"I stayed next to you for three hours. I thought about how fucking furious I was that someone had hurt you."

Her heart was beating faster.

"And I thought about how much I'd like to take all of your pain away. How I'd like to only give you pleasure." His eyes were so bright. "Wouldn't you like that pleasure, sweetheart?"

She opened the bathroom door and pretty much fled inside. Her shaking hands dropped the bags and then those hands slapped against the sink. A big, marble-top sink. *Get a grip, woman.* Jane stared at herself in the mirror. She had to stop letting the wolf get to her.

But his voice rolled through her head.

How I'd like to only give you pleasure.

Jane stripped. She tossed her ashy smelling clothes to the floor and then hurried toward the shower. She yanked the faucet and had water streaming out—from two different locations in the shower. A very massive shower. Easily big enough for two...

Wouldn't you like that pleasure, sweetheart?

She hadn't been with a lover in a very long time. Her job had been her goal—she'd busted ass to move up the ranks, and so, yeah, okay, maybe she sucked at the dating scene. Small talk and flirtations weren't her thing. Busting perps and solving crimes—that was what she lived for. Trying to interact with someone on a romantic level, oh, jeez, but that was beyond her scope.

She got too nervous. She found men who wanted commitment—and she wasn't ready for that—or she found men who only wanted fast hook-ups, and she didn't want that, either.

She wanted...

I don't know what I want.

Jane stepped into the shower. Steam rose around her.

You're a liar, Jane. A sly voice seemed to whisper to her. *You know exactly what you want. And he does, too. He just told you...he can smell what you feel.*

The water slid over her skin. Her eyes closed. Then she just whispered... "Aidan."

Could he hear her? Was werewolf hearing that good, that strong? That he could hear her over the pounding of the water? Through the door?

"Aidan, I want you."

The door banged open, hard enough to have her head snapping up. She saw him through the glass door of the shower. He stood in the doorway, his eyes locked on hers.

"Don't fucking tease, sweetheart. Teasing a werewolf is a *very* bad idea."

The big, bad beast had heard her whisper.

I won't back down this time.

She opened the shower door. Cold air slid against her skin, making her nipples harden.

One of his hands grabbed the sink and clenched around its edge. "Mary Jane…"

"Sometimes," she confessed as she stared at him, totally nude and vulnerable as she bared her darkest truth, "what I fear most is myself." Trusting the wrong man. Not going for what she wanted. Letting life pass her by.

The dead are all I know.

She lifted her hand toward him. "I don't remember ever wanting someone the way I want you."

With his eyes on her, he took a step forward. One, another. His feet were bare as he approached her. Then, stopping right in front of the open shower, he stripped off his shirt and dropped it onto the tiled floor. His hands went to his jeans and the button at the top. He unhooked the button and slid down the zipper. Her gaze fell and when those jeans dropped —

Aidan doesn't believe in wearing underwear. Check. I'll remember that.

His hand reached for hers.

"Will it hurt?" Jane blurted.

His gaze widened.

"Being with — with a werewolf. I mean, are you different from a man?" No, no, she was screwing this up and sounding like a complete idiot. He *looked* like a man. A man with a seriously big dick. Big and long and wide and she really wanted to touch that long length, but…what if werewolves had sex differently? What if there was biting involved or, hell, something *else*? She wasn't a biter.

"I'm very different from any man you've ever been with before." His voice roughened. "And I don't want to ever hear about those fucking bastards again, okay?"

"Aidan —"

"As far as hurting you…" He lifted her hand to his mouth and pressed a kiss to her knuckles. "Never."

Unless I become a vamp. Then he'd have to kill me. Worry slid through her. He'd said —

"I don't like the smell of your fear," Aidan murmured. "So why don't we focus on desire?"

She gave a quick nod and he stepped into the shower with her. Immediately, that huge space seemed way, way too small. The water poured down on them from the left and the right, the twin jets sending warm water and steam out as Aidan brought his body against hers. Her hands lifted and curled around his shoulders.

Jane could think of a million reasons why she should *not* be doing this.

He was a werewolf.

They'd just met.

She wasn't a risk taker, not when it came to relationships.

And—

Aidan kissed her. Her mouth was open, her lips lightly parted, and his tongue swept right inside. And all the reasons not to do this, not to be with him, faded away. Because all that really mattered was that she wanted him. Wanted him more than she could ever remember wanting anyone else.

The kiss started easily enough. He was sampling. Seducing. She rose onto her toes so that she could get closer to him. Their bodies were slick now, and the long length of his cock pressed against her.

What will he feel like inside of me?

Soon enough, she'd be finding out.

A low growl built in his throat and the kiss became harder. More demanding. She could practically taste his desire, and she loved that wild flavor. Her hands slid down his arms. Down, down…she pushed them between their bodies because she wanted to touch his cock. And as soon as her fingers curled around that broad length, he gave another groan. Rougher. Wilder.

Yes, please, more of that. Was it so wrong that the sound of his lusty growl turned her on?

But he pulled back. No, he pushed *her* back. Her shoulders brushed against the tiled wall of the shower. Steam was all around them. "Touch me too much…" Aidan warned. "And I won't get to savor *you.*"

She wasn't really about savoring right then. Passion and need were churning inside of her, and she wanted to act — right then — before the feelings stopped. Before sanity came back.

But he bent before her. She felt the light rasp of his breath and then he'd taken her nipple into his mouth. A surge of pure fire raced through Jane and her sex clenched because that licking he was doing — it felt *so* good. His tongue laved her nipple and, a moment later, she felt the light edge of his teeth. The sensual tug had her arching toward him even as his fingers slid down her stomach. Down and between the spread vee of her thighs.

No fair. I'd wanted to touch him. I'd wanted —

His fingers didn't push into her. Instead, he stroked over her clit. Touching with sensual skill, a man who knew *exactly* what he was doing. She was on her toes, biting her lip, her body shuddering, just with a few strokes over her clit. "Aidan!" So close to an orgasm. So incredibly close.

His strokes turned more demanding. Faster. She was going to come like that, Jane knew it. Come just from a few touches of his fingers right over her clit. *Never* had she done that, not so fast, but she was already on the razor's edge, and she just wanted, "More!"

His mouth kissed a trail to her other breast. He licked her nipple. His fingers kept strumming her clit.

"Aidan…" It was hard to talk. Her eyes had squeezed closed.

He pushed a finger into her, drove it in deep, then pulled back, his fingers swiping over her once more, rougher, harder.

Her breath caught in her throat.

That finger pushed into her again. Fast. One finger, two, then he pulled back, going toward her clit, spreading the cream from her sex over her as she climaxed on a quick scream, her whole body becoming bow tight in an instant as the wave of release hit her and surged through Jane, rocking her core. Her eyes flew open and she saw him watching her, a faint glow lighting his gaze.

His fingers were still sliding over her, making that orgasm last and last, wringing every last bit of pleasure from her.

"So beautiful," Aidan whispered.

He made her feel that way.

The pleasure faded and his fingers slid away from her. Her heartbeat drummed in her ears and little aftershocks had her sex contracting every few moments. She felt the delicate inner muscles give a little shiver.

That was good. Better than good. Way better.

He put his fingers to his lips. With his eyes on her, he licked those long fingers, tasting *her*.

Oh, wow.

"Delicious," he told her. A muscle flexed in his jaw. "I think I need more."

She didn't know —

He picked her up. Moved so fast that the world seemed to spin. His hands were tight around her waist as he knelt before her — and put his mouth on her sex. She was still sensitive from her release and the feel of his mouth on her was almost too much — *in a really, really good way.* Her fingers sank into his wet hair and she pushed her hips against his mouth. What a wicked, wonderful mouth. She could feel the swirl of his tongue against her. In her. And another climax bore down on her. It should have been impossible to need again that quickly, to have her body aching already, but it was happening.

Actually, if she didn't stop him, she would be climaxing again any moment. But this time… "I want you, in me," she said.

He licked her again.

She bit her lip so hard she nearly drew blood. Jane was trying to hold off her second climax because when she came again, she wanted to be riding him. She wanted that hard cock in her as she went insane with her release.

Her fingers tightened on his hair. "Aidan, please."

He moved again—that way too fast movement that she couldn't quite follow. A werewolf thing. Then he was in front of her, still holding her against the wall, still lifting her up and acting as if she didn't weigh a thing.

Supernatural strength.

"My kind…we don't carry human diseases."

It took a lust-filled moment for his words to sink in.

"You're safe…" Aidan added, voice so rough and dark. "With me."

No condom. She knew exactly what he meant. She'd never gone without a condom before. Never been flesh to flesh with a lover. But Aidan wasn't like her other lovers. "I'm…ah…on birth control." It was hard to get those words out. He couldn't carry diseases, she didn't have any diseases, and there was no risk of pregnancy.

Do it. Take him in. Skin to skin.

Her head moved in a small nod. His eyes locked on hers. He held her with one hand as he moved to position his cock with the other.

Jane circled his hips with her legs. The broad head of his shaft pushed against her. She sucked in a quick breath.

He drove into her, sinking deep with one strong thrust. He stretched her. He controlled her. He pretty much wrecked her with pleasure. Because when he withdrew and thrust back into her, Jane came. There was no more holding back, she just erupted. Pleasure hit her, and she squeezed the full length of his cock as she rode out that wild wave.

He kept thrusting. "So good, love the way you feel…perfect…*Perfect for me.*"

In and out.

And then he was coming.

She was *still* coming. The pleasure just wouldn't stop. It kept hitting and hitting and every movement of his body inside of her just heightened the intensity of her feelings. Pleasure, pain—they were almost the same. It was just *so* strong. Incredible.

Freaking fantastic.

Her nails raked over his back. And she kissed his shoulder, hard, trying to muffle her cries. Her mouth opened and she bit him.

"Fuck, yes. I like that." He was still coming, too. Thrusting hard inside of her and she felt the rush of his release filling her.

For a minute, the pleasure was so strong that she thought she might pass out. And that would be way embarrassing.

So she bit him again.

He gave that sexy growl and held her even tighter. Jane could hear the frantic pounding of his heartbeat. It was oddly reassuring.

For a time, she just listened to that heartbeat and she let the pleasure course through her.

Never like this. Never.

Then another thought followed…

I can't believe I've been missing out on this.

His heartbeat slowed. She became aware of the water then, still hitting them. She blinked groggily as he pulled out of her. Her body protested a bit, clamping down harder because she had enjoyed the hell out of him, but she made herself settle down.

Get your control. One fantastic time in a shower wouldn't turn her into a sex fiend. Maybe.

Her legs slid down his body. He took a step back. For a moment, her legs nearly buckled as her knees did a little jiggle, but he wrapped a hand around her waist, steadying her. "I've got you." His words were a deep rumble.

She looked up at him.

His touch seemed to scorch her. He was touching her on her right side. His fingers were on her scar, the scar she'd hated for so long. His gaze was on the scar, too, and she followed his stare. His fingers traced over the lines, white lines now—not the angry red they'd been before—yet still so distinct after all of this time. His touch was so careful, as if he feared hurting her, but the mark didn't hurt anymore.

Only in her dreams.

The mark was almost shaped like a horseshoe. The top was circular, a wide circle, but at the bottom, the circle didn't close. Instead, a leg seemed to go out from each side of the circle, one toward the left, another toward the right.

"Omega," he said, voice rough.

She frowned. "What?"

But he gave a grim shake of his head. Aidan turned from her and opened the shower door. A flick of his hand had the water turning off and cold air slid inside of the door. Her body still hummed with pleasure but something was different now. A new tension had entered his body, only that tension had nothing to do with desire.

He left her a moment and came back with a big, fluffy white towel. When she slipped from the shower, he wrapped that towel around her, then dried her gently. She could've dried herself. Could've pulled away, but she didn't. She rather enjoyed having someone take care of her because it didn't happen that often.

Aidan was much rougher as he dried his own body, jerking the towel over his abs — seriously amazing abs. The guy had a twelve pack, at least. And she didn't think that hot bod was a werewolf thing. Aidan was just...Aidan.

And his gaze kept straying to the scar on her side. "What did you say before?" Jane asked as she wrapped that towel around her body and tucked an end between her breasts, securing it in place — and covering her scar. "When you saw the mark, you said..."

He waved it away. "Nothing. I just hate that anyone ever hurt you."

She hated it, too. She also hated it when people lied to her. "Liar."

He turned toward the door. He hadn't dried his broad back very well, and water drops slid over his tanned skin.

"You said something," Jane persisted. "Do you know what that mark is?"

His shoulders stiffened. "What do you think it is?"

Now that he wasn't looking at her, Jane stepped toward the mirror. She lifted up the towel so that she could see the curving lines of the mark. *After great sex, this is what we talk about? No cuddle time?* "I think it's some kind of hack job. The guy was coming back to add more, but...I got away." The mark was glaring to her. Nearly as big as her hand, and the raised flesh was even whiter than normal right then—probably because her body had pinkened in the warm shower.

She looked up in the mirror and found that Aidan was staring at her reflection.

Jane let the towel fall back into place.

"You're sure the guy was going to add more?"

"He left his...pen...next to me." The thing had looked like a pen, but it had been fire hot. No, it had been hot. "He said we'd take a little break." Her laughter was bitter. "I'd screamed until my voice broke. I think he wasn't giving *me* a break. He was giving himself one." The scent of burning flesh would haunt her forever. Her fingers moved over the towel, over the spot that covered her scar. "One lover told me it was a lucky horseshoe." After that lame line, she hadn't ever seen that guy again. Lucky? She'd been savagely burned while her parents were murdered. There had been nothing lucky about the mark.

"Fucking idiot," Aidan snarled. "And...sweetheart..."

In the mirror, she saw that his hand had clenched around the doorknob. No, not just clenched around it—the doorknob had broken off in his hand.

She whirled around to face him, her jaw dropping in surprise.

"Don't tell me about your other lovers," he added as he tossed the doorknob toward the garbage can. "I really can't handle that shit."

She forced her gaping mouth to close.

"Not a horseshoe," Aidan rasped.

"I-I didn't think—"

"Omega," he gritted out. "It looks like the Greek letter Omega."

She knew *nothing* about Greek letters, but she'd be finding out everything possible about them immediately.

His gaze slid to the bags she'd dropped in the corner of the bathroom. The faint lines near his mouth tightened. "You should get dressed. We have witnesses to interview."

We?

And was he still not going to talk about the sex? Or maybe it hadn't been so mind-blowing on his end. Maybe it had been normal, run-of-the-mill pleasure for a werewolf.

But for her…

I think I may be totally ruined for other guys.

She swallowed, took a deep breath, and as he walked out of the bathroom, Jane called out, "What does Omega mean?" It had to stand for something, right?

He stilled.

"Aidan?"

He glanced over his shoulder at her. There was no expression on his face. No desire. No anger. No emotion at all. "Omega is the last letter of the Greek alphabet."

She nodded. For some reason, breathing was a little hard. Her fingers skimmed over her scar, as if she could feel it through the towel.

"It means…the end."

CHAPTER THIRTEEN

"So you're telling me that Melanie Wagner had no friends, no family, no associates at all?" Jane asked, her voice tight with anger as she grilled the club owner who stood—sweating and shifting nervously—in front of the Bourbon Street strip club where Melanie had worked.

Correction...*dancing* club. The guy—Jimmy Cross—had been fast to point out the difference to Jane. Though Aidan knew there wasn't any damn such difference.

When Jimmy had sputtered and rambled about his hole-in-the-wall business, Jane had just narrowed her phenomenal eyes on him.

Aidan crossed his arms over his chest and continued watching the exchange. He hadn't really expected this human to be much help in Jane's investigation, but if she was determined to interview witnesses, he hadn't been about to let her head out into the city alone.

Yes, she was a capable detective. More than capable. And her trusty gun was back in her holster. But...

I need to stay close to her.

He'd seen her scar, recognized it for what it was, and fear had blasted through him. It was odd. Aidan hadn't known fear, not until he'd known her. She'd stirred too many dangerous emotions inside of him.

If word got out about her scar, if other werewolves found out about the mark…werewolves who actually knew the old stories like he did…

We are screwed.

He had to figure out a way to protect Jane. To keep her alive. Because when the others learned what he had, what she *truly* was…it wouldn't be about preventing a violent death for her…

They would want her eliminated as soon as possible.

An assassin would be sent after Jane. A painless, easy death. A professional who knew just how to end a life, without bringing Jane back as the monster that she may become.

His claws stretched from his fingertips and Aidan made sure to keep them hidden from the still-sputtering human, a man who reeked of drugs and addiction.

"I want her employee files," Jane snapped.

"I don't—f-files?" Jimmy stammered.

"Jesus save me," Jane muttered as she threw her hands into the air. "Yes, employee files. You know, those forms you are *supposed* to have people fill out when they start working for you? Melanie's emergency contact should be on them."

Jimmy just blinked.

Sighing in disgust, Jane took a step toward him. "I've got a woman lying cold in a morgue— a woman who has a family out there, somewhere. They need to know what happened to her."

A search of Melanie's tiny apartment had turned up no clues.

I don't know…Maybe she didn't have any family looking for her.

Maybe there was no one.

And maybe that's why the vampire targeted her. With no one to miss Melanie, she would have been the perfect victim.

"I-I don't have any employee files."

"How did you even know the woman was of legal age?" Jane fired back at him.

Jimmy's cheeks were fire-engine red. "She said she was, okay? She wanted to work here. The tips were good."

"I'm sure they were," Jane said, voice icy. "And guess what else I'm sure of? I'm sure that if you didn't check her age, you didn't check ages for any of your other employees, either. I'll be making a phone call and getting this place investigated, *count on that.* If you've got underage girls here, consider your ass shut down, Jimmy." She spun on her heel, marching back toward Aidan.

There was fury in her gaze. The woman was sexy when she was enraged.

Actually, she was rather sexy all the time. He thought so, anyway.

"Let's go," Jane said, her voice tinged with her fury. "This joker is—"

"Wait!" Jimmy called out frantically. He surged after her, his hands outstretched.

Before the guy could touch her, Aidan was in his path. "You don't want to do that." A lethal promise.

Jimmy looked at his hands, looked at Aidan, and looked at his hands again. "No, no, I wasn't—wasn't gonna hurt her!"

Hell, no, he hadn't been.

"I just—just needed to tell her…" Jimmy licked his fat lips and then smoothed a hand over his sweaty brow. "I *did* see Melanie hanging with someone af-after work one night." He spoke quickly, the words spilling over each other. "I remember 'cause…I thought she was finally loosening up a bit…hanging out with customers…"

Jane pushed Aidan back. "You know the customer's name?"

Jimmy shook his head. "He was a…pay in cash only guy, if you know what I mean."

"I know," she said with a roll of her eyes. "Tell me more about him."

"Big." Jimmy cast a glance up at Aidan. "About his size, but blond. Kinda pale."

When he didn't say more, Jane shook her head in frustration. "Anything else?"

Jimmy just shrugged. "He was an average white guy, okay? Good lookin', I guess. Melanie seemed to like him." He scratched his chin. "You know, I think she might have left with him the night she…" His voice trailed away.

Jane squeezed her eyes shut. "The night she died?"

"Uh, yeah." Jimmy's fingers were shaking a bit.

"Can you talk to a sketch artist?" Jane prompted when her eyes opened again, after she'd done with what looked like some kind of fast counting/cooling down technique. "Get me a better idea of who the hell this guy is?"

Jimmy rubbed his sweaty forehead once more. "I can do better. I-I think I got him on video." He turned and headed toward the back of the club.

Jane strode after him, and since Jane was following him, so did Aidan. They passed at least five stripper poles and two golden cages on their way to the back. Then the hallway snaked to the right, and Aidan saw that the area was filled with small, private dance rooms. Jimmy led them past those rooms and into a little office.

In that closet-sized office, two computer screens sat on the desk. Jimmy keyed up the computer. "I had the feed runnin' when she left..." Jimmy muttered.

"You *recorded* your guests?" Jane demanded. "Jimmy, that shit is illegal!"

He curled his body over the keyboard. "You want the video or not?"

"Yes, I want it! Give me the damn video!"

His fingers tapped over the keyboard. "And, for the record, copper, I wasn't videoing the rooms...this was right outside my place. A freakin' public alley. People shouldn't fool around out there if they don't want others seeing them..."

The video popped up on the screen.

Melanie was there, waiting, pacing. Alone.

And then...

A man closed in. He was tall with blond hair that swept back from his face. When she saw him, Melanie raced into his arms. She also immediately offered her neck to him.

Aidan saw the flash of the guy's teeth.

Same fucking vampire from the alley. Same jerk who tried to end me. Thane Durant. I knew it...

And the guy's description...shit, Aidan hadn't wanted to scare Jane unnecessarily, but when she'd been telling him about the vampire asshole who'd killed her family...*that guy's description had sure matched up with the bastard in the alley who sent his little army after me.* But there could be plenty of blond vamps out there. There could be—

"Freeze it, right there," Jane ordered, her voice shook a bit and she'd paled as she stared at the screen.

Jimmy's fingers tapped on the keyboard once more. "Weird freak is biting her."

Yes, he was. But Aidan's gaze left that video feed and slid toward Jane. Her pupils had turned to pinpricks as she stared at the image.

Fuck me. She recognizes him. Thane is the vamp who killed her family. He's been after Jane…all this time? He marked her.

Aidan couldn't wait to tear that sonofabitch apart. It took all of his self-control to stop his claws from bursting out right then.

"I'm confiscating that video," Jane said. Her gaze was still on the man. Her breathing was coming too fast. Aidan could smell her fear. *Hate that scent.*

Aidan knew, without a doubt, that he was looking at the vamp who'd wrecked Jane's life so long ago. But Jane wasn't falling apart. Wasn't freaking out. She'd wrapped herself in steely control as she stood there, her chin up, her face cold.

She is one hell of a woman. His respect for her notched up even higher.

"I'll take the video footage," Jane continued, "and you *will* be getting a visit from my buddies at the PD. No underage girls, Jimmy. *None* had better be found here."

Jimmy's sweating just got worse as he saved the footage onto a flash drive for her. Then Jane's fingers curled around the drive. Aidan could tell that she wanted to say more, but Jane clamped her lips closed. She stormed out of the bar and Aidan quickly followed her. The place was dead quiet right then.

Just like a tomb.

When they left the club, Jane turned to the right and hurried toward the alley they'd seen in the grainy video. The alley was empty then, just the faint scent of old garbage lingering in the air.

"She knew what he was," Jane said, her breath exhaling in a hard rush. "You saw her — she *offered* her throat to him."

Yes, she had.

Jane paced in the alley, looking for clues that just weren't there. The ground was wet — not surprising really, since the city washed the streets every day. Any clues were long gone.

"Why the hell would she do that?" Jane stopped and her hand automatically went to her right side. A habit that he now understood. "Why run to a man who could kill you as easily as he embraces you?"

Aidan had to glance away. "Maybe she thought she loved him."

"She loved a vampire? You said they were monsters."

"That doesn't mean that someone can't love a monster." He looked down at his own hands. His claws were gone. Not gone, just beneath the surface. His beast was always beneath the surface, waiting for a chance to come out and attack. "Especially if he did a good job of hiding his darkness on the inside." *And I know all about that.*

"The vamp who attacked her — the vamp who sure seems like he was Melanie's lover — you know him."

Aidan stiffened. *I know him. And you do, too, don't you, sweetheart?* He wanted her to tell him, to confide in him…

I want Jane to trust me.

"I saw your face when you looked at the video." She tapped her foot on the cement. "Spill it, Aidan. If we're partners on this, you share with me."

He advanced toward her. "Partners?" He tasted the word. And wished he were tasting her again. *Nothing had ever tasted so sweet.* "Is that what we are?"

She squared her shoulders. "You tell me."

Ah, she was a tricky one. His hand lifted and he brushed back the hair that had fallen over her cheek. "I thought we were lovers."

Her pupils expanded, making her eyes go even darker. "We had sex. Once."

"But you came for me more than just once, sweetheart."

Her hand flew up and pressed frantically over his mouth. "You did not just say that to me!"

Her reaction—her flush, her frantic movements—she was just so cute that laughter rumbled from him.

Jane dropped her hand. "You don't say things like that," she muttered, "not in public."

He laughed harder. "We're in an alley."

"Aidan…" A warning edge entered her voice.

So he choked back the laughter. "We're in a dirty alley, not a public place." His head tilted as he studied her. "And who says one time with you is enough for me? You asked what we were, so I'm saying…we're lovers." *You're mine, Mary Jane.* "I rather thought you enjoyed being with me." He had the delicious bite marks and scratches on his body to prove it.

Her gaze flew to the mouth of the alley. "You're talking about this now? Here? You have shitty timing, wolf."

His lips twitched. "I have been told that." Paris had always said he had shit for timing and tact. Alphas weren't really known for tact, though. More for brute strength and animal cunning. Paris was the guy with the tact. He could charm his way out of any situation.

That charm saved our asses when we were kids. Aidan had wanted to fight and claw, but Paris had always used his head.

Still did.

That's why I know I can count on him. Paris would bring him the information that he needed, Aidan was sure of it.

But for now… "Don't you want to be my lover?"

She threw up her hands and spun away from him. "Okay, we are not talking about this now." She paced to the right and peered up at the side of the building. "I can see the video camera. I'm guessing some of Jimmy's clients liked to bring the dancers back this way after the, um, show was over. A piece of crap like Jimmy probably used the videos for blackmail, especially if the creep has underage girls working for him." She pulled out her phone and, a few seconds later, he heard her start talking to someone else. By the sound of things, the guy on the other end of the line had to be another cop. A few more terse words were exchanged, and Aidan realized Jane was definitely keeping her word. Cops were going to be swarming at Jimmy's place soon.

Good.

She shoved the phone into her pocket. Jane glanced toward him once more. "Okay, that's done. So spill it."

His brows climbed.

"I need a name. Tell me who the vampire is. Tell me what you know about him."

Fine. He could do that. "When I knew him before, he went by the name of Thane Durant. Rumors are the guy is very old, so I figure he probably adopts a new name every twenty years or so." That was the usual game that vampires played. "And he's one vicious sonofabitch."

"I figured that." But there was a deeper knowledge in her voice.

"Thane Durant killed Garrison's parents. He and his newly turned vamps attacked them. Had a gorge fest. See, vamps like werewolf blood because it gives them a power boost. They killed Garrison's parents, tortured them for hours until there was no blood left."

Her flush had faded. She wasn't even blinking as she stared at him.

Shit, this is too much like —

"That's what they did to my parents," Jane said, her voice hoarse. "They didn't kill them outright. They…I heard noises. Laughter. My parents were begging…" Her gaze fell to the cement. "Then they brought them in to me. And I-I was the one who started begging. Asking them to let my parents go. They didn't." She swallowed and the faint click was painful to hear. "They killed them in front of me."

In an instant, he moved toward her and wrapped his arms around her body, pulling her close. He'd wanted her to confide all in him, but now Aidan wished that he could take her pain away. Nothing would make him happier than easing her sorrow—

Or giving her some much deserved vengeance.

"How did Garrison survive?" Jane asked as she held herself still in his embrace. He wished she'd hug him back.

"I got there. Vamps scented me, and they hauled ass." And he'd walked into a bloodbath. "Garrison can be a dick, I get it. But once upon a time, he was a scared kid, crying over his parents' broken bodies." So when he wanted to kick Garrison's ass—and after the fool had shot at Jane, that ass kicking had been foremost in his mind—Aidan would have a flash of the wolf as that young kid.

Even werewolf alphas could feel empathy. Actually, they could feel a fucking lot. He pulled Jane closer. "How did you get away?"

"It was *him*."

She was breaking his heart. And when the fuck had he gotten a heart?

"There are some faces that you never forget, and I haven't forgot his." Her body trembled against his. "When I saw the video, I-I knew. I just couldn't say, not in front of Jimmy. Freaking Jimmy." She shook her head in disgust.

"Jane…"

"His jaw, his nose…his eyes…they're all the same. The vampire in that video—Thane—he was the vampire who killed my parents. He hasn't aged a day," she murmured. "As soon as I saw that video, I felt the punch right to my gut. He was the one who did this to me. All of this time, it's been him."

"How did *you* get away?" Aidan asked again as he bit back his rage. He hated to think of her being scared, alone, hurt. *It won't happen again. I won't let you face him alone ever again.*

She pulled free of his arms. "I told you, he stopped burning me. Took a break. When he went upstairs, I got out. H-he'd left me in the basement, and I crawled out the window."

Her voice had hitched the faintest bit.

Werewolves couldn't smell lies, despite what some rumors said.

But he recognized hers. And he wondered just what she was holding back from him. But he'd already pushed enough, and the last thing he wanted was to cause her more pain. "Partners," he said.

Her head nodded jerkily. "We can be. I actually think we'd make a pretty good team."

If she stopped lying to him. If he stopped lying to her.

"You have paranormal connections that we can use. I have human sources." Her chin notched up. "We know the vamp we're after, we can shake this town apart and find him while he's weak. We can stop anyone else from getting hurt and give justice to Melanie Wagner."

"And to your family."

She blinked fast and Aidan knew Jane was trying to stop her tears from falling. When would she get it? She could let go with him. She could cry or scream or fight…he would take all of her.

Always.

"We can do this," Jane said determinedly. "I know we can."

If he was her partner, then it would only be expected that he'd stay close to her. He nodded. "I know our next stop."

Her eyes widened. A tear slid down her cheek but she quickly brushed it away with the back of her hand. "That was, ah, really easy. I expected more of a fight."

When they were talking about her life? About giving her justice? No fight from him. He caught her hand. Kissed her knuckles. He liked to do that, with her. She wouldn't realize that it was a claiming thing, of course, a werewolf thing. Whenever she met someone new—a new paranormal, anyway—she'd probably offer her hand. It was what polite society dictated. A handshake. But when any paranormals took her hand, they'd catch his scent and know to back the hell off.

She had his protection. She had him.

"Sweetheart," he told her softly, "I'll be your partner. I'll be your lover. I'll be anything you want."

"My executioner?"

Ice slid straight into his heart. "It will never come to that." *I won't let it.* He'd already decided not to make the same mistakes that other alpha wolves had made in the past.

The same mistake his father had made.

Jane will never be turned.

"Because I won't die violently." She nodded and pulled her hand from his. "Right. I'd actually prefer to die when I'm ninety-eight, sitting in my rocking chair as I fall softly to sleep."

His chest hurt. "Jane…"

But she gave a brisk shake of her head and squared her shoulders. "What's the next stop? Who do we see?"

He glanced up at the sun. They couldn't afford to waste more daylight. "You familiar with the voodoo shops in town?"

She laughed. "Who isn't?"

"The shop we need is just a short walk away." And at this time of day, it should be closed down for business. The perfect time to pay a little visit to a shop that dealt in secrets. He turned and she immediately fell into step with him.

"And...*why* are we going to the voodoo shop?"

"Because the fire that ate up your apartment last night wasn't natural. It shouldn't have burned so fast and so hot."

"Okay." She sounded a little breathless. "Not natural. That's because it was *supernatural?*"

"A special fire blend I've seen before. Only normally it's used *on* vampires. They shouldn't have access to it, not unless someone sold me out." A seriously bad mistake.

"And that someone would be?"

"Annette Benoit, the best damn voodoo practitioner I've ever met." He paused. He liked Annette. Respected her. But if she'd sold that fire to Thane...

That's the wrong damn team to play on. Aidan yanked out his phone and called Hell's Gate. Graham answered on the third ring. "Get a team to Annette's," Aidan ordered.

A stark pause. "Is she...okay?"

Once upon a time, Graham and Annette had been close. Very close. "She may have betrayed us." *May have...I know she did.* "Can you handle guard duty on her or do I need to call in someone else?" A blunt question.

"I've got it." Graham's response was flat. "You know pack always comes first for me."

"Then get to the shop. I need you."

His footsteps thudded as Aidan and Jane headed down the street.

***

Jimmy Cross raced around his office, sweat soaking his clothes and his stomach knotting painfully. He had his phone to his ear as he snapped, "You said this would never happen! That no cops would come banging on my door." With his left hand, he spun the dial on his safe. "You were so wrong. Detective Hart just walked out, and the bitch is sending in a whole team of cops! They are going to shut me down!" He grabbed the money inside the safe and started tossing it into his duffel bag.

"What did you tell her?"

"*Not* that I'd been letting you feed on my girls. Shit, man, why'd you have to take an interest in Melanie? You changed her! Of course that crap is gonna bring the cops around. Cops and werewolves." But he'd played it cool. Mostly. He hadn't let on that he knew just what Aidan Locke truly was.

I'm lucky I didn't piss myself. Freaking alpha…right there. When Aidan had grabbed him, Jimmy had nearly lost it.

"What did you tell her?"

"I didn't give her your name!" *I just showed her your face.* "I'm cutting out of this town. By the time the cops get here, I'll be long gone." He was really sick of vampires. "You forget me, and I'll forget you." He'd sure made a good pile of cash with the guy, though. And all he'd had to do was look the other way while some girls vanished. It wasn't as if anyone had cared about those girls anyway. They'd wanted to make money with their bodies. They had.

"Where are you going, Jimmy?"

He strained, trying to see if he heard cop cars coming. "I'll go to my uncle's place in the swamp. Lay low there just a bit." That was as far as he'd planned. "Forget me, man. Believe me, I've already forgotten you." He hung up the phone and raced for the back door.

***

Jane had visited the Voodoo Shop before. If you lived in New Orleans, you pretty much had to visit the shop. It was just…well, a thing.

But when Jane knocked on the door, she didn't hear any movement inside. And the CLOSED sign hung at a slightly diagonal slant on the front window, a window that also featured a grinning skull wearing a black hat. Jane glanced over at Aidan with raised brows.

"She's in there," he said. "Let's go around back."

Well, that was easier said than done. Because there *wasn't* a way to get to the back, not unless you scaled a six foot wall and managed to avoid the broken bottles that rested on top of said wall. Those bottles were a mainstay in New Orleans. Security that dated way, way back. You didn't want someone climbing your wall and sneaking onto your property? Put some broken bottles up there. That way, the would-be intruder couldn't get a handhold without slicing himself deep and hard.

"Don't worry," Aidan assured her. "I've got this."

Good to know. Truly but—

He leapt over the wall. Seemed to *fly* over the thing.

She spun around, her gaze frantically searching the street to make sure no one had just seen that crazy move. He couldn't freaking bound up over six foot tall walls like that in public! But, luckily, no one else seemed close enough to see him. She rushed toward the front of the shop. Jane put her ear to the glass. There was a crash inside and then a woman screamed. Fear and fury were in the cry.

She screamed a second time, and the sound held only fear.

Hell. *What is happening in there?* Jane kicked at the door. Her second kick actually got it open. "Police!" Jane yelled as she raced through the shop. It smelled strongly of incense and…beignets? "Police!" She rushed through the beaded curtain to the back.

And that was when she found Aidan…and the woman she guessed had to be Annette Benoit. Aidan had his hands up—his *clawed hands* – and the woman was trapped between Aidan and the back wall.

Beside them, what looked like a dozen beignets—all covered with gobs of powdered sugar—littered the floor.

"Stop!" Jane yelled. She hadn't meant to have a partner who'd go off into crazy town at the drop of a hat. "Move away from her, Aidan!"

"She's working with Thane."

The woman's light brown gaze flew toward Jane. She gave a frantic shake of her head.

"She was eating beignets for goodness's sake. Not working with a Master Vamp." Jane put up her gun. "Back away, Aidan, *now.*"

Growling, he did.

Relief flooded across Annette's face. "Glad someone can control the beast."

"Annette…" Her name was a dark rumble from Aidan. "You think I can't smell him here? Can't scent the fire you the made for him?"

Jane peered closer at Annette. She couldn't scent any of that stuff that Aidan was talking about, but her attention had been caught by the green scarf that the woman had around her neck.

Annette was, quite simply, stunning. Her hair was long, black, and perfectly straight. Her eyes deep set and exotically tilted at the corners. Her skin was a soft cream, smooth, totally unlined. Her chin curved gently, her cheekbones stretched high, and her full lips trembled a bit with fear.

Jane's gaze drifted over the scarf. And there, right at the upper edge of the silken material, she saw the faint mark on Annette's throat. "He bit you."

Annette's hand flew up and she repositioned her scarf. "I don't know what you're—"

"You've got vamp bite marks on your neck," Jane said flatly. "Thane was here. You made fire for him."

Thane. Just saying his name made Jane feel sick. When she'd seen that video—seen the monster from her nightmares on the computer screen—she'd nearly lost it.

Her knees had shook. Bile had risen in her throat. And deep inside of her, the girl she'd been had been screaming.

He's real. He's real…Not a nightmare.

A monster who was back in her life once again.

But she'd kept her shit together, barely. She hadn't freaked out in front of Jimmy and even though her stomach was still in knots, Jane was doing her job. Later, when she was alone—maybe she could break apart then.

I've been holding it together for so long. I'm scared to let go.

"Jane?"

She blinked. Aidan was frowning at her, and that was definitely a beast glow lighting his stare. Crap. He was probably scenting her fear and thinking that the woman caused it.

As if having the same fear, Annette cast her a desperate stare. "Control the beast!"

It wasn't an order. More of a plea. Like Jane was supposed to be able to magically keep Aidan from going all wolf. Jane cleared her throat. *Keep that shit together longer.* "Your fire nearly killed me last night!"

"But it didn't!" Annette spoke quickly. "Because Aidan was there. I knew he'd be there. I knew he'd get you out. And I knew…" She exhaled on a deep sigh. "That he'd eventually come to me." She twisted her hands in front of her body. "What was I supposed to do?" Annette asked, eyes flashing. "Thane would've killed me if I hadn't given it to him. He left me alive only because I'm useful to him. If Thane can't use you, then he eliminates you."

Thane. Jane's heart raced in her chest. "You seem to know an awful lot about him."

Annette gave a nod. "About him. About Aidan. About what's going to happen to *you*, Detective Hart." She inched toward a table in the middle of the room. A black mirror rested on that table. A broken mirror. "I saw a lot of death today when I scried."

"*You should have called me immediately!*" Aidan threw at her.

Annette swayed a bit on her feet. Her hands curled around the table. "He took too much blood. I passed out after he left. When I woke up, the fire was over and I was just happy the sun was up." Her fingers slid over the broken glass. "Do you know how many people are going to die before midnight?"

What kind of question was *that?* "Tell us where he is," Jane said. "Tell us where this Thane is and we can stop him." She wanted to find the bastard and make him pay for all his crimes. *Personal? Hell, yes, it is.*

Annette glanced at Jane's right side. "The end," she said, her voice suddenly sad. "It never looks the way we expect, does it?"

Omega means the end.

Annette picked up a piece of glass, then she sliced the broken shard over her hand.

"*What are you doing?*" Jane shot forward. She yanked the woman's scarf from her neck and started to quickly wrap her wound. Blood was dripping everywhere. "That's crazy! Why are you—"

Annette's blood had hit some of the broken mirror. Annette leaned over the table staring down into the glass. "Others know," she murmured, her voice strangely hollow. "Others have figured it out. You were missing, but now you're found."

"Um, okay…" Jane started to edge away from the other woman. *Creepy-ville.*

Annette's hand flew out and locked around hers. Her grip was tight, almost painful, and Annette's gaze never left the mirror. "There isn't an escape. Death *will* come for you."

"I wasn't really looking to have my fortune read," Jane said. Especially not such a shitty fortune. Why couldn't happiness come for her? A long life? Wealth?

"Easy or hard, that is the only choice. Which do you want, Mary Jane Hart?"

Unease slithered through Jane. *Okay, so she knows my full name and we just met.* Apparently, the woman was very, *very* in the know. "I've never been one to do anything easy, and as for hard—if you're talking about some kind of violent death…" And she totally thought that was what Annette meant. "Then I'll just pass on that option, too. Give me what's behind door number three."

Candles had been lit around the table. Thick, white candles with flames that danced, but at Jane's words, the candles sputtered out.

Annette exhaled on a shuddering sigh. "Then door three is yours." Her fingers fell away from Jane's. "Though I don't think you will like what you find there."

"You're a creepy woman, you know that, right?" Jane murmured, deciding to be straight-up honest with her impression of the lady.

Annette laughed, the sound tired. Bitter. "You think I asked to be this way? Spirits have been haunting me my whole life. I talk to the dead more than I do the living." She finally looked into Jane's eyes. "I didn't ask for this life, just as you didn't ask for yours. But we're both screwed and we just have to make the best of it."

Jane glanced at the broken, black mirror. "Were you talking to the dead then? When you did the whole blood dripping thing?'"

"They were showing me the way. Just like my guides always do." Her voice was heavy with weariness. "I hope you're ready for what's coming."

"Just what *is* coming?" Jane wanted to know.

"Betrayal. Blood. Death."

"Lovely." Jane paced toward Aidan. He'd been quiet during the exchange, but she could feel a feral intensity practically burning off him.

"So she's the contact who was going to help us?" A proclamation of death was hardly helpful.

"Where is Thane?" Aidan asked Annette.

But Annette shook her head. "I don't know. Probably out someplace, planning her death." She pointed one ringed finger at Jane.

Only fair, I'm plotting his downfall, too. He won't get away from me. Justice will come for him.

Before Jane could speak, her phone began to vibrate in her pocket. She picked it up and read the text there. "We've got another body," she said, body tensing. "An anonymous caller phoned it in. Warehouse district. A whole lot of blood at the scene."

Which probably meant — not a knifing, not a shooting…

A vamp attack.

"Captain wants me there," Jane continued. She nodded toward Annette. "I, um, may have broken your door earlier."

"You were trying to save me." One of Annette's slender shoulders rose and fell. "You always wanted to be the hero, didn't you? It's that trait that will destroy you in the end."

She could really live without hearing more of Annette's predictions. *Doom and gloom, much?*

"My men will fix the door," Aidan told her. "And they'll also make sure you have a guard, just in case Thane pays you another visit."

Annette backed up a step. "Guard..." She tasted the word. "Does that mean I'm a prisoner? Because prisoners have guards."

"It means my men are already outside. I caught the scent when they arrived. You won't be making another move without the pack knowing just what you're doing."

"A pack betrayal means death," Annette said simply, as if stating a fact that everyone knew.

Since Jane wasn't aware of that particular pack rule, she stared at Aidan with wide eyes. "She's not serious."

He didn't speak.

"Aidan, you *aren't* killing her!"

"She was ready to have *you* die, Jane."

"She was attacked by a vampire!" Now Jane put her body in front of Annette's. "She's still got the bite marks on her neck to prove it! You don't kill a victim—you help her!" Seriously, shouldn't that be obvious?

His face was implacable.

"Wanting to be a hero," Annette said, voice nearly whisper soft. "That's a flaw that you have. Be very careful, Mary Jane Hart. Don't let it kill you."

Jane didn't move. "It's just Jane, okay? And since I'm trying to save your ass, maybe try to be a little more grateful and a little less doom and gloom."

Annette gave that faint, husky laugh again.

"She doesn't die," Jane said flatly. "Got me, *partner?* Your men can keep an eye on her—some protection sounds great. But you give the order that they aren't to hurt her."

Behind her, Annette cleared her throat. "No one orders an alpha."

"I wasn't ordering." Okay, she had been. "I was asking." She stared at Aidan. "Don't do this. I get that there are different rules in your world, but just…don't, okay?"

He closed in on her. "If I do this for you, what do I get?"

"Um, the joy of *saving* a life?"

"That won't cut it for him," Annette warned darkly. "Be careful making deals with the wolves. They're slyer than foxes."

Aidan's warm fingers closed around her chin. "What do I get?" Aidan asked her again.

They had a murder victim waiting. "What do you want?"

His eyes heated.

You.

He didn't even have to say the word. She just knew.

"I don't trade sex for favors," Jane snapped at him.

Annette grabbed her shoulder. "You are playing with fire."

"You're one to talk," Jane muttered back to her, never taking her gaze off Aidan. "You're the one selling fire to vamps."

Annette's hand fell away. "True…"

"So name something else," Jane told Aidan flatly.

"Blind trust."

She knew her eyes widened. Talk about asking the impossible.

"There will come a time when I want you to trust me. No questions asked. You just do what I say. *One time.* That's the deal. You agree and we're done here."

"Fine." Easy enough to say.

He smiled and his expression softened. "Thank you."

His whole face changed when he smiled. He became way less intense, not so scary and just…sexy. Jane cleared her throat. "You're welcome." She actually wanted to throw her arms around the wolf and hug him. *Crazy.* "We have a body waiting, so let's go."

He nodded and turned to leave the back room. Before Jane could follow him, Annette had reached out to her again. Annette came in close, putting her mouth to Jane's ear and barely whispering, *"Trusting him is a terrible mistake."*

Goosebumps rose on Jane's arms.

"Annette!" Aidan stood in the doorway, his smile gone. Even though Annette had whispered

her warning, Jane knew Aidan had still heard the other woman. And he was pissed.

Jane shrugged away from Annette and headed out with Aidan. She reached for his hand. Curled her fingers with his. "Don't worry, wolf," she told him. "I make my own decisions about who I trust." And so far, Aidan had been there for her. He'd saved her ass. He'd given her more pleasure than she could stand and—

He was her partner. For now. So, for now, she'd trust him.

And she sincerely hoped she wasn't making a fatal mistake.

Hello, door number three.

CHAPTER FOURTEEN

Her captain was at the scene before Jane arrived. The captain, several patrol cars, and even Dr. Bob were already on hand.

And the scent of death was strong.

"Stay back here," Jane said to Aidan as she slipped under the line of yellow police tape that had been put in place to section off the crime scene. "I'll go see what's happening."

He caught her wrist. "I know his scent."

She waited, brows raised.

"The victim. It's the guy who stole the body last night. He's dead in there." His lips tightened. "I'm guessing he might have been the new vamp's first meal."

Jane glanced toward the entrance to the warehouse. "But...but they were working together."

Keeping his voice low, Aidan said, "I already told you. When a person becomes a vamp, the bloodlust takes over. Doesn't matter if it's a friend, family—your own kid, the bloodlust is in control and all the vamp does is feed."

Yes, but being told that and finding a *body* that was proof…Two different things. "Stay here," she said, making sure that her voice was steady. "And if you happen to scent any vamps around, let me know before you go off chasing them."

"Will do."

She hurried toward the open warehouse. Her captain had just stepped outside, and the light glinted off her dark sunglasses. Captain Vivian Harris was in her late forties, but her smooth coffee cream skin belied that age. She was dressed in a suit, with her badge clipped to her hip. The holster of her weapon was just barely visible beneath her well-cut jacket. As Jane rushed toward her, Vivian lifted a hand.

Jane stilled in front of the captain.

"I hear you've had quite a few…incidents within the last twenty-four hours."

"You mean my apartment fire?" She didn't look back at Aidan. Jane kept her focus on the captain, but with those tinted glasses that Vivian wore, she couldn't tell exactly where her boss was looking. At Aidan? The crowd? "I actually think that attack—as well as the attack behind the cathedral—is related to the death of Melanie Wagner."

"So I've heard."

Wait, what?

Vivian smiled at Jane, and for an instant, Jane saw that Vivian's eye teeth were…long. Like, longer than normal.

"I'm in his pack," Vivian said simply.

Shit. Holy *shit*. Her captain was a werewolf, too?

"There are more of us than you realize," Vivian continued. "Supernaturals hide best in plain sight. If you're stepping into this world, you need to realize that. Never believe what you see on first glance. Always, *always* look deeper."

And in a blink, the captain's white teeth were back to normal.

"When I got promoted to captain, that promotion took me out of the field," Vivian said. "I need a detective who can handle our cases."

Our cases. Paranormal cases.

"You think you're up for that job?"

Jane didn't know, but she wanted to find out. "I want to try." Because everyone deserved justice.

"Good." Vivian gave her a nod. "Because it's a real freaking bloodbath in there, and most of the cops on scene went green when they walked inside. *You* are the one we'll be calling for these cases. You're the one who'll handle things, and it will be so much easier because I won't have to bring in the alpha to make everyone forget shit all the time."

So Vivian knew that Aidan's power didn't work on her. Did she also know what would occur if Jane happened to—oh, say get shot in the chest?

"You'd better start suiting up with a bullet proof vest more often," Vivian added, as if she'd just read Jane's mind. And Jane sure hoped her boss didn't have that talent. "Makes the likelihood of you being staked later on much less, you know?"

"Bullet proof vest, check," Jane agreed.

Vivian nodded briskly. "Glad to have you on board. It will be nice not to have to bullshit with at least one of my detectives." Then she gave Jane a little salute and marched away—straight toward Aidan.

For an instant, Jane wished she had enhanced hearing. She'd love to eavesdrop on their conversation.

"Detective Hart!" Dr. Bob called. "I'll be transporting the remains soon."

Jane squared her shoulders and headed into the warehouse. Dr. Bob was someone else she needed to have a little one-on-one chat with. A real Come-To-Jesus and Clear-The-Air meeting. *Later*.

Right then…

An ambulance was *inside* the warehouse. She rounded the back of the abandoned ambulance and saw that its rear doors still swung open. A smashed gurney lay on the cement. And a dead man stretched out in a pool of his own blood. His throat had been savaged, nearly ripped open.

Her lips thinned. *I hope this one won't rise again later as a vamp.*

It was starting to seem as if no one could just die in this town anymore.

***

"I like Jane," Vivian said as she closed in on Aidan.

Jane had just disappeared into the warehouse. Being very careful with his words, Aidan replied, "I'm finding that I like her, too."

"I didn't realize what she was," Vivian told him, the sunlight glinting off her glasses. "Not when I put her name out for promotion."

"Only an alpha would have caught her scent." It was too faint for other wolves to know. He hadn't even been sure himself, not when he first met her. Hell, he'd never come across another like her, so he'd just thought her scent was extra sweet. No, he hadn't realized what she truly was — not until he'd been unable to control her mind.

"She could be an asset to us," Vivian continued, her voice mild. "She doesn't have to be a threat."

His head tilted to the right. "Who said she was a threat?"

"There are whispers. Rumors. You know they can spread fast." She glanced at the warehouse, then back at him. "Others know what she is."

They can't know about her scar. Only Paris knows, and he doesn't even realize what it is. Aidan hadn't given him any specifics on the mark.

But...

Annette knew. Fuck. As soon as she'd started talking about "the end" then Aidan had known she'd gotten a premonition. One of those hellish visions that came to her when she looked in her dark glass.

Betrayal. Blood. Death.

"She's different," Vivian continued thoughtfully, "and different isn't always good — not in the paranormal world. Different is power. Different is death."

"Jane isn't a threat, and she's under my protection."

"Some are calling for her end. The only end she can possibly have."

The end. Omega. Hell, maybe other werewolves *did* know. Maybe Annette had been spreading whispers.

Annette...or someone else?

Vivian gave a sad shake of her head. "If the vamps get her — especially this bastard who seems intent on hunting her — you know she'll wake up."

As a vampire.

"Someone like her hasn't been around in a long time. Word among the wolves…they're scared she may be too strong to handle. That even you can't take her down."

"No one is too strong for me." His voice was mild.

"Aidan…" She sighed his name. "We have been friends for a very long time."

He waited.

"So I am telling you this…as a friend…there are whispers that you aren't in control with her. That her scent—" She broke off, waving her hands in the air, and then finally said, "You know the stories…You, better than anyone else."

He did know the tales. Fuck, yes, he did. One story in particular had been carved into his freaking memory. Once, there had been an alpha that fell too hard for his lover — a lover just like Jane. Aidan had grown up hearing the damn story, again and again. A warning for all alphas. In the fucking story, the alpha had loved his mate too much, and when she'd changed, when she'd become a vampire. He hadn't been able to take her head.

He'd hesitated.

And she'd killed him. Killed their two children. Been ready to attack the baby that slept in his crib—

But she'd been taken out by the remains of the pack. They'd swarmed her—and wound up losing four more members before she'd eventually been stopped.

Never lead with your heart.

Hell, yes, he knew the warning. Intimately well.

Because he'd been the baby that survived that bloody night. The child who had never known his mother or his father. Only a pack that hated vampires. "I know all too well the dangers."

"They'll be coming tonight for her."

Anger ate at his gut. "I *gave* her my protection." And werewolves *dared* to come after her anyway? They were going to challenge him?

Why hadn't Graham warned me? Paris was out of town, so he probably hadn't heard the whispers. But Graham…Graham was in the thick of things. He should have known.

Why didn't he come to me?

"Some say that your protection isn't good enough. They'll be coming." She reached for his shoulder. Gave it a squeeze. "I *won't* be with them. I stand with you. With her. I truly think she can help us. Jane said she'd take the paranormal cases. Tell the others what she can do. We can use her. They just have to understand that. You make them understand that."

But when fury and fear were involved, logic didn't always work.

"I will be at your side," Vivian promised.

It didn't matter who stood with him, not in the werewolf world. An alpha was expected to fight his own battles. Always. To show strength, never weakness. To win this battle, he would have to act and act alone. "Don't get caught in the crossfire," Aidan warned her. It wasn't the first time he'd been challenged as an alpha, and it wouldn't be the last.

Vivian squeezed his shoulder before slowly walking away.

Aidan pulled out his phone. A moment later, he had Graham on the line. Graham—the wolf he'd left guarding Annette. Now he understood more about that woman's whispered ramblings. Perhaps she'd been trying to warn him, too, of the danger that was coming.

Or maybe she was the one who'd set up the whole damn thing. Soon enough, I'll know the truth.

Graham answered on the second ring. "Everything is secure here, Aidan," he said right away. "Don't worry."

Easier said than done. But at least a plan had formed for him. "Get Annette to make me a Sleeper's Spell."

Silence.

His hold tightened on the phone.

"Are you…sure about that?"

"Have you heard werewolves are coming for Jane?" He threw that out as a test. Was Graham on his side or—

Graham swore. "Hell, no, she's under your protection! They wouldn't dare!"

Yeah, some of them fucking would. "They're coming. They want her dead."

"But a Sleeper's Spell *will* kill—"

"Tell Annette to make it for me." Because sometimes, he had to make hard, brutal choices in life.

I will know my enemies. I will know my friends. I will know my lover.

He wouldn't make the same mistake his father had made. It wouldn't be his heart that led him.

Jane stepped out of the warehouse. Immediately, her gaze swept toward him. When she saw him, some of the sadness seemed to slip from her expression.

"I'll need you to take Jane tonight," Aidan ordered. As a leader, he often had to make the hard decisions. Nothing was harder than this. *Jane will fight.* But she didn't know what was coming. If he failed…

I won't fail. "We're going to the mansion." A place in the middle of the Louisiana swamps. A perfect spot for the werewolves to run, to fight, to kill. If there was to be a battle, Aidan wanted it there. *His* home turf. Where he could see the traitors coming. "Keep her secured, understand?"

"I will." Graham didn't ask any questions. He understood an order from an alpha, and an order from his friend. "And for what it's worth, I never doubted you."

Aidan's eyes turned to slits. "Good to know." Jane was closing in. Aidan lowered the phone and ended the call. "Any news?" he asked Jane.

"Only that you're right. It was the ambulance thief." She bit her lip. "Will he change, too?"

"If he got the vampire's blood in him, yes."

"Then I guess we'll be staking out the morgue later, huh?"

There were plenty of cops on the scene. And it was day time. Vamps wouldn't hunt then. "Keep your gun close."

"Aidan?"

"You go ahead and stake out the morgue. If the guy so much as twitches, stake him and take his head." He turned away.

But, faster than he'd expected, Jane slipped under the yellow police tape and grabbed his arm. "What about you? Where are you going?"

"Pack business." More like a pack clusterfuck. He needed to find out who'd been stirring up the wolves, and he needed to figure out that shit, ASAP. Before someone made the wrong move and death came calling.

"Oh, right. Should have realized…you have a whole pack to run." But she looked…hurt. "I'll call you when I find out—" She broke off and gave a little laugh. "I don't have your number."

Yes, she did. "I programmed it in your phone while you slept at Hell's Gate."

"You did what?"

He shrugged. "If you needed me, I wanted you to be able to reach me." The way she was eyeing him told him that Jane thought the move had been more stalkerish than thoughtful.

"That's—that's a serious invasion of privacy."

"I promise, I didn't look at your emails or your texts." Though he'd been tempted. "But if you want, you can scroll through mine later."

"Aidan…"

He bent and pressed a quick kiss to her lips. So what if cops were around? He wanted everyone to know.

She's with me. Simple. Deep.

Quite possibly, deadly.

"I just want you safe." He stared into her eyes. Savored her taste. "And I'll do anything to make sure you stay *safe*. Remember that."

She nodded once, briskly. "I need to canvas the area. Maybe someone saw something…" Though she didn't sound hopeful. They both knew the area was deserted. The warehouse looked as if it had been shut down for years.

"I'll see you soon," Aidan promised her.

Jane nodded again.

Sooner than you think, sweetheart.

"Be careful. I get that you're a werewolf and all, but even werewolves can be hurt." She turned away from him.

She cared what happened to him? Progress. And...it felt good, knowing she worried. Not many did worry about him. "Don't forget our deal." He had to say it. "You owe me trust. Once, blindly, no matter what else happens."

After a small pause, Jane glanced back over her shoulder at him. "I keep my word, Aidan. That's something you should know about me."

And I break mine, sweetheart. That's something you should know about me, too.

***

Graham put his phone down on Annette's scrying table. She sat a few feet away from him, her body tense, her gaze directed at the wall.

She hadn't said a single word to him during the entire time he'd been there. He totally got that the woman was pissed.

But he had a job to do. "The alpha wants a Sleeper's Spell."

Those words had her gaze flying to him. "That's—that's not a good idea."

Graham glanced down at the broken mirror on the table. When he looked into the glass, he saw nothing. But Annette—she saw everything.

She told me once that Aidan would command power longer than any other alpha. That he would be feared, more than any other.

"Has Aidan's future changed?" he asked quietly. "When you look in the darkness, do you still see the same fate for him?" *And what about for me?* He had to tread so carefully with her. Yeah, once upon a time, he and Annette had been lovers, but he'd started to wonder if she saw too much. If she *knew* too much.

He didn't want a lover who knew his every secret.

Even a lover as sexy as Annette.

"Everything is changing," Annette said. Her hand rose, touched her scarf. He knew she had bite marks there, and they pissed him off. *Vamp shouldn't have touched her.* "Can't see clearly. I just know…"

Her words trailed off.

"Don't leave me in fucking suspense."

"The end," she said, sadly, softly. "It's here."

For some of them, it was. Aidan wasn't going to take lightly to any werewolf betrayal, and a Sleeper Spell…that wasn't some toy.

The night was going to be brutal, and when dawn came…who would be left standing?

***

The hospital had been a fucking dead end.

Paris Cole slammed the door of his SUV as he turned to look at ranch-style house that sat at the end of Magnolia Lane.

A cute name for the street — and sure enough, magnolias lined the sidewalk. But Paris figured magnolias and Mississippi kind of went hand in hand. And he was in Mississippi right then — Biloxi, Mississippi. He'd visited the hospital that Jane had been taken to after her attack so many years ago. No one had been able to give him any intel at the facility. None of the staff members he'd met had even worked there fifteen years ago.

So he'd turned his attention to the shrink who'd sent a very young Mary Jane Hart to a psych ward. The shrink's name had popped up easily enough in a search of Jane's past.

Dr. Judith Farley, a child psychologist who'd retired just a year ago. The lady had ditched her condo and her practice and moved to this small piece of property on the outskirts of town.

The little lane was dead silent as Paris made his way up the steps. A welcome mat lay just in front of the door. He was counting on Dr. Farley to help him out with Jane.

Because he sure didn't want to return to Aidan as a failure. He lifted his hand and knocked on the door.

A few moments later, he heard the shuffle of footsteps inside. Paris pasted on his friendly, *I'm-harmless* smile as he waited. The door creaked open and a woman with red hair — cut to her chin — and big, brown eyes stared up at him.

He'd been told Dr. Farley was in her fifties. But this woman…

She barely looked thirty-five.

His nostrils flared as he fought to drink in her scent. *Plastic surgery or —*

"May I help you?" she asked.

"Dr. Farley?"

Her eyelids flickered, just a bit. "Why, yes, I'm Dr. Farley."

He wasn't sure any plastic surgeon was this good. "I'd like to speak with you about one of your former patients." He let his smile widen a bit, keeping the whole *I'm-harmless* vibe going. "It's about a book I'm working on…"

"I don't discuss my clients. Not with anyone." She started to close the door.

He moved his foot, a quick, casual slide, and the toe of his boot blocked the door from closing. "Mary Jane Hart." He threw the name out because he wanted a response.

Her gaze went arctic. "I don't discuss clients." She glanced down at his foot. "Now you need to back away before I call the cops."

Paris held up his hands. "I'm sorry!" And he made sure his voice sounded that way. Terribly apologetic. He didn't move his foot, though. "Actually, I've misled you."

A furrow appeared between her brows.

"Mary Jane is a friend of mine. She's having a really hard time lately, talking about monsters left and right, and I…" Paris let his voice roughen. "I'm worried about her. Worried that she may be losing her grasp on sanity. She mentioned you to me the other night. Said you'd helped her before. I was really hoping you could help her again."

"Mary Jane." Dr. Farley leaned forward a bit. "She's talking about monsters?" Sadness flashed on her face. "Poor thing. She did that before, you see. I always knew…Come in, come in…" She opened the door and let Paris step into her house. She waved him toward her den and he strode forward as she shut the door behind him. "I always knew," Dr. Farley continued, "that she would turn out to be everything we'd hoped."

Everything we'd hoped.

Paris tensed. He turned to glance back at the doctor.

Too late. A thundering blast sounded just as the jarring impact thudded into him. Paris flew forward, his hands sliding over the hardwood floor, his claws scraping out in instant response to the burning pain that seared him.

Silver. She shot me with silver! And it damn well hurt. He tried to roll over—fought to move his body and—

Dr. Farley aimed her gun straight at his head. "Did you think I didn't know you'd be coming? Thane said it was time to move. She's the right age now. No more waiting. She'll be everything she was meant to be. The end is here, and the werewolves will die. The dominoes are falling, just like we planned."

He lifted his hand. His jacket sleeve hung low, skimming over the edge of his wrist. "Knew…what you are…too…smelled it…"

She blinked at him, then laughed. "Doubtful. I have a wonderful new perfume, a special batch that was made for me by a certain voodoo seller that is *the* best. It cloaks a vampire scent and—"

He threw the stake that he'd hidden in his sleeve. *Never leave home without one.* His motto since he'd been a kid and vamps had taken out his family.

His throw was perfect. Aidan had taught him how to attack just the right way. Aidan had taught him how to pick up the shattered pieces of his life and move the hell on. So when Paris threw that sharpened stake, he didn't miss. It sank into Dr. Farley's chest even as Paris jerked to the right, anticipating that she'd fire that gun before she drew her last undead breath.

Her bullet missed him.

And then she fell to the ground, gasping.

His head sagged back against the floor. That silver was burning like a bitch. Fumbling, he managed to pull out his phone and call Aidan. The alpha answered on the second ring. "We've got a big problem," he gasped. "Big." *And I'm gonna need a pack rescue out of here.*

CHAPTER FIFTEEN

"So…are you a werewolf?" Jane asked Dr. Bob as she paced near his exam table. The room was icy and she shivered as she posed the question to him. It made sense, though. Maybe he was just like the captain, maybe he was—

"Hardly," Dr. Bob snorted, sounding highly offended.

She blinked. "Um, but you *know* about werewolves?"

"How do you think I bought my last beach house in Gulf Shores?"

He had a beach house in Gulf Shores? *Gulf Shores, Alabama?*

"Werewolves pay me well."

She stopped pacing. "You're on the take?" Aidan wasn't using his mojo to make the guy forget. Instead, he was just *bribing* Dr. Bob?

How annoying. How…boring?

Six hours had passed since she'd last seen Aidan. She'd canvased the area near the warehouse and turned up a big pile of nothing.

Then she'd headed to Bob's office so she could learn more about the victim.

And to finally have it out with good old Dr. Bob. When she'd spoken with him before, they'd both carefully dodged the issue. Jane wasn't in the mood to dodge anything any longer.

Bribery? Seriously?

"That's a harsh assessment." His bloody fingers—covered in latex gloves—lifted from the body he was examining. "I do my job. I examine the bodies. I try to figure out who the killer is…but when my findings show that a supernatural being is involved, it only makes sense to go to the supernatural authorities, not the human ones."

She shook her head. And wished she had a good drink handy. Aidan's whiskey would have been good right then. "How long have you known about the supernaturals?"

"When a werewolf crosses your table, you know. Once the autopsy starts, there is no way to miss the signs."

She was awful curious about those *signs.*

"And vampire attacks are pretty apparent. Puncture wounds. Missing blood. Not so hard to connect the dots." He pointed toward her with a bloody index finger. "It was your captain who first connected me to Aidan Locke. I followed her orders. I started turning the paranormal cases over to him, and well, so maybe I *did* get a nice little bonus for my work. Is that so wrong?"

"You tried to make me think I was going crazy the other night!" Jane sputtered.

He winced. "Sorry about that. Thought you'd forget, like all the others." For an instant, his gaze darkened. "One day, I want Aidan to make me forget it all, too. Maybe when I retire…" Sadness flickered in his eyes. "There are some things we're all better off not knowing." His attention turned back to the body in front of him. "Like I'd enjoy forgetting just how much damage a vampire's bite can do to a human's neck. How savagely the bite can cut and how deeply." He pointed to the bruises on the victim's chest and arms. "I'd also like to forget how much stronger they are than humans. How easy it is for them to hold us down and kill us. I'd like to forget all of that," he added. "Because one day, I would enjoy being able to sleep all night long."

Okay, so maybe she was starting to soften toward the guy a bit. "I always liked you, jerk."

His lips curved in a faint smile. "What will it take for you to forgive me?"

"For making me think I might be crazy? One hell of a lot." Especially with her past and the ghost of Dr. Farley always haunting her. "But you can start by helping me find this vamp. He killed Melanie Wagner and then this guy —"

"Different vampires killed those two."

Jane blinked. "You're sure?"

He tossed his gloves aside then moved toward the storage locker. Melanie was in that locker, Jane knew that. He quickly donned more gloves and pulled out Melanie's slab. When Jane saw the other woman, she lost her breath for a moment.

She just looks so young.

"Melanie had bigger bite marks on her neck, despite her attacker's attempt to hide them. Male vamps always have bigger teeth," Bob told her. "The guy on the table — my money says he was attacked by a woman. Smaller fangs and, um, a whole lot less control. She made a real mess of him. So I'm thinking she was either one seriously pissed off vampire or…"

"Or a newly made one," Jane said, thinking of the body that had been taken from the hospital. She'd wanted that woman to live. She'd worked so desperately to save her.

Aidan had wanted to make sure she didn't rise again. I stopped him. Jane kept her voice calm as she asked, "Is he going to change?" Because if he did, Aidan had said she had to stake him. "Will he become a vampire?"

Even as she asked the question, there was a brisk knock at the door.

"No, he won't change. I already looked at his blood under the microscope. There's no sign of mutation."

Her shoulders sagged as relief filled her.
The knock came again.

"Mutation?" Jane prompted, curious now
that she wasn't going to be driving a stake into
the dead guy.

"After about three hours, if the victim is
going to change, the blood cells mutate. They
become something…new."

That was scary shit. "If Melanie's cells were
mutating, then why'd she get out of here? If you
knew what she was, why didn't you stop her?"

Bob straightened his spine. "I don't kill, not
humans and not vampires. I just examine the
dead. That's all. Once I got the lab results in, I
called Aidan's clean-up crew. Aidan *had* been in
here before, but I didn't have the information for
him yet. As soon as I had the results, I grabbed
some coffee and I made the call." His lips
thinned. "Only she vanished while I was getting
that damn cup of coffee."

Melanie had gotten free and Aidan had
found her in the alley. *Death, two times.*

Another knock came again. Seriously,
someone was damn persistent out there. Jane
slanted a fast glance at Bob and she made sure
not to let her gaze dip to Melanie's body. Melanie
was going to be transferred out soon. No family,
no friends—the city would pay for her burial and
provide a plain headstone to mark her grave.

What a fucking terrible end for her.

Jane headed toward the determined knocking. Bob's office door was made of frosted glass, so she couldn't clearly see who was out there. She hesitated, wondering if she might have been tailed to Dr. Bob's. Vamps and werewolves seemed to be everywhere these days.

No, they were always out there. I just didn't realize the full truth.

"Aidan sent me." A rough voice said.

She still didn't open the door.

"I recognize the voice," Bob told her as he closed the cold storage locker. "That's Graham Faulkner. He's Aidan's left-hand guy."

Left-hand? That was a rather odd turn of phrase. Usually a right-hand—

"A fellow named Paris Cole is his right. Two tough bastards that you don't want to meet on a dark night."

Jane opened the door. A tall, blond man stood on the threshold. He wore a white t-shirt and dark jeans. He smiled at her, flashing dimples. For some reason, his smile didn't reassure her too much.

Probably because I know he's a werewolf.

"Hello, Jane. We haven't formally met yet. My name's Graham Faulkner."

So Bob had just told her.

Graham pushed his hands into the pockets of his jeans. "Aidan needs to talk with you."

She lifted a brow. "And he didn't pick up the phone because…?"

"Because some things can't be said on a phone call." His smile slid away. "And because it's getting late, close to vampire hunting time…so he wanted me to come and escort you to the wolf mansion."

A mansion? Sounded awfully fancy.

"You *did* agree to stay with him, didn't you?" Graham pushed and he looked a bit worried. "He said—"

Jane waved away whatever he was about to say. "I don't know you. You seem like a semi-nice werewolf, but I'm not just going to walk out of this place with you and go vanish to some werewolf mansion. Sorry, not happening." She crossed her arms over her chest. "If Aidan wants to talk with me, he can give me a call. Or better yet…" She pulled out her phone and called Aidan. She was going to need more than Blondie's assertion that it was safe to leave with him.

Aidan answered on the second ring. "What's wrong?"

"Why is there some six foot plus blond guy saying I have to go for a ride with him?"

A pause. "Graham is there."

There and currently frowning at her. "I said I would trust *you*," Jane told him. *Not any other werewolf.*

"Graham will bring you to me. We...need to talk, Jane. Things have changed."

Okay, now that edge in his voice was making her nervous. "Changed how?"

"For starters, I found out that your old child psychologist, Dr. Farley—she's a vampire."

Jane automatically shook her head, then realized he couldn't see the move. "Not possible."

"Very, very possible. They've been watching you for a long time, Jane. Making plans. I can't let those plans come to fruition. I *won't*."

Dr. Farley had told her never to mention monsters. That people would think she was insane. *Stay quiet. You're just trying to make a tragedy into a nightmare.*

No, no, everything *had* been a nightmare.

"Go with Graham."

Her grip on the phone was way too tight. "Fine, but you'd better give me a full update when I see you."

"I will." His voice thickened. "Jane?"

"Yes?"

"You were not what I expected. But you are exactly what I want."

Warmth bloomed in her chest. "Werewolf, I assure you, you were the *last* thing I ever saw coming." She turned away from Graham and dropped her voice. "But I want you."

He growled.

Love that sexy growl. Jane cleared her throat. "Goodbye." She put the phone into her pocket. "Okay, Blondie, let's go."

He inclined his head toward her. "Your chariot awaits."

***

The hunger was growing within her once more. It burned, and slithered in her guts, like a hot snake. A whimper slipped from her lips.

"It's all right, love," he told her.

He. The blond vampire. The man who'd done this to her…Thane.

The vampire she needed.

He strode into the room with a young girl cradled in his arms. Not too young, probably around eighteen or so. She had on a too-short, red dress and as he carried her, one of her dress straps slid down her arms.

"I caught Lisa before she could sign in at work. Guess she didn't hear her boss Jimmy wasn't coming back to town. He couldn't, not after you and I got through with him…"

Lisa was out cold, but her pulse—it beat in such a tempting rhythm. Virginia could hear that sweet beat. She barely understood Thane's words because she was so focused on that beat.

The bloodlust grew.

"I'll let you drink her," he promised, his green eyes hooded. "But first, I need you to do something for me."

She wanted that woman's throat.

No, no, stop. You'll hurt her. This isn't you. You don't…

But she'd always been a killer, right? Taking jobs that she knew were shady. And this wasn't so bad, really. It was…survival.

"You're going to use that amazing voice of yours, and you're going to make a phone call."

She couldn't. Virginia couldn't do anything but hunger for blood.

"I have a recording that you'll listen to. A certain alpha asshole's voice. You'll listen to his voice, then you'll *be* him. You'll make a call and you'll bring my prize to me."

She was salivating, unable to look away from the woman's throat.

Thane sighed. "Here, take a few sips…"

Virginia pounced on the woman. She pounced even as a voice in her head cried out…*No, no, don't bite her! Don't tear her! Don't —*

Blood flowed over Virginia's tongue. Her eyes rolled back into her head because it was just so good. So amazing. She stopped worrying about hurting the other woman. She stopped worrying about anything but blood.

Then he yanked away her meal.

"No!" Virginia tried to reach for Lisa once more.

The vamp punched Virginia in the face. "Get back."

She flew across the room and slammed into the wall.

"The taste calmed you down, right? You've been gorging all fucking day on the prey I brought you, so have a second of control, got it?"

Her breath sawed out of her lungs. Had she been gorging? She…she didn't remember. Surely she hadn't…eaten other people.

But then she had a flash of a sobbing redhead.

And…a man. He'd smelled of sweat and fear and he'd been begging…saying he hadn't told the detective Thane's name.

Wait. That man, he was…

Jimmy?

For an instant, she remembered. The vamp had said that Jimmy wasn't getting away from them. Then he'd said…*Go ahead, love. Rip out his throat.*

And, dear God…she had.

"You're going to make a call for me," Thane said, his voice strong and commanding. "You have to do it *now*. My intel says the alpha is trying to move her. He may be killing her. We have to stop him."

Virginia nodded. "I-I'll do what you want…"

"Good," he said grimly. Lisa was sprawled at his feet. He pulled out his phone and swiped his finger across the screen. A few finger taps later and a man's voice came from the phone. The recording said, "There will come a time when I want you to trust me. No questions asked. You just do what I say. *One time.* That's the deal. You agree and we're done here."

Virginia fought to push back her bloodlust.

"Can you imitate that voice?" the vampire demanded.

"*Yes.*" She could imitate any voice.

"Prove I made the right choice in keeping you alive. Do what I want. Get me my prey." He tossed his phone to her. "I'll give you the number, and you'll repeat *exactly* what I say, using the alpha asshole's voice, got it?"

Her fingers trembled around the phone. Her gaze dropped to the woman on the floor. Lisa was bleeding. "I-I do it…" Virginia whispered. "And I…drink?" The thirst was burning her again. A snake, slithering…

"Do it and you can drink as much as you fucking want. Drain her, for all I care."

Virginia licked her lips and nodded.

**

They'd left the city. The bright lights of New Orleans were in the distance as Graham and Jane headed toward the swamp. Jane wasn't a particularly big fan of swamps. Alligators lived in swamps. So did snakes—water moccasins. She *hated* water moccasins. Their fangs were way too much like a vampire's for her peace of mind.

She turned in her seat, studying the man—werewolf—who was driving the car. "Want to share with me why we're going into the middle of nowhere?" Because her cop brain told her a swamp was good for one thing—making a body vanish.

She wasn't in the mood to vanish.

"Werewolves can't run free in the city," Graham said. "Out here, though, it's our land. Pack land. When the beasts need to take over, they come here."

That wasn't particularly reassuring. She didn't want to find herself in the middle of some werewolf madness. "I thought only Aidan could shift fully."

His fingers tightened around the steering wheel. "That doesn't mean the rest of us don't still carry a wolf. We have enhanced speed and strength—and sometimes, we need to just *run*."

She filed that bit of information away. "What made you pick this particular place as your running ground?"

"We have a house out here," Graham said as he focused straight ahead.

"A mansion," she murmured. Because that was the way he'd described it before.

"Yeah." Graham laughed. "It's been in Aidan's family for years. Fucking huge place. Locals think it's haunted. Maybe it is."

"Or maybe it's just overrun with werewolves," she said. Howling wolves. Her phone vibrated and she pulled it from her pocket. Jane didn't recognize the number on the screen but because of her job, she always had to answer her phone. Always. "Jane Hart," she said as she put the phone to her ear.

"Don't trust him."

Her breath stilled in her lungs. That was Aidan's voice. She'd know him any place.

"Get out of the car, now. Run—get away from the werewolf driving."

And even as Aidan said those words, Graham's head shot toward her. *Oh, hell. Werewolf hearing. He knows what Aidan just told me.*

"You owe me, remember?" Aidan blasted in her ear. Graham was frantically shaking his head even as Aidan snapped, "Blind trust—*get away from him.*"

But the car was thundering down the road. Going way too fast. She couldn't just jump out.

"Jane...I don't know what the fuck is happening," Graham began.

She pulled out her gun and shoved it into his side. "I know what's going on. Aidan found out something about you. Something bad. So stop this car right now and let me go…or I'll shoot."

He slammed on the brakes. Hard. Far harder than she'd anticipated and her head jerked forward. He tried to take her gun in the next instant, but she slammed it into his face, and Jane heard the crunch of bones.

Oh, crap. I just broke the werewolf's nose.

She'd also dropped her phone.

"What in the hell!" Graham snarled.

"Change of plans," Jane threw at him, keeping her tight grip on the gun. "I'm not getting out. You are." Because she needed the car in order to get back to town. "Get your wolf ass out, Blondie, or I will start shooting."

His eyes glowed in the car's dim interior.

"These are silver bullets." Just so he knew she wasn't screwing around.

"This is a mistake," Graham said, voice rumbling, but he was opening his door. He was backing out of the car. Jane scrambled across the front seat. "I was trying to protect you."

She didn't buy that. Not with Aidan's words ringing in her ears. "Get away from the car."

He backed up.

And she spun out of there. The wheels kicked up mud and gravel as she turned that ride back around as fast as she could. Her foot slammed down on the gas pedal and the car shot forward. A quick glance in the rear-view mirror showed that Graham was running after her. Just how fast could a werewolf run? She freaking hoped not fast enough to catch her. Her gaze whipped back to the road and the car's headlights hit on the man there. A man with hunched shoulders who'd lifted his hands, as if telling her to stop.

The lights flashed so bright on him. She could see his face clearly in those lights.

Garrison—it was *Garrison.*

He was in her way. The car was about to hit him. He needed to move, but he wasn't. He was just standing there. She slammed on the horn, but he wasn't moving.

This wasn't some game of chicken. This was life or death. This was—

I can't kill him.

She swerved to the right. A hard swerve. The car careened toward the trees there, narrowly avoiding a crash with a twisting cypress. She yanked again on the wheel, trying to whip left, but then there was a terrible groaning, a sucking, and the car's wheels just spun and spun.

And the car didn't move forward. Or back. *Stuck. Probably in thick swamp mud.*

Jane jumped out of the car.

Both Garrison and Graham had closed in on her. It was so dark, she could barely see them. The moon had slipped behind the clouds.

"I'm sorry," Garrison said, actually sounding it. "I couldn't let you leave. My job is to keep you safe. I'll do that job from now on."

She swung her gun away from him and aimed at Graham. "*You* stay away from me. Aidan told me that I had to get away from you. That you couldn't be trusted."

"I heard him," Graham said, voice thick. "But I don't know why the hell he would tell you that. I've never betrayed my alpha."

Her phone was back in the car. And it was ringing once more. She should get it—it could be Aidan calling again, but she was afraid to lower her guard with Graham.

"Aidan told me to make sure you got to the mansion," Garrison said as he edged closer. "As far as I know, there has been no change in orders."

She could hear another engine coming toward her, moving fast down that windy road. And the phone was still ringing. Hell. "Don't come any closer to me," she warned Graham. "I will shoot. Garrison, tell him—*I will seriously shoot his ass.*"

"She will shoot your ass," Garrison said immediately.

She lunged for the phone. Jane saw the same number from before lighting the screen. Her fingers swiped over it.

"Jane!" Aidan's voice sounded frantic. "Where are you? Did you get away?"

"No, the car crashed. The wolves are here, and I don't think I'm going anywhere."

The sound of that approaching vehicle was closer.

"Where are you? *Tell me.*"

"The werewolf mansion, just like you told me to be. Outside of it anyway, somewhere in the damn swamp."

A big SUV had just come to a jarring halt a few feet away from her.

"More wolves are here," she said, her breath rasping.

"Shoot them," Aidan ordered her, his voice blasting in her ear. "They can't be trusted. They are there to kill you. *Shoot them on sight!*"

Her weapon was up. She was half in and half out of that car, a vehicle that was sinking deeper into the muck with every second that passed. Footsteps raced toward her. The open door of the car let light spill out and she saw the first werewolf to close in on her was—

Aidan?

No, that wasn't possible.

Because she was talking to Aidan on the phone.

"Shoot or die!" Aidan yelled in her ear, his voice roaring through the phone. "Don't trust them! They will kill you! Get away, get—"

"Jane." This soft whisper of her name came from the Aidan in front of her. Real. Strong. Her wolf.

*If he's standing right there…"*Who the hell is this?" Jane snarled into the phone.

Silence.

Then…

Laughter. Aidan's laughter. And it was Aidan's voice who told her, "You're going to die." Right before the line went dead.

Then the man in front of her — *her* Aidan — he stepped closer. "I don't know who the hell that was," he said, obviously having overheard the conversation with his werewolf hearing, "but it wasn't me."

Obviously, because he was standing right there. She knew about voice distorting software, but how could someone else sound so *exactly* like him?

Aidan offered his hand to her. "Come with me, Jane. I need you to come with me."

You're going to die.

She looked down at his hand, then back up at him. His eyes glowed faintly.

"A war is brewing," Aidan said. "I can help you. I *will* help you."

She believed that. She believed him.

Who was on the phone?

Jane holstered her weapon and reached for Aidan's hand.

***

Hunger. Blood. Need blood. "Sh-she's at some werewolf mansion. In a swamp." Virginia reached out with greedy hands toward Lisa.

"You didn't get her away from the werewolves."

Thane stood between her and Lisa.

"I said—said everything you told me." Her fangs hurt. She needed *blood.* "She's at the werewolf mansion!" Those words were almost a shout.

He hit her again. The blow was even more powerful this time. "I needed Jane away from them."

She crawled toward him. "I said—said the wolves would kill her!" The woman should have listened. "She's with them...couldn't get away." The hunger made it hard to think.

His eyes glinted. "You're lucky...I know where this mansion is. Got a wolf on the inside, though I had hoped to cut him out of the game."

They were playing a game? Since when?

"If you want something done right...you have to fucking kill and do it all yourself." His fangs were out. "I'll go get her."

Then he whirled away.

Lisa moaned.

"Drink her, but don't change her," he ordered. "But be fast. I may need you, so you're coming along. You and every other vamp I made in this city."

Virginia grabbed for the woman. *This is wrong. I have to stop. I'm a monster.*

Her fangs sank into the woman's neck, and Virginia couldn't think of anything else but that sweet, sweet taste of blood.

"Gulp her," Thane urged. "She's just food. Doesn't matter at all..."

CHAPTER SIXTEEN

Play it cool. Stay in control. Aidan knew he didn't have much time, not before the pack assembly was called.

When midnight came, he'd have to leave her. Once he'd learned of the brewing discontent, Aidan had been the one to organize the assembly. He wanted every damn member of his pack there to witness the battle that would go down.

If someone is going to challenge me, everyone will see it.

"Who was on the phone?" Jane asked, voice strained.

"I don't know." Aidan shook his head as he paced his bedroom. The mansion was his, the old antebellum that so many claimed housed ghosts — it was his. And the memories there had haunted him for his entire life. "I heard the bastard's voice, though." *He sounded just like me.*

"He wanted me to leave the werewolves. To get away."

His hands were fisted. "So you'd be unprotected. Thane is pulling strings, playing tricks as he tries to get you."

She stood near the foot of his bed, staring at him with wide eyes. She had no idea what the night was going to bring, and he didn't want to tell her. He didn't want her to fear more. Didn't want her to fear him.

Aidan walked to her, and his knuckles brushed over the softness of her cheek. "I never expected you."

Her hand lifted and caught his. Staring into his eyes, she said, "I don't like it when you're afraid."

For an instant, Aidan couldn't breathe. Alphas weren't supposed to be afraid. Not of anything or anyone.

But I am afraid. Afraid I won't be strong enough to keep her safe.

"You're holding back with me, Aidan. I can see it in your eyes. *Tell me.*"

He didn't, though, because this was a burden he'd carry. If this was to be there last few moments together, so be it. He brushed his mouth over hers. So very carefully. Memorizing her sweet taste. He wanted to touch every inch of her. He'd carry her scent on his skin.

And her mark on his heart.

He pushed her back onto the big, four poster bed. Then he stripped as he stared down at her.

"I know…" Jane murmured, "that you didn't bring me all the way out here just to have sex with me."

His shirt hit the floor. He kicked away his shoes and his jeans. Soon he was completely naked and he crawled onto the bed. "Don't be too sure. I would do just about anything to have you."

She smiled at him. A slow curve of her lips that made him want her all the more. "In case you haven't noticed," Jane's voice had gone husky, "I want you, too. So you don't have to go to any desperate extremes for me."

Yes, he did. Aidan lifted her shirt over her head. Tossed it. Her breasts were pushed up by a black bra that was sexy as hell, and when he pulled the jeans down her long legs, he saw that she wore a matching pair of black panties.

"You got to do all the exploring last time," Jane said. "When do I get my chance?"

His eyes closed. He would fucking love to feel her hot mouth on his dick, but if she touched him with her lips, with her tongue — he would be gone.

And he needed to savor this time with her. To make it count.

Because it could be his last time with Jane.

He caught her hands in his and lifted them above her head, stretching her and getting Jane to arch her back. Her breasts thrust toward him and he put his mouth to the curve of her right breast, just above the silk of that bra.

"Aidan…"

One of his hands kept her wrists pinned and the other pulled down her bra, exposing her nipple. Already pebble-hard and flushed. So very perfect for his mouth. He took that nipple. Sucked and licked and lightly used the edge of his teeth because he knew that Jane liked that.

He thought that Jane might quite enjoy his rougher, wilder side. And if they had a *next* time…

She will get all of me.

But for now, he was keeping his control.

Her hips arched against him and the scent of her growing arousal made his cock harden even more. He wanted in her, balls deep. Her sex was heaven and he'd been in hell too long.

He licked his way to her other breast. Yanked down the bra enough to have her nipple spilling into his mouth. He loved her breasts. He could lick her nipples forever.

Her hips were rocking against his, and she lifted up her legs, putting her sex flush against his cock. Every movement of her hot core sent her sex sliding over him. She was wet already. Only fair, considering how damn hard he was for her.

"Come…in!" Jane demanded.

No, not yet.

"Keep your hands up here," Aidan ordered her. Because if she touched him, he would be a fucking goner.

He freed her wrists, but only so he could push her legs farther apart. Then he feasted. His lips and tongue took her as he tasted her sex. A growl worked in his throat because she was so good.

Her hips slammed up to meet him. "Aidan!"

He loved it when she got demanding.

But her hands flew down and curled around his shoulders. Her nails bit into his skin. Ah…his Mary Jane wasn't so good at following orders. Unfortunately.

He pulled away from her, sliding back on his haunches.

"Wh-what are you doing?"

He flipped her over. Jane immediately pushed up onto her knees, putting her in the absolute perfect position. Did she have any idea just how fine her ass was?

His fingers curled around her hips once more.

She looked over her shoulder at him. "Like this?"

Hers hand locked around the headboard. She arched back even more.

And he drove his cock into her. Her hot, tight sex closed around him greedily. So good that he didn't even move for a moment. Just savored the feel of her all around him.

But then Jane moved, surging forward, then back. Demanding.

His.

He withdrew and plunged deep, moving in perfect time with her. And this angle let him slide his hand around her body, let him find her clit and stroke her with every pounding surge of his hips.

"Yes!" Jane yelled.

He liked it when she yelled. Fuck who might overhear.

They'll all know soon enough. There is no going back from this. And, no, he hadn't told Jane all that tonight meant. She could be pissed later. If there was a later.

Then he felt the contractions of her release. She cried out and her neck arched. He kissed her shoulder. Drove into her again and came — a pounding, roaring thunder of his release.

And as that pleasure nearly fucking annihilated him, his mouth opened over the curve of her shoulder. Aidan bit her. Not the gentle nips he'd given her before, but the hard bite of a werewolf who wanted to claim his mate.

He was afraid she'd pull away.

She didn't.

Her moan was pleasure-filled and her release just kept going, heightening his own climax. He licked the wound he'd made on her skin, a wound that was faint but detectable to all others of his kind.

He'd made his choice.

His drumming heartbeat slowed. He kissed the mark again. Jane turned her head just a bit, and he kissed her lips.

Yes, he'd made his choice—and he'd deal with the fucking death and pain that followed. *It will be on me. Not her.*

***

The sex had been incredible. Quite glorious really. Spectacular. Only now—Aidan was climbing from the bed.

Way too fast.

Jane rolled over and watched him as he dressed. Her shoulder throbbed a bit and she should probably say something about that. Tell him not to be so rough next time...

Unfortunately, she'd liked the roughness. A lot. What did that say about her?

He zipped his jeans. Didn't bother to put on his shirt. Then he turned away from her.

Okay. So he was still awkward when it came to the whole after sex business. Jane glanced around, spied her panties at the end of the bed, and she hurriedly put them back on. Her bra was semi in place, so some quick adjustments had most of her lady parts concealed. Now, if she could find her jeans and her shirt…

Aidan stood in front of her. Jane blinked. She hadn't seen him move. That creepy fast thing he did would still take some getting used to on her end. He had her shirt in his hands. Her jeans, too.

Carefully, he slid the shirt over her head. His touch was oddly gentle—incredibly so—and his fingers seemed to linger on the faint bite mark that now marred her shoulder.

She put on her own jeans, *thank you very much.* Then they stood, facing each other. Jane tried to figure out what she was supposed to say. Tried to figure out how to get them back on track in this crazy tangle of—

"There are werewolves who want you dead," Aidan said, voice quiet.

Um, not so great.

He reached into the nightstand. He was pulling out something—wait, holy hell, those were handcuffs. She started to back away—

Too slow. Always too slow when there is a werewolf involved.

Because in a flash, he'd snapped one handcuff around her left wrist and another around the post of the bed—the narrowest part of that tall, wooden post.

Her mouth dropped.

"They're made of silver," Aidan told her, voice still soft. "We have to restrain the werewolves sometimes, and these work best."

Her gaze was on his fingers — fingers that had smoke coming from them as he still touched the handcuff that circled her wrist.

"They won't hurt you, though," Aidan added quickly. "Just keep you here."

No, this wasn't happening. "You don't have sex with a woman," Jane forced out the words through a haze of red fury, "then lock her up. That shit is not done." Unless you were a serial killer.

Or a werewolf?

He stroked her inner wrist. "This is the moment I was talking about before. I need you to trust me."

Trust was hard when handcuffs were involved! "Aidan..."

He pressed a kiss to her forehead. "It will be over soon."

"What will be over?"

He glanced toward the clock on the wall. "He'll be coming any moment."

She yanked at the cuff. It bit into her wrist and did *not* give. And the bed was sturdy as all hell. That wood wasn't just going to break apart for her. It wasn't as if she was a werewolf with super human strength.

A knock rattled the door.

"Come in!" Aidan yelled.

The door opened. Garrison stood there, looking pretty damn miserable as he slinked inside with a tray in his hand. There was a drink on that tray. Looked like wine.

"Put it on the table." Aidan motioned toward the table that waited near the window.

Without a word, Garrison put down the tray. Then he looked at Jane, regret in his eyes.

"Buddy, I saved your ass," Jane reminded him as she yanked once more on the cuffs.

Garrison's gaze darted to Aidan.

Aidan nodded. "You can report that the delivery has been made. Then you stay outside of the room. No one else comes inside, got it?"

Garrison gave a quick nod. When he scrambled from the room, Jane glared after him. This shit was not cool.

Her gun was in the chair near the door. She'd put it there after she followed Aidan inside. She'd foolishly thought she wouldn't need a weapon in his bedroom. Now the gun was too far out of her reach.

Aidan's fingers slid over her cheek once more. "There's poison in that wine glass."

What? *What?*

"I'll come back, and you *won't* drink it."

"Hell, no, I'm not drinking poison!" She grabbed his shirt with her right hand. "And if you think you're leaving me like this—"

He already had. Before she could even blink, he was at the door and Jane was holding nothing. "Aidan!"

"Trust," he said. "Give it to me this one time." He looked…sad.

He should be sad. She'd give him plenty to be sad about. "This isn't how partnerships work," Jane yelled at him.

He turned away.

"This isn't how *relationships* work!"

He hesitated.

"I *did* trust you!" Jane shouted. "Then you cuffed me! You brought me poison! *What in the hell is going on?*"

Aidan looked back at her. "I will do everything to keep you safe."

Holding her prisoner wasn't some kind of safety thing.

"I…need you," Aidan confessed. "More than I realized. More than—" He broke off. "I will be back, I swear it. I'll always come back for you."

Then he shut the door. Locked it. She saw the lock turn. "No!" Jane yanked on the cuff, frantic. "No, Aidan, get your furry ass back in here! You can't do this to me! *No!*" With every yell, she pulled harder and harder on that cuff. But it didn't break. It didn't give.

And Aidan didn't come back.

Always come back my ass.

***

"No, Aidan, get your furry ass back in here! You can't do this to me! No!"

Aidan froze just outside of his bedroom, Jane's yells seeming to echo around him. Paris strode down the hallway toward him, his movements a bit slower than normal because he was still healing.

Silver could be such a bitch.

"So that's her?" Paris asked as he drew closer. "I must say, she's got a rather healthy set of lungs on her."

"Aidan!" Jane bellowed.

Paris inhaled. "You're wearing her scent like armor."

"I want everyone to know where I stand." There could be no doubt.

Paris nodded. "And I stand with you. You know that."

He did.

Garrison strode back toward them. The guy was sweating. "They—they're all outside."

Because it was midnight. A wolf's time. Aidan tossed the handcuff keys to Garrison. "You watch from up here. When it's decided…"

Garrison gave a grim nod. "I will remember my vow."

To protect her.

Then it was done.

Aidan strode away even as Jane called for him. His insides felt as if they were fucking shredding with every single step that he took, but Aidan kept going. An alpha never hesitated.

Never ran from any battle that waited.

Soon he was outside. The clouds had passed away, and the sky was filled with a million stars. This far from the city, the stars always shined their brightest.

Other wolves waited outside. Fifty. Sixty. They'd come from far and wide for this night.

Vivian watched from the left. She'd been correct when she told him that word had spread. Someone had made sure the wolves were riled up.

They'd formed a circle. Aidan went to the middle of the circle. He braced his feet apart, kept his arms at his sides. And he waited.

They would all detect her scent. He'd made love to her because he needed *her*. But also so that these wolves would know exactly where he stood.

With her.

"She has to be stopped!" Someone yelled out. Some dumb fool.

"She'll turn! She'll attack us — we know what happened before!"

There were murmurs from the crowd. Agreements. Nods.

They were working themselves up to a fury. But who had started this fury? Who had begun to stir the beasts?

"She is the enemy!" Another werewolf yelled.

The circle was closing in on him.

Aidan smiled and he let his claws come out. "Which asshole is gonna be first?"

***

She could hear howls. Screams. Terrible roars.

Jane stopped yanking on her handcuffs and her gaze flew to the window. What in the hell was going on out there?

A blood-chilling scream split the air.

Oh, hell, that was *not* good. She yanked harder on the cuffs. Dammit! *Dam —*

The bookshelf to her right swung inward. It moved so suddenly that Jane let out a shocked cry. The thing had seriously just swung out like some old school secret passage, all Scooby-Doo style. Now that it was open, Jane could see inside to a narrow corridor. And — Annette was there. Rushing out toward Jane.

"Am I in the Twilight Zone?" Jane demanded. It sure felt that way.

Annette reached her. "You're about to be in the dead zone." She pointed to the liquid that looked way too much like wine. "You can't drink that. It's a Sleeper's Spell."

Aidan had told her it was poison.

"You get more than two sips down you, and you will never wake up." Annette frowned down at the cuffs. "That's how they're going to end you. Not a violent death. You just go to sleep, all nice and easy, and suddenly, you aren't a problem for the werewolves any longer."

But Aidan had told her not to drink it. If he wanted her to slip into some easy death, then why tell her to stay away from the poison?

"Where are the keys?" Annette cried out as she glanced around frantically.

"If I had them," Jane retorted, "don't you think I would have used them by now?" Her wrist was bleeding because she'd been yanking so hard on the cuffs. "Do some of your magic mumbo jumbo and make them break!"

"It doesn't work like that," Annette fired back at her. But her voice was a whisper — and Jane's had been, too.

Jane cast a desperate glance toward the door. Was anyone out there? "Look for something I can use to pick the lock. Like…a writing pen, a nail file, a hair bobby pin —"

Annette handed her a bobby pin.

Relief nearly made Jane dizzy. "That will totally be our magic trick." Because she'd seen a fellow officer accidentally get locked in cuffs

before—a really bad Christmas party one year—
and the guy had popped out of them with his
wife's bobby pin. Jane had watched his
movements closely, and she'd even got him to
show her later how he'd done the escape routine.

So she *maybe* had an escape artist issue.
Houdini had always been her favorite magician.

A few twists of her fingers, a desperate push
to reach just the right spot, and that cuff sprang
open. "Voila," she muttered.

Annette grabbed her wrist. "Come on, we
need to get the hell out of here." She tugged Jane
toward the bookshelf.

But Jane stopped.

Annette spun around and stared at her as if
she were crazy. "They are going to *kill* you! I saw
it in my mirror. You're going to die, so I have to
get you out of here, now!"

The howls and screams were still coming
from below. She had to go and look…

Jane hurried toward the window. Her hip
bumped into the table there, sending the wine
glass bobbing a bit. She stared through the glass
and saw a giant circle of men and women down
below. That circle was tight and…

Were there bodies on the ground?

"Werewolves get freaking crazy!" Annette
told her as she pulled on Jane's hand again.
"When the beasts take over, you can't stop them.
Hurry. They had me locked up, too, but the fools

got distracted by the fight. I got loose and found my way to you."

She'd just *found* that secret passage? By chance? Like Jane believed that bull.

"I had a vision of this place," Annette told her, her voice was still hushed. "A vision of you. I knew I had to save you! You can change things. Nothing has to end the way they plan!"

The circle of bodies parted just a bit and Jane saw—

Aidan.

He was right in the middle of that throng. Bloody and fighting, slashing out with his claws as if his very life depended on the battle.

Maybe it does.

Jane inched ever closer to the window. The wine glass bobbed again. Bobbed and fell over, shattering. Wine soaked the floor.

So much for being quiet.

The door flew open. Garrison was there, staring in shock at her and Annette. "What—how did she get in here?"

Annette turned and ran for the open bookshelf/passage.

Jane ran, too—right toward Garrison. She grabbed his shirt. "What is happening down there?"

He clamped his lips together.

"Why are they fighting? Why are they all attacking Aidan?"

His Adam's apple bobbed. "Not…all."

It had certainly looked as if they were *all* attacking to her.

"It's…It's a Blood Battle. Any who want to challenge the alpha can have a turn…he has to face them all, until none are standing."

That circle had been *huge.* "Why do they all want to challenge him?"

Once more, his lips clamped together.

She shook him. *"Why?"*

"You!"

It had been the answer she feared.

"Word has spread about you! They want you dead. Only, in an, um, preferably non-violent way."

The poisoned wine. Aidan's orders *not* to drink.

"If he dies, then…so do you. Pack law." He exhaled again. "He marked you, claimed you. And he went to the Blood Battle with your scent on him. If he wins, then you will always be protected from the werewolves. If he loses…"

She could figure this out for herself. With a sinking heart, Jane said, "He dies."

"You *both* die." But Garrison shook his head. "Only I'm not supposed to let that happen. Graham and I were going to take you out the secret exit. I don't know how that Voodoo Queen found out about it…"

Jane let him go and grabbed her gun. She checked it real quick. Yep, the silver bullets were ready to go.

Then she tried to push past Garrison. The guy proved stronger than she'd anticipated, though, as he jumped in the doorway, blocking her. "You *can't* go down there!"

"Watch me."

"He can't protect you and fight them all! Why the hell do you think he locked you up? To keep you safe!"

She shook her head. "I'm not the kind of girl who lets someone else fight her battles." Jane stared into his eyes. "Since I saved you, I figure you owe me. So how about moving that werewolf ass."

"Shit." He moved.

She brushed past him and then—

He was following her.

Jane looked back, frowning.

"I've got your back, detective," he muttered, looking all determined. "The way I figure it, you and I both have the same enemy."

Thane.

"He took what we love, and one day, we will make him pay."

They came to the top of the spiral staircase.

"And I will do my absolute best to keep you safe out there," he said as they ran down the steps. "But just be warned, werewolves fight dirty."

The howls and screams were louder.

"So do I," Jane told him grimly. They burst outside.

At first, the werewolves kept fighting. Jane saw Captain Vivian Harris. The woman started running toward her.

A few of the others glanced Jane's way, frowning.

But the main focus stayed on Aidan. Aidan—who was kicking ass and not bothering with names as he took down werewolf after werewolf. He was bleeding and bruised but positively lethal as he battled.

A battle for her.

That was oddly sexy. Way fierce, too. But *entirely* too dangerous. The last thing she wanted was her werewolf dying for her.

"Stop!" Jane yelled.

The wolves didn't stop.

So she lifted her gun and fired.

CHAPTER SEVENTEEN

The roar of that bullet echoed around Aidan. His beast was ready to full-on shift. Ready to go for every throat he saw. Ready to have a fucking river of blood around him because these fools would not hurt what was his.

They would never touch Jane.

Jane.

"I said…" Jane's voice rang out. "*Stop!*"

The attack had stopped, for a stunned moment. The werewolves — those who'd been attacking still had their claws out — turned toward her in surprise. And Jane just walked right through the center of the pack.

His muscles strained, jerked. His scent was on her, so no one would be foolish enough to touch her. *They'd better not be. I will rip them apart.*

"I figure none of you jerks can kill me right now," Jane suddenly said as she placed her body right in front of Aidan's. "Because if you did, then I'd die all violent-like, and that's what you want to prevent, right? That's why you're having this blood fest? 'Cause you want me to be put down? Poisoned? A death that's all nice and *easy?"*

No, it won't happen.

"You can't attack me right now because then I might turn into some kind of super monster. So you're stuck." She laughed at them. "But guess what? I *can* attack. I've got silver bullets in this gun just waiting to find their way into some unlucky werewolf hearts. Anyone who makes a move at Aidan again is going to get one of those bullets. *Because you don't hurt him, got it?"*

She was protecting him? Him?

That was...

Jane.

"I might be pissed as hell at this wolf but—" She looked back at him, seemed confused and muttered, "But he's mine."

Always. Did she have any clue what she was doing? Probably not. A human wouldn't understand a werewolf bond. Wouldn't know that she'd just made a public declaration linking them.

He knew.

So did a few of the others who suddenly backed away.

He felt Paris at his back. His friend had been there the entire time. Fighting off any attackers who'd tried to jump Aidan from behind. A Blood Battle was supposed to be fair. Come at your attacker from the front, but not everyone wanted to play by those rules.

So Paris had been making sure those assholes were taken down.

"Told you she wouldn't be captive for long," Paris murmured.

"Who the hell is he?" Jane said and she lifted her weapon toward Paris.

"My best friend." Aidan made sure he stood between Paris and Jane's gun. "Paris. And, like me, he'd protect you until death."

"Can we all stop talking about death?" Jane's voice was nearly a shout.

No, they probably couldn't.

"Pleasure," Paris said. "Though I wish we'd met at a different time."

A time when he wasn't fighting his own pack.

Vivian walked among the wounded. So far, none were dead. He hadn't been trying to kill them, just incapacitate them.

Garrison stumbled to Jane's side, and he turned, glaring at the crowd. "Everybody, stay back!"

There were snarls. Glares. But no one else attacked, not yet.

"I get that you all think I'm some kind of threat," Jane said, her words carrying easily. "Trust me, I get it. But I am not your enemy. And Aidan — he's definitely not. He's your alpha. He protects the pack. Why would any of you even think that he'd ever do anything to hurt you all?"

Because someone had been planting the seeds of doubt in their minds. Someone had been working to make them believe that Aidan shouldn't be in charge.

But it wasn't the wolves he'd faced that night. They were weak. They had their fucking emotions on their sleeves. No, it was someone else…

Before Aidan could say another word, a new scent reached him. The scent of blood and death. The scent of…*vampires.*

Not just one. It seemed as if a virtual army of vamps were coming their way.

And the other werewolves had scented them now, too. There were sharp cries of distress. The flash of more claws and then those werewolves surged past Jane and Aidan. As one, they turned to face the paved road that led to the werewolf mansion, and those wolves—the same wolves who'd been lining up to attack Aidan before— now formed a solid wall blocking him and Jane off from the vampires who were coming their way.

"Um, what just happened?" Jane asked, confusion rich in her voice.

"A new threat," he told her. "One that their beasts can't ignore." One that his couldn't ignore. *When a vamp gets close, the primal instinct kicks in.*

Kill. He wrapped his hand around the nape of her neck and brought her in close, then he kissed her. Hard and deep. *My Mary Jane.* "Vamps are coming this way."

"Vamps?"

"Coming in fast and coming in hard." He would shift fully for this battle. He'd held back with his pack. He would show no mercy to the vampires. His beast wouldn't let him. "You have one job to do—"

"Actually, if vamps are attacking, I think I have several."

"They're coming for you. Stay the fuck alive, got it? That's your job. Do it, for me." He kissed her again, because he had to do it. "I won't lose you. I can't."

Her left hand locked around his neck before he could pull away from her. "Careful, wolf," Jane murmured. "Talk like that will make me think that you're starting to care."

"I do care." No starting about it. She'd gotten to him, and, soon enough, they'd both have to deal with the consequences of that shit. But for now... "Get back in the mansion."

"Uh, how about I watch your ass? And your pack's back?"

The vamps were already there. He whirled around and saw the vampires collide with the line of werewolves. Blood and claws, teeth and battle. Death.

What had Annette told him?

Betrayal. Blood. Death. Yeah, he had it all that night.

His beast took over. Aidan lunged forward. His hands flew out, and when they hit down, they were powerful paws. The change burned through him, ripping away his humanity and leaving only his beast. He could attack better in this form. Could hunt, could kill, so easily.

The vampires had come onto *his* land. There would be no mercy.

***

She was in the middle of a war. Jane knew it. The vamps and the werewolves fought savagely and getting back into the house might have been a good idea, after all —

A vampire tackled the wolf Aidan had called Paris to the ground. The vamp went right for Paris's throat.

Aidan had said Paris was his best friend.

Jane shot that vamp. The bullet ripped right into his chest and he fell back. The vamp wasn't dead, not yet, though. Paris jumped on top of him. His claws slashed down.

He may be dead now…

Jane whirled around. Aidan was in wolf form. A truly terrifying sight because he wasn't a normal wolf — he was like three times the size of a wolf she'd once seen at a zoo. His fangs were enormous and when he swiped with his claws—

Vamps went down.

Her gaze darted to the left. Garrison. He was—actually, holding his own. He'd just thrown a vampire a good ten feet. Impressive. And that was—

"Jane!"

Her head whipped toward that scream. Her captain was on the ground, struggling desperately. A vamp had his teeth in Vivian's throat.

Jane ran forward, firing at the same time. The bullet hit the vampire in the shoulder. High and hard. The impact spun him back, freeing Vivian. The captain jumped up and drove her claws into the vamp's chest.

Hard hands grabbed Jane around the waist. She spun, ready to fire, but she saw a tall blond standing there.

Graham.

He lifted his claw-tipped hands. "Not a vamp! *Not!*"

A vampire was running up behind him, though. Jane aimed, fired. The vampire screamed when he fell back.

"You are one fucking good shot," Graham said, sounding impressed. "Didn't realize just how good…"

She strained to see around him. Where was Aidan? *Please, please, not at the bottom of that pile of vampires.*

"Aidan can't focus with you in danger! We have to get you inside!"

Aidan *was* under that pile of vampires. At least five had jumped on top of him. She fired her gun again, hitting one in the back.

Just as the werewolf — her Aidan — threw the vamps off him with a ferocious howl. Hell, yes, that was —

Something sharp stabbed into her side. She looked down, saw Graham's hand at her waist and realized that his claws hadn't cut her. No, not claws. He'd just jabbed a needle into her side. Jane blinked, confused. "Wh-what —"

Her knees buckled. He caught her before she fell, lifting her over his shoulder and running for the mansion. Her whole body had gone heavy, and her eyes wanted to sag closed but Jane forced them to remain open.

Graham was moving so quickly. In just seconds, they were in the mansion. The door clanged shut behind them. Graham turned to the right, held tight to her, and began running down the stairs to a lower level that she hadn't even noticed before. Were there supposed to be basements in swamp houses? She didn't think so — but hell, thinking at all was hard then.

"He'll be waiting," he muttered. "Have to hurry. Have to hurry…"

She needed to fight that jerk but her body wasn't listening to her mind's commands. She was too sluggish and why did her limbs feel so thick and heavy? Just what had been in that shot he gave her?

A musty scent reached her as he opened another door—the hinges creaked. Then they were in a tunnel, not a hallway. And she felt like they were still going down. "L-let go…" Jane managed, her voice weak and husky.

"Hell the fuck no," Graham responded as his hold tightened on her. "Do you have any idea just how much money you're actually worth?"

What?

Then he turned, moved down another tunnel. Just what was this place? Why were there *tunnels* everywhere?

Tunnels…and another light. A light right up ahead. Someone was there. It was—

Graham dumped Jane onto the ground. "What the fuck are you doing?" Graham demanded.

Jane couldn't push herself off the ground, but she did manage to turn her head so she could see the person who was in that tunnel with them. Annette. Annette held a glowing lantern in her hand.

"You're working with the vampires," Annette said, her voice sad, but not shocked.

"You shouldn't be down here. Dammit, I let you *go*. I'm the one who arranged for all your guards to suddenly be distracted." He grabbed her arm. "That meant you needed to get the hell out of this place before the shit went south. You knew all the passages in this place. You should have taken one and left *before* the vamps arrived."

But Annette hadn't left. Instead, she'd gone to Jane. Told her not to drink…

Annette's gaze slid to Jane. "You injected her with the Sleeper's Spell."

Wait—shit, what?

Jane shivered. *Am I dying?*

"Don't worry, I didn't give her enough to kill her. Barely a drop."

"It only takes two drops to kill."

"I said *one* fucking drop. Just to make her easier to handle. The woman is a freaking hellcat, for a human. I had to get her away from Aidan and down here for the exchange." He roughly shook Annette. "But you have to get out of here! The vamps won't let you go a second time!"

Annette yanked free of him. "You sent Thane to me the first time. I wondered how Thane had gotten past my safeguards. But you told him how to get to me. How to get in my protected shop. You set all of that in motion. You *used* me. I thought you cared, but all along—"

"I don't have time for this shit!" Graham yelled. He looked back over his shoulder, staring into the darkness of the tunnel.

Jane wiggled her fingers. She *wiggled* them. That was good, right? Maybe she was getting control back. Maybe.

Please.

"You made a deal with Thane," Annette said. "Don't you know you can't deal with a devil?"

"I know I'm *sick* of being Aidan's dog on a leash. Fucking third in power. That's not me. So what if I wasn't born with freaking alpha blood? I have saved this pack time and again. But Aidan won't get out of my way. Aidan won't let *me* have a shot—"

"Because you're not…as strong as…him," Jane huffed out the words.

Graham's stare flew down to her.

"Dirty…betraying…asshole," she muttered. In her shoes, her toes wiggled. *Yes.* She just needed a little more time.

"I'm starting my own pack," Graham bellowed at her. "With the money and power I'll get for you. The vamps will be doing *my* bidding. They'll jump at my commands. I'll be the most powerful wolf in the whole freaking U.S."

Annette sat her lantern down on the ground. "That isn't how it works. The vamps won't follow any orders from you. They'll just kill you. You should know that."

"Wrong." His voice was frantic. Wild. "Thane swore a blood oath to me. He'll give me two million for her—vamps are freaking rolling in the cash because they've been around so shit long. They do nothing but grab wealth. *And* he'll make me the leader of my own pack. He'll get rid of Aidan." He laughed and pointed down at Jane. "Actually, *she'll* get rid of him. Once she turns, Thane plans to lock her in a cell with Aidan. Aidan won't fight her. Fool went soft for her. Thinks she's his mate or something. He'll die just like his father did, then no one will be in my way! I will rule!"

Okay, so the guy was definitely a two-faced lying piece of crap.

And that bit about Aidan's father…she stored that away for later.

Jane was now pretty sure she could control her body—mostly, anyway. She just needed the perfect moment to attack.

"I'm in your way," Annette said quietly.

"Baby, *no…*"

"You came to my bed. You said you loved me…You said we'd have a future."

"We *can*. You can be at the side of the most powerful werewolf in—"

"Then you sent that vampire to attack me. He ripped into my neck. He said he'd kill me. *You* sent him."

"I knew he wouldn't kill—"

"Consider us fucking broken up, Graham." And she yanked out a knife from beneath the skirt of her dress.

Nice. Jane was definitely liking Annette now.

"It's silver," Annette told him flatly. "And I will use it to cut out your worthless heart. My loyalty is to the pack. They saved my family. They saved me. I was nine, *nine*, when my family came under attack. Humans with hate in their hearts. Humans who didn't understand magic. Who hated anything or anyone who was different. I was beaten and left on the streets and—"

"Blah, blah, blah…" Graham mocked. "Great old Aidan came to save the day. I know this story. I've heard it a thousand times from a thousand different people. I am so sick of him!"

"I'm not," Jane whispered.

"I'm taking her," Annette said as she lifted that knife higher. "I know these tunnels. I'll get her away and Aidan can deal with you."

"That's not happening," Graham said, his voice sad. "Sorry, baby."

"It *is* happening—*ah!*"

Her words ended in a scream because someone had come up behind her. Not just someone—a big, tall, blond vampire had grabbed her from behind and tossed her against the side of that tunnel. She slammed into it, hard, and her knife flew from her fingers. Before Annette could right herself, the vampire grabbed her again, yanking her close to his gleaming fangs as he prepared to rip out her throat.

No! Jane grabbed the knife and jumped up. So maybe her knees jiggled—she was upright and she sliced that knife along the vampire's side. *"Let her go!"*

And he did.

He just dropped Annette right on the ground, but another woman shot forward from the depths of the tunnel. That woman grabbed Annette, yanking her up by the hair. *That woman — she has fangs — fangs stained red with blood.* Annette was barely keeping the female vamp's fangs from sinking into her neck.

Recognition surged through Jane. *Oh, my God, I know her.*

That attacking female vampire—she'd been the one Jane wanted to save behind the St. Louis Cathedral. The woman she'd fought so hard for. *And this is what she'd become.*

Jane lunged to help Annette, but the blond male vampire laughed and, in a flash, he'd knocked the silver knife from Jane's hand. He locked an arm around Jane's throat and yanked her against his body. He was big and muscled and Jane swore that he smelled like death. *Because he was death.*

"It's been so long," he whispered in her ear as he yanked her neck to the side. Her back was to his stomach and he held her in an unbreakable grip. "But I have been patient."

Graham—that asshole—just stood there watching them. Annette was fighting for her life. Jane couldn't get that vamp bastard to let her go. And Graham...*watched*.

"Do you have my money?" Graham demanded.

The vampire had been sniffing Jane's throat, but at those words, he glanced up.

"I did *everything* I promised," Graham went on, shifting his weight slightly from his left foot to his right. "So I want my pay-off."

"Don't worry," the vampire—Thane—assured him. Jane knew it was Thane. She knew him. *I never forgot the monster in the dark.* His voice seemed to roll right over her as he told Graham, "You'll get exactly what you have coming."

***

Jane wasn't there.

Trapped inside his beast, Aidan raged and fought his growing fear. He couldn't see Jane. Couldn't find her anywhere.

The vampires were retreating. As they fucking should. Their dead littered the ground. They had been far outnumbered by his pack.

Why attack now? Why come like this?

They had to know their numbers were too small to face his entire pack.

His wolf drew ragged breaths and slowly, so slowly, the man took control once more. His bones popped and snapped. The fur melted from his body. He soon crouched on the ground, not as an animal, but as a man. His fingers sank into the dank earth. The scent of blood filled the air.

Blood, but no Jane.

"Your lady was pretty incredible." Garrison—he was there, walking up with blood dripping down his face. Paris was just a step behind him. "I'm damn grateful for her shots. She was pulling some serious Annie Oakley shit."

"Where is she?" His voice was guttural.

"Graham was taking care of her," Paris said. "Saw him with her…" But his words trailed off. "Maybe they went to the house?"

Aidan scanned the battlefield once more. Vivian was tending to the wounded and already giving orders about disposing of the dead vamps. He could count on her to handle the clean-up now that the battle had been won but…

Why come at us when they knew we had stronger numbers?

It didn't make sense to him unless…

Distraction. Vampires were such master fucking manipulators.

Where. Was. Jane? He surged to his feet and ran for his house. Her scent was there, and he followed it, but...

Not upstairs. She hadn't gone back to his bedroom.

"Here." Garrison tossed him a pair of jeans. They kept those handy, just for the times Aidan had to shift and kick ass.

He yanked them on in an instant and he kept following Jane's scent. Not up, but down...down below into the secret sections of the mansion. He yanked open the old, heavy wooden door. A door that led down to the tunnels.

Once upon a time, his family's home had been part of the Underground Railroad. The tunnels ran for miles and miles, and they spit out far away from the house.

Those tunnels were perfect for werewolves who might need to vanish from an attack.

But Jane shouldn't go out in those tunnels. They opened in the swamp. And the vampires could be *waiting* out there. She would have been safer inside the house.

He stepped forward, and another scent hit him.

Vampire.

Maybe the vamps had already found the tunnels. Maybe they'd blocked Graham and Jane from escaping.

His claws were out.

Or maybe…*maybe I've just found the wolf who stirred up the others.*

Annette had told him that she saw betrayal. She just hadn't told him which member of his pack was going to try shoving a silver knife into his back.

I can protect my back…but if anyone hurts Jane…

They would find out just how vicious of an alpha he truly was.

No one will hurt her and live. No fucking one.

Pack mate or not, he would rip apart any fool who so much as bruised her skin. Jane mattered. Jane was *his.* His life, his hope, his chance at something more. And he would do anything to keep her.

He bounded through the old tunnels, the earth hard beneath his bare feet. The scent of blood grew stronger and he could tell that it wasn't just one vamp up ahead.

The tunnels turned, branched off. His nostrils twitched. He dove low—

Just as Graham fired with his gun. No, *with Jane's gun.*

The bullet missed Aidan. And Graham—the traitorous bastard—didn't get a chance to fire again. Aidan swiped his claws over the man's wrist, cutting deep, cutting him open, and the gun dropped to the ground.

In the next second, he had his claws at Graham's throat.

"No!" Graham begged. "Don't, I—"

Laughter. A woman's wild laughter.

"Help me…"

Aidan's head turned. Annette was on the ground and a woman was crouched above her, a woman with dirty, blood-soaked hair, vampire fangs, and wild eyes. Blood dripped down the female vampire's chin.

Annette's blood.

"Fucking hell," Garrison said as he rushed around that curve. Aidan had been aware of the younger wolf following him, and he'd been too distracted with worry over Jane to tell the guy to stay the hell back.

Aidan inhaled again. Jane wasn't there. She wasn't in the tunnel. Just Graham, Annette—and that female vampire. A vampire he'd wanted to end at the hospital.

While Aidan held his claws at Graham's throat, Garrison hurried past him. Garrison tackled the female vampire, rolling with her. She let out a loud, desperate scream and Aidan saw that Garrison had a wooden stake in his hand—a stake that he'd just shoved into the woman's chest.

She looked down at her chest. Then back up at Garrison.

She tried to smile at him.

And then the vampiress went still.

"He betrayed you!" Annette yelled as she stumbled to her feet. She put a hand to her throat, but blood pumped through her fingers. "Graham—he made a deal with Thane! H-he set all of this up!"

Aidan's gaze had jerked toward her, and at her cries, Graham surged forward with a burst of strength, momentarily breaking free of Aidan's hold.

The tricky bastard drove his claws into Aidan's side. Like that was supposed to hurt him. "You forget," he said, his voice lethally soft. "I'm the alpha. I can *destroy* you." And he attacked with his claws. Graham tried to block him, but Aidan was too fast. He sliced left, right. He tore into the wolf who'd dared to betray him. *"Where is she?"*

But Graham wasn't telling him. Just smiling. Sick freak. Still fighting and—

Trying to stop me from going after her.

Screw that. Aidan slammed him into the wall, as hard as he could. There was a sickening thud as Graham's head connected on impact.

Paris burst around the curve of the tunnel. Figured he'd join the party. *Always trying to watch my back.*

"Hold the bastard!" Aidan roared.

The tunnel branched again up ahead, splitting into two paths. He had Jane's scent now, a fresh trail, so he could follow her easily, even without Annette shakily pointing to the right.

"Too late!" Graham yelled. "She's…gone." He laughed. "Gone…gone…*gone*…She'll be the one to kill you. No more alpha…"

Aidan didn't spare him another glance. If he did — he'd kill Graham. Right there. And he didn't want to do that because he had to get to Jane. No more time could be wasted. Faster, faster he ran though those tunnels. Vamps had enhanced speed, just like werewolves. The vamp could be so far ahead.

Can't let him get away with her. Jane has to live. She has to stay with me.

A wooden ladder appeared up ahead, leading to the surface. He climbed it quickly and grabbed for the trap door above his head. Aidan threw it open. He leapt out just as —

"No, Aidan, no!" Jane yelled.

Gunfire exploded at the same instant. Fire ignited in his chest and Aidan fell back, tumbling down that ladder.

Silver. Fucking silver bullets. Two to the chest.

His eyes began to sag closed.

Jane. My Jane.

CHAPTER EIGHTEEN

"Aidan, no!"

Thane laughed. Jane's ears were still ringing from the gunshots. The bastard—the sick bastard had just waited up there for Aidan to appear. He'd covered her mouth with his hand until that last moment, stopping her from calling out a warning until it was too late.

Aidan had fallen back down into the tunnel. He could be dead. Right the hell then, he could be dead. Fury pounded through her, surging past her pain. She hit back with her elbow, as hard as she could, and Thane actually let her go. Maybe he'd been caught off-guard by her move or maybe—

Screw why.

She lunged forward and tumbled down into that tunnel. She hit the ground, her knees slamming into the earth, her palms thudding with a bruising impact, but Jane didn't care. She crawled forward, desperate to reach Aidan.

And then Thane jumped into the tunnel with her.

"He's not dead yet. His body is fighting the silver. He'll live a bit longer, I'll make sure of it."

Jane's hands were flying over Aidan's chest. So much blood. And…she could feel one of his wounds. The spot where one of those silver bullets had driven into his chest.

Get it out.

Aidan could heal, damn fast, but she had to get the silver out of him. Hadn't he healed up fast enough before when he'd dug that bullet out of his chest? Jane didn't even give herself time to think. She just shoved her fingers into that gaping hole. *Find it. Find it.* Maybe the bullet had shattered on impact. What she was doing could be completely useless. She was—

Thane's fingers locked around the nape of her neck and he yanked her back. But even as he pulled her, Jane's fingers curled around the bullet she'd ripped from Aidan's chest.

"He'll live longer," Thane said again. "After all, he has to live long enough to be your first victim. I have to provide you with a strong meal, one that will give you plenty of power."

Thane walked backward with her until she slammed into the dirt wall of the tunnel. His fingers were tight bands around her neck. He leaned in close and she felt the rough lick of his tongue along her neck. "I would love to taste you."

Bile rose in her throat.

"But that isn't how it works." His hand went to her right side, and he yanked up her shirt. His left hand was locked around her neck, but the fingers of his right hand traced her scar. "You *are* the end. The one we've been waiting for. Humans and werewolves—they won't stand a chance. Not when you rise."

Jane tried to shake her head.

"I'm going to strangle you," Thane said, as his fingers tightened on her throat. "I thought about breaking your neck, but well…we want to be sure your death is nice and violent, don't we? A snap would be entirely too quick."

He was squeezing her throat, compressing her airway. Her temples were throbbing. And Aidan—

Aidan let out a long groan. *Yes. Yes.* He was coming back to her. She just needed that wolf to heal one hell of a lot faster.

Her hands pounded into Thane. Asshole Thane. He wasn't letting her go. *I can't get a breath!*

"Did you know you were special before that night? Did you realize it?" Thane asked her.

I'm not special. Some freak vampire just decided to burn me—and that same freak thinks he's killing me! But she wasn't ready to die. No way.

"The perfect instrument of death," he murmured.

The pressure was so intense. Her eyes were aching. She stopped pounding at his chest and desperately clawed at his hand. She could hear the blood pounding in her ears. He was crushing her throat, squeezing tighter and tighter and she couldn't get free.

"Your mother thought by hiding you from your real father, you'd be safe. She was wrong. You are his blood. The only one who can become more."

Her real father.

Jane hadn't...

No. Dear God, no!

"He's dead now, werewolves killed him. Werewolves like that sick freak you took as a lover."

She couldn't see Thane any longer. Black dots covered her vision. And she wasn't clawing at his hands any longer. Her arms had fallen limply to her sides.

"It will only be fitting that you rip out his throat when you wake back up. You are *the end*. The one who we've all been waiting for. Show the world just what hell looks like—"

He was dragged away from her. His bellowing scream echoed in the tunnel.

But...

Jane fell. She didn't gasp for breath. She just fell. And even though darkness surrounded her, in that one terrible moment, she thought of Aidan.

Her werewolf.

Her lover.

The one man who'd made her wish…made her want more. Made her want the happiness that other people seemed to have.

Aidan.

As her body hit the ground, she said a silent prayer.

Please, God, please, don't let me kill him. Not Aidan. If I wake up, don't let me hurt him.

Such a pity…Jane thought that maybe…maybe she could have loved him.

Or maybe I already do.

***

"The alpha is a dead man!" Graham snarled.

Paris drove his fist into the guy's face. "Bastard! We *trusted* you! You were our friend!" Shit—he'd known Graham for years. Fucking years. And the guy had sold them out to a vampire?

"Our turn for power," Graham said, licking away the blood from his busted lip. "You and me. We can take over this pack. Let me go…let's go after him, together. Make sure the job is done. Make sure Aidan is *dead*. His vampire-to-be piece of ass is going to rip his throat out."

Paris shook his head. "No, she isn't." But he wanted to run after Aidan to make absolutely sure of that fact. Dammit.

Annette staggered closer. Annette Benoit. He knew her. Had always thought she was fucking gorgeous.

And powerful. Everyone knew...you didn't mess with the Voodoo Queen.

Annette lifted up a small doll. *Where the hell did she get that from? Wait...*it looked as if it had been made from the dirt of that tunnel. Dirt held together with her own blood. "You betrayed me," Annette said to Graham.

"I—"

Her fingers fisted over the doll, and the pieces of dirt crumbled. Before Paris's eyes, Graham crumpled, too. He let out a long, loud, inhuman scream of pain and he fell to the ground, shuddering.

Annette stared down at him with a pitiless gaze. "That's what betrayal feels like to me," she whispered. Then she glanced up at Paris. "You can go now. He won't hurt anyone else."

"Um..."

"I-I'll keep guard," Garrison offered, though he looked as if he were afraid of Annette, too.

Smart man.

"Go," Annette said again.

"I sure as hell hope I never piss you off," Paris muttered to Annette.

Her eyelids flickered.

But Graham was obviously not a threat to anyone right then. Her magic had done something to him, and Paris rushed after Aidan, knowing that if his friend needed him, he had to be there. Aidan had saved his ass before and now—

Now it's my turn. Because unlike Graham, Paris would never betray his friend. He just wasn't made that damn way.

***

Thane was laughing. Laughing so hard even as Aidan drove his fist into the fool's chest.

That stopped the laughter.

But Thane didn't go down. "She's dead," he whispered. "Dead, dead, dead…"

And Aidan felt as if someone had just tried to cut out his heart. He sliced up with his claws, going for Thane's neck this time. He would cut the bastard's head off and be done with him. But at the last moment, Thane managed to stumble back. Aidan cut the bastard—sliced him deep enough to send blood spraying—but he didn't get Thane's head.

Dead, dead, dead…

Instead of attacking Thane again, Aidan leapt for Jane because he knew every second counted. Maybe he could bring her back. Do CPR. Give her his blood. *Something*. If he acted fast enough, he could stop this. He could save her. It didn't have to end this way.

Please, don't end this way. He pulled her limp body into his arms. And he felt it right then…his heart stopped. It just stopped because Jane wasn't moving. The pain ripped straight to his soul. He hadn't realized what was happening with her. With them. He'd thought he was just reacting to her scent, to what she was but…no.

All along, everything had happened between them because she was, simply…*Jane*. His Jane. His beautiful, strong Jane.

Jane…who made him ache. Who made him want. Who made him need.

Who made him love.

I fucking love you. Don't leave me. Don't.

He hunched over her, grief nearly tearing him apart because this was too soon. He needed an eternity with her. He pushed on her chest, wanting her to breathe. His lips found hers and he gave her his air. "Please," he begged, but she was so still. "I love—"

She shuddered. Her eyes flew open and she gasped, sucking in a deep breath.

Hope held him still. Fear controlled his body.

"Not…dead…yet…" Her voice was a broken rasp, and it was the most beautiful sound he had ever heard.

He squeezed her tight. *Jane. Jane. Jane!* He hadn't lost her. She was his. They had a chance. They had—

"Vamp…" Jane whispered. "Behind…"

He leapt up just as Thane came at him. The bastard had ripped one of the wooden support beams right out of the tunnel's wall. He slammed the board into Aidan's chest. It splintered.

Aidan didn't go down.

Jane was alive. He would *not* let that bastard get to her again. His only job was to keep her safe. *Keep her safe. Protect her. Love her for all my days.*

So he attacked with claws and fury. Again and again, he hit the vampire. But Thane was strong. And he struck back. They slammed into the walls, they rolled across that damn tunnel. Blood and pain. Aidan called forth his wolf, knowing he had to shift completely so that he could take out this vamp. Thane was powerful, ancient, and he wouldn't go down without a—

"Thane."

Jane's voice. She was on her feet. Weaving a bit. Behind her, he saw Paris running down the tunnel.

"I've got something for you," Jane whispered.

Thane lunged for her.

Before Thane could grab her, Aidan grabbed *him.* Aidan caught Thane's arms, yanking them back.

And Jane lifted the broken chunk of wood she'd hidden behind her body. She slammed it into Thane's chest, sending it straight through his body. Right through his heart.

"One of us...is dying tonight..." Jane said, her voice hoarse and broken. "But it's...n-not...me..."

Thane sagged to the ground, his knees hitting hard.

"Look away," Aidan ordered Jane.

She didn't.

"Paris..." Aidan snapped.

Paris grabbed Jane and pulled her behind him just as Aidan let his claws fly one more time. This time, it was Thane's head that hit the ground. *No coming back from that, you sonofabitch.*

His breath heaved out. His shoulders shook. Blood was all around him, but that last vicious swipe from his claws — that blood spray hadn't hit his Jane. Paris had protected her.

Paris had stopped her from seeing Aidan *enjoy* the kill.

Because he knew he'd been smiling when he took Thane's head.

Silence beat in that tunnel. Heavy and thick. He stepped over the body. Paris looked up at him. "Guessing you want her now?"

I want her always.

Aidan took Jane into his arms. He lifted her up, a tremor going through him because he was so grateful and happy that she was alive. Her sweet scent filled his lungs and the fear finally faded enough that he could draw a full breath.

He carried her up the ladder and out into the night. Stars glittered overhead.

She was so still in his arms. "Is it…the end?" Jane asked him, her broken voice making him ache.

He pressed a kiss to the top of her head. "No, sweetheart, it's the beginning." For them, this night was a turning point. He knew exactly how much Jane meant to him.

Everything.

And he knew that he would face any battle, kill any foe…for her.

"The beginning," he said again and tightened his hold on his Jane.

***

She looked like hell.

Jane glared at her reflection. She'd slept for ten hours. Okay, maybe twelve hours. She shouldn't have woken up with circles under her eyes and too pale skin, but she had.

And she'd also woken up with some wicked blue and black bruises all around her neck, courtesy of a now rotting vampire.

"You are so beautiful."

At that low rumble, Jane turned around. Aidan stood in the bathroom doorway. His gaze drank her in and Jane forgot about bruises and stupid bags under her eyes.

He stepped toward her. Kissed her so carefully. He'd been careful with her all night. Taking care of her. Coddling her.

She wondered if he was going to make that a habit.

If so, she'd have to stop that shit. Care was all well and good, but she liked her rough wolf, too. Especially...at certain times.

"I have an in with your boss," Aidan rasped against her lips. "So I've been told that you get the next few days off. Nothing but time to rest and relax."

She sincerely hoped that resting wasn't the only thing on the agenda.

Aidan pulled back and stared down at her. "I am so sorry."

"For what?"

"Graham was *my* pack. My responsibility. And I didn't see the threat that he was. I brought that danger to you."

Jane shook her head even as her fingers tightened on the fluffy white robe that she wore—a robe of Aidan's that totally swallowed her. "Not your fault. You can't control other people's crazy."

His lips tightened. "My pack."

And he thought he had to shoulder the burden of their sins? Not the way the world worked. "What's going to happen to him?"

"He's dead."

Jane blinked. "What?"

"Not by my hand," he said, shaking his head. "Seems that he…he grabbed a silver gun while he was in Paris's custody. He shot himself, screaming that he had to stop the pain that was ripping him apart."

Jane rocked back on her heels.

"Paris said that he thinks Annette worked a spell on Graham when they were in the tunnels."

"A spell to make him take his own life?" That was…terrifying. As terrifying as everything else that was going on.

"I don't know. I'll find out."

"Is she okay?" Because Annette had tried to help her. Was Annette bad? Good? Maybe both?

Maybe we're all both. A little bad. A little good.

Except for Thane. She figured he'd just been one *Straight A Devil* to his core.

And he knew my real father. But she didn't mention that tidbit to Aidan. Perhaps he hadn't heard those words of Thane's. And she didn't want to tell him. Because if she told him about her father, there would be so much more that she had to reveal.

And she couldn't, not just yet.

It wasn't just her life that she was protecting, after all.

"Annette is recovering. She's weak, but Dr. Bob said she'll be just fine."

Now her brows rose. "Since when does Dr. Bob work on the living?"

His fingers curled around hers as he led her into his bedroom. They'd made love in that big bed before…before the nightmare that had exploded around them. Now though, he just eased her under the covers. Held her.

So careful.

Not my style. And it's not his, either.

"When I have emergencies," Aidan said quietly, "I call him. I wanted to make sure Annette was all right." He pressed a kiss to her cheek.

Jane turned to face him. "You have to stop."

A furrow appeared between his brows.

"I'm okay. Don't treat me like I'm some kind of—"

"Victim?"

She didn't like that word, mostly because it was so true.

"Your voice is still hoarse," he said, eyes glinting. "Every time I hear it, I think of how close I came to losing you."

She caught his hand. Brought it over her heart. Let him feel that strong beat. "You didn't lose me." Because she hadn't been about to give up. She'd fought with all of her strength to live. She had *felt* him calling to her.

And she'd known that she had to get back to him.

I love him.

It was strange how death could make some things so very crystal clear.

So Jane took a deep breath, she licked her dry lips, and she stopped being afraid. "I love you, Aidan Locke."

His eyes glowed. A good glow? She hoped so.

"Did you hear me?" Jane continued, though she knew he must have heard her. Werewolf hearing and all of that. And the fact that she was *right in front of him*. But he hadn't responded, so she tried again. "I love—"

He kissed her. Not carefully. Not gently. But hot and hard and wild and she *adored* it.

"Love you," Aidan bit off against her lips. "Want you. Need you. Love you *always*."

And happiness exploded in her chest. She grabbed him and held on tight. It was her turn to be wild as she kissed him. There was no way to hold back because the joy Jane felt was too strong.

He loved her. She loved him. They had challenges coming their way — secrets and no doubt, more vamps — but they had each other.

To Jane, that was all that mattered.

Everything else…they'd deal with it.

She pushed him onto his back. Stripped his clothes away because she needed him naked. When he shoved down her robe, Aidan groaned his pleasure at finding she was nude.

She started to slide right over his cock. That big, thick cock that was fully erect. For her.

And she was already wet for him.

But first…

Jane bent and put her lips around the head of his arousal. She licked him, then took him into her mouth deeper, stroking him with her tongue and savoring him. Aidan had said he liked her taste. Well, she *loved* his taste. Jane was pretty sure she could get drunk off it.

"Jane. Fuck me *now.*"

Her impatient, perfect, sexy wolf.

Jane rose over him. She straddled his hips, then she surged down, taking that heavy cock into her. Their hands linked together. Their eyes met. Then she started to move. *He* moved. Thrusting hard and lifting her off the bed. Their breaths heaved out. His gaze began to glow, in that hot way that she loved so very much.

And then the climax hit her. She fell forward and Jane bit him lightly, right on the curve of his shoulder. She marked him, just the way he'd marked her before.

You're mine, Aidan Locke. And Jane didn't plan to let him go.

Her sex quivered and contracted as he pounded into her. So good. So incredibly good.

He shouted her name when he came. The pleasure blasted through every cell in her body, and Jane never, ever wanted it to end.

She didn't want fear. She didn't want doubt. She didn't want anything but a life with her werewolf.

A life in which she knew she was loved.

Always.

By him.

Jane kissed her werewolf once more.

And he held her tight.

***

The sun was setting. Jane walked out onto the balcony at Hell's Gate so that she could watch the night come for her.

Three days had passed since the attack at the werewolf mansion. Three days that she'd spent with Aidan, secured away at his home in the swamp.

But a girl couldn't hide forever and, besides, hiding wasn't exactly her style.

Her holster was under her arm. There were wooden bullets in that gun. And a silver knife was strapped to her ankle. A cop could never be too careful.

"Are you afraid?" Aidan asked as he came up behind her. His hands covered hers on the railing and he pressed a kiss to her neck.

The bruises were gone.

Afraid. The one word seemed to slice right through her. Was she afraid?

Of dying? Of changing?

Of the monsters that waited out there in the darkness?

She stared out at the city. Aidan felt so solid. So secure.

"I'm not afraid," Jane said. Truth. She wasn't. Because whatever else might come her way— *whoever* else—she'd face the threat. With Aidan at her side, they could do anything.

They *would* do anything.

She wasn't afraid of the monsters.

Not even of the monster that might lurk inside of herself.

THE END

###

Ready for the next Blood & Moonlight Novel? Jane and Aidan will be back in BETTER OFF UNDEAD.

Lust. Love. Monsters.

BETTER OFF UNDEAD

BLOOD AND MOONLIGHT BOOK 2

New York Times and USA Today Bestselling Author

CYNTHIA EDEN

A NOTE FROM THE AUTHOR

Thank you for reading BITE THE DUST. I hope that you enjoyed Jane and Aidan's story.

If you'd like to stay updated on my releases and sales, please join my newsletter list www.cynthiaeden.com/newsletter/. You can also check out my Facebook page www.facebook.com/cynthiaedenfanpage. I love to post giveaways over at Facebook!

Again, thanks for reading BITE THE DUST.

Best,

Cynthia Eden
www.cynthiaeden.com

ABOUT THE AUTHOR

Award-winning author Cynthia Eden writes dark tales of paranormal romance and romantic suspense. She is a *New York Times, USA Today, Digital Book World,* and *IndieReader* best-seller. Cynthia is also a three-time finalist for the RITA® award. Since she began writing full-time in 2005, Cynthia has written over fifty novels and novellas.

Cynthia is a southern girl who loves horror movies, chocolate, and happy endings. More information about Cynthia and her books may be found at: http://www.cynthiaeden.com or on her Facebook page at: http://www.facebook.com/cynthiaedenfanpage. Cynthia is also on Twitter at http://www.twitter.com/cynthiaeden.

HER WORKS

Paranormal romances by Cynthia Eden:
- THE WOLF WITHIN (Purgatory, Book 1)
- MARKED BY THE VAMPIRE (Purgatory, Book 2)
- CHARMING THE BEAST (Purgatory, Book 3)
- DEAL WITH THE DEVIL (Purgatory, Book 4)
- BOUND BY BLOOD (Bound, Book 1)
- BOUND IN DARKNESS (Bound, Book 2)
- BOUND IN SIN (Bound, Book 3)
- BOUND BY THE NIGHT (Bound, Book 4)
- BOUND IN DEATH (Bound, Book 5)

Other paranormal romances by Cynthia Eden:
- A VAMPIRE'S CHRISTMAS CAROL
- BLEED FOR ME
- BURN FOR ME (Phoenix Fire, Book 1)
- ONCE BITTEN, TWICE BURNED (Phoenix Fire, Book 2)
- PLAYING WITH FIRE (Phoenix Fire, Book 3)

- ANGEL OF DARKNESS (Fallen, Book 1)
- ANGEL BETRAYED (Fallen, Book 2)
- ANGEL IN CHAINS (Fallen, Book 3)
- AVENGING ANGEL (Fallen, Book 4)
- IMMORTAL DANGER
- NEVER CRY WOLF
- A BIT OF BITE (Free Read!!)
- ETERNAL HUNTER (Night Watch, Book 1)
- I'LL BE SLAYING YOU (Night Watch, Book 2)
- ETERNAL FLAME (Night Watch, Book 3)
- HOTTER AFTER MIDNIGHT (Midnight, Book 1)
- MIDNIGHT SINS (Midnight, Book 2)
- MIDNIGHT'S MASTER (Midnight, Book 3)
- WHEN HE WAS BAD (anthology)
- EVERLASTING BAD BOYS (anthology)
- BELONG TO THE NIGHT (anthology)

List of Cynthia Eden's romantic suspense titles:
- WATCH ME (Dark Obsession, Book 1)
- WANT ME (Dark Obsession, Book 2)
- NEED ME (Dark Obsession, Book 3)
- BEWARE OF ME (Dark Obsession, Book 4)
- MINE TO TAKE (Mine, Book 1)
- MINE TO KEEP (Mine, Book 2)
- MINE TO HOLD (Mine, Book 3)

- MINE TO CRAVE (Mine, Book 4)
- MINE TO HAVE (Mine, Book 5)
- FIRST TASTE OF DARKNESS
- SINFUL SECRETS
- DIE FOR ME (For Me, Book 1)
- FEAR FOR ME (For Me, Book 2)
- SCREAM FOR ME (For Me, Book 3)
- DEADLY FEAR (Deadly, Book 1)
- DEADLY HEAT (Deadly, Book 2)
- DEADLY LIES (Deadly, Book 3)
- ALPHA ONE (Shadow Agents, Book 1)
- GUARDIAN RANGER (Shadow Agents, Book 2)
- SHARPSHOOTER (Shadow Agents, Book 3)
- GLITTER AND GUNFIRE (Shadow Agents, Book 4)
- UNDERCOVER CAPTOR (Shadow Agents, Book 5)
- THE GIRL NEXT DOOR (Shadow Agents, Book 6)
- EVIDENCE OF PASSION (Shadow Agents, Book 7)
- WAY OF THE SHADOWS (Shadow Agents, Book 8)

36185610R00202